WISHFUL THINKING

BOOK ONE

HOW TO BE THE BEST DAMN FAERY GODMOTHER IN THE WORLD (OR DIE TRYING)

HELEN HARPER

BOOK COVER DESIGN BY YOCLA DESIGNS

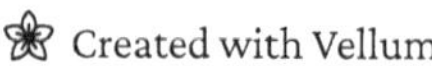

CHAPTER ONE

The monster was bloody massive. Despite the soupy fog surrounding us, his features were still clear. His angry red eyes glowed, almost laser sharp in their intensity, while his green skin glistened wetly in the drizzle. He opened his mouth, jaws yawning wide. The roar which ensued just after was in equal measures ferocious and terrifying. I beamed proudly.

The bolder of my three trainees raised his hand. Normally, I wouldn't countenance questions in the middle of a client session. For now, however, I'd allow it. I had a few seconds to spare and I was feeling generous.

I nodded towards him. 'Yes?'

He swallowed. 'Isn't it rather derivative? I mean, giving him green skin and all. It's not very original.'

The kid deserved to go to the top of the class. I snapped my fingers at him. 'Exactly! It's not supposed to be innovative. You have to ensure that you are creating something which is connected in some way to reality. If you stray too far and let your imagination run riot, then you run the risk of either at worst turning your client psychotically crazy or at best making him completely dismiss your conjuration and forget about what he's seen.' I pointed at the hunched over figure in the doorway. 'If *he* can believe that his own mind created that monster, then *you*'ll have more success in your endeavours.'

'I thought that as dope faeries we are supposed to give them the best trip possible.'

'We are.' I explained further. 'And the best trip possible is the one that your client can believe in. To a certain extent anyway. You can't give them more than their own minds can cope with. When Duncan Smith here properly sobers up, he'll believe that the mushrooms he ate were fantastic. He'll think that he hallucinated a monster akin to the Incredible Hulk because last week he saw part of the film when he sneaked into the local cinema. He'll be more inclined to have mushrooms again, instead of progressing to harder substances which will only lead to his eventual demise. And,' I gestured to his expression, 'he'll continue to enjoy himself.'

All three trainees stared at Duncan's glazed expression. His mouth was indeed curved up into a goofy smile, with his tongue lolling out happily. The trail of drool curling down from his bottom lip was somewhat off-putting but fairly par for the course.

'Is the boogeyman coming?' Duncan whispered.

I knelt down next to his ear. 'The boogeyman is here, Duncan.'

'No.' He shook his head. 'The other one. The real one.'

'What's he talking about?' asked Sarah, the only female out of the three of them.

I shrugged. 'Probably a previous hallucination which he's confusing with this one.' I held my index finger up to my mouth, indicating that they should stop talking. 'Now be quiet. You can't leave your conjurations alone for too long or...'

I didn't manage to finish speaking. The green monster, irritated at being left on its own, snarled loudly and stomped forward, shoving me out of the way. The thing didn't realise its own strength. I went flying, smacking with a painful thud into a nearby brick wall. While I picked myself up, feeling somewhat dazed, the monster lunged for Duncan, grabbing him by the collar and hefting him up.

'What do we do?' Sarah screamed.

I dragged myself up to my feet. 'Stay back,' I said calmly. 'That's what you do.'

I raised my right hand up into the air and twirled my dope faery wand three times. Initially, nothing seemed to happen. Then, however, there was a scuttling sound. The three trainees drew back. That was a wise decision. The scuttling sound grew louder and louder until it was almost a deafening roar. While the green monster craned its head down, prepared to quite happily gnaw on Duncan's exposed neck, from the shadows, hundreds of tiny creatures suddenly appeared. Each one was about the size of my thumb and each one was charging towards the monster. Some wore kilts; some wore suits of armour; some were completely naked. They all carried weapons, however, and they were all directed at Duncan's monster. Within scant seconds they swarmed up its body, engulfing it until it was no longer visible. Duncan fell to the ground, landing badly on his side. I winced. He'd have an inexplicably painful bruise when he woke up tomorrow morning. I rubbed at my spine. He wasn't the only one.

I raised my hand once again and twirled it anti-clockwise this time. The tiny army vanished. A split second later so did the monster.

I shook out my hair, brushed off the dirt from my t-shirt, and turned to my cowering trio. 'So,' I said with a smile, 'what can you learn from that episode? Dean?'

He ran a shaky hand through his hair and blinked at me. 'Er ... stay on your guard at all times?'

I nodded. 'Yes. What else?'

Sarah swallowed. 'Keep a close rein on your incantations.'

'Yes.' I cast a glance at Duncan. Mild confusion was reflected in his face but he didn't appear unduly perturbed by his near brush with death. 'Although you can easily control whatever you conjure up, if you become distracted then disaster can ensue.' My tone darkened. 'Make no mistake. Serious injury and even death can and does occur. We are already dealing with vulnerable clients. The last thing you want to do is make their lives worse than they already are.' I stepped out of the shadows so that Duncan would finally notice my presence, and knelt down in front of him. 'How are you feeling, Duncan?' I asked softly.

His dilated pupils fixed on me. 'Good.' He frowned. 'Great, in fact.' He stared at me more closely. 'Do I know you?'

'I'm a friend,' I told him.

'Ah.' He bobbed his head in understanding. 'Did you see the monster too?'

'I did.' I smiled at him. 'It was pretty scary.'

'I wasn't scared,' he quickly declared. 'Monsters don't scare me.'

I patted him on the shoulder. 'Good for you. I'll see you around.'

'Be careful,' he muttered. 'You don't want to get hurt.' He lifted his feet, using them to push himself against the wall. Then he began to fumble in his pockets for a cigarette. I left him to it. My work, at least as far as Duncan was concerned, was done for now.

'What happens,' Sarah asked, 'if he does move onto more potent drugs? Will he still be your client then?'

'Yes.' I sighed. 'But the hallucinations I create will affect him more deeply. It will become harder to maintain control over his moments of lucidity. Some clients manage to pull back from that. Some don't. You can nudge them towards the right path but you can't choose it for them.' I touched my chest. 'That sort of motivation has to come from within.'

All three of the trainees looked rather dubious. Dean's colour still hadn't returned to his cheeks. It wasn't easy starting out. They'd learn soon enough though.

'Will he remember us?' Dean asked.

I shook my head. 'The memory magic covers you as well as me. He won't remember a thing.'

All three of them looked relieved at that. They were clearly still nervous about their new jobs. I smiled sympathetically. 'It's not glamorous being a dope faery,' I told them. 'A lot of other faeries in other professions will look down on you. But make no mistake about it. You are giving some small amount of joy to your clients. What they then do with that afterwards is up to them.'

'He doesn't look very joyful,' Dean pointed out.

That was the trouble with specialised language, I reflected. Unless you were in the loop, it rarely made sense. 'When I say joy in this context,' I said, 'I'm actually referring to a number of possible emotions. All positive and all with the potential to lead to genuine joy, as you understand it.' I thought a little more about it before continuing, choosing my words carefully so that my three students would grasp my actual meaning. 'In Duncan's case it's about bravery. He's too scared to pick himself up and move on from the trauma that put him in this position. I've been working with him for months to build up his confidence. Last year he wouldn't have been able to cope with a monster such as the one I just conjured up. It's taken a lot to get him to this point. Being a dope faery isn't only about giving your clients happy drug dreams. It's about giving them the tools they might need to survive beyond this existence.' I waved a hand around to illustrate my point.

'It's a lot more complex than I'd realised,' Sarah said, as much to herself as to anyone else.

'You'll grasp the ins and outs more quickly than you think,' I told her. Then I smiled at them all. 'Let's head home to Colchester and clock off. You can spend the evening remembering that, no matter what anyone else tells you, this is a great job and you'll gain immense satisfaction from it.'

'I FUCKING HATE MY JOB.' I gazed morosely into my beer. 'Three hours I've spent in crappy rain with crappy clients and crappy trainees.' I gestured towards my hair. 'You do realise that no amount of conditioner is going to calm down this frizz now, right?'

Harry grinned at me. 'I think the frizz kind of suits you.'

'Piss off.'

'I'm telling the truth. It makes you look like a poodle.'

I looked up from my drink and stared at him.

'A very cute poodle,' he said.

I snorted. Most other faeries were blessed with perfect locks and unblemished skin. I, on the other hand, had the sort of hair which wouldn't look out of place on a circus clown and I was prone to repeated acne break outs. No-one ever said life was fair.

'Anyway,' Harry said, 'you're ridiculously good at your job. You take it seriously and you help out lots of people. Very few of your clients have died from overdoses.' He paused. 'You won employee of the month three times in a row! So stop whinging about it. You're just having a bad day.'

'More like a bad year,' I muttered. I took a swig of my drink and sighed. 'Alright. I don't really hate my job. I'm just bored as hell.'

'Isn't that why your boss has been giving you all those trainees?' Harry asked. 'To keep you on your toes?'

I grimaced. 'Jacob is trying to keep me busy. I'm sure he thinks that I want his job. The last thing I want, however, is more sodding dope faery paperwork. I don't want to be sat behind a desk. I want to be out there,' I gestured aimlessly in front of me, 'helping people.' Not to mention being the best dope faery there was. That went without saying.

'You do help people.' Harry scratched at an old scab on the back of his hand. 'And at least you don't have to hang around waiting for it to rain like I do. This dry spell we've been having is driving me nuts. I've not been able to create any decent rainbows since April. And even then I was told the last one I made wasn't good enough because my blues were too insipid. Blues by their very nature are insipid!'

I gave him a commiserative look. 'You've still not been given the London contract then?'

'No.' He grunted in irritation. 'The dippy twins have it instead. And that's only because their uncle is Philip Vasterson.'

My mouth curved into a sympathetic smile. 'Remember when we were students and we created FAN? We should never have abandoned it.'

'We didn't have much choice in the matter,' Harry reminded me. ' Besides, 'Faeries Against Nepotism was never going to gain any traction when all the powers that be enjoy their position because of that very nepotism. We were young and optimistic and now we're tired and over-worked. This is how it will be until we retire, draw our pensions and then drop dead immediately after.' His eyes danced. 'So we should forget about our jobs and just party harder.' He clinked his glass against mine and drained it dry. 'Let's do shots. Then clubbing.

And maybe a kebab before a quick vomit into the nearest drain.'

I smirked. 'That's very tempting. But I've been called into for an early meeting tomorrow. I have no idea what Jacob wants but I reckon I'll need a clear head. Especially if he's going to call me out for making that client last walk into the lake last week. He doesn't realise that it was a carefully planned operation designed to help my boy get over his fear of water. If he thinks that he can give me an official warning for almost drowning the man then he's got another thing coming.'

'You go, girl.' He nudged me. 'You see? You do care about your job.'

'Of course I care about it.' I sighed. 'I'm still bored though.'

'Only one shot then. Vodka.'

I couldn't deny that I was tempted. I shook my head firmly. 'No. There have been whispers that there's a new task force being created to deal with people who are taking that synthetic drug that's recently come onto the streets. I think it's called Wings.' I shrugged. 'Anyway, if it does come about I want to be the one to head it up. I've got the experience and the expertise.'

Harry raised an eyebrow. 'Not to mention the ambition.'

This was a conversation we'd had many times. 'Why have dreams if you're not willing to work to achieve them?'

'Saffron, your dream isn't to head up the Wings task force.'

My mouth twisted. 'No, it's not. But right now it's about all I've got that's achievable.' I leaned over and gave him a quick peck on the cheek. 'I'll see you later.'

'Count on it.'

Jacob wasn't a bad boss. In fact, I rather respected and admired him. He ran a tight ship and didn't take fools gladly. Admittedly, he had a disturbing penchant for implementing new initiatives from his various middle management training courses with unbridled enthusiasm, regardless of whether they were smart ideas or not. Unfortunately, I couldn't fault him for possessing the same ardent desire to do well that I did. I simply wished I had more opportunities to shine. Modesty aside, it was all very well being a big fish in a small pond but I was quickly running out of room.

'Take a seat, Saffron.' Jacob pointed at the chair in front of his desk. 'Thank you for coming in so early. I know you had a busy day yesterday.'

'It wasn't too bad.'

'Your trainees were impressed. You've done a good job of firing them up. Not ever faery wants to come to this department. We can always count on you to show the newbies what things are really like. The magic you weave with them as well as with your clients is nothing short of wonderful. Complex tapestries shot with gold. That's what you do.'

I frowned at him. Jacob wasn't normally prone to flowery language. Neither did he tend towards effusive compliments. Something was definitely up. 'I do what I've been told to do,' I said slowly.

'And you do it very well. Lots of other dope faeries look up to you.'

His expression was remarkably earnest. That had me worried. 'Alright,' I said, 'enough already. What's this actually about?'

His nose wrinkled. 'This department was never your first choice.'

'No.'

'You applied to the luck faeries, I believe?'

I nodded. I was growing more suspicious by the second.

'And the dream faeries?'

'Yes. What of it?'

Jacob ignored my question. 'On three occasions, you also applied to the faery godmothers. You were not long listed.'

I tilted my head. 'Is this your attempt to tell me that I was lucky to get any kind of job at all?'

His gaze was steady. 'No. It's my attempt to tell you that we saw your potential even if the other departments did not. You do good work here, Maisie. If you remain on this trajectory, you could head up the entire department one day.'

There was definitely a 'but' coming. I folded my arms.

Jacob sighed. 'An opening has come up in another department. They have suggested that you would be a good fit. They would like to interview you.'

I stared at him. 'Me?'

He sniffed. 'It's far from ideal. You'll go right back down to the bottom of the heap. You'll have all sorts of new things to learn and you'll be considerably older than any of the other new starts. It might seem appealing but you have to remember that not all that glitters is gold.'

'Which department?' I asked.

'Just because somewhere has a good reputation doesn't mean that it's actually going to be an amazing place to work. And just because they've asked for you to attend an interview doesn't mean that you'll get the position.'

'Jacob, which department?'

His mouth moved and the words came out but for some strange reason I couldn't actually hear him. What he said did not compute.

'I'm sorry,' I said. 'I didn't catch that. Which department?'

He remained calm but there was an odd glint in his eye. 'The same one you applied to three times. The supposed top of the faery tree.' A hint of sourness coloured his tone.

'The faery godmothers?' I asked stupidly. 'The faery godmothers have asked for me?'

'You don't have to do it,' he said. 'You don't have to attend the interview.'

I was already on my feet. 'When?' I asked, my blood fizzing in delight at the very thought. 'Where?'

Jacob's mouth tightened. 'Their Assistant Director would like to talk to you as soon as possible. In fact she's waiting outside. She'll interview you here. You don't have to use the Metafora to transport yourself to their building. She is,' Jacob added darkly, 'a remarkably humourless person.'

My feet were already propelling me towards the door. Why hadn't I put on smarter clothes this morning? Damn it. There was no time to go and change. I didn't want to give the faery godmothers the chance to change their mind. They'd asked for me. For *me*. This might turn out to be the best day of my entire life. 'Thank you, Jacob! Thank you so much!'

'You don't have to take the job,' he called out once again after me.

I barely heard him. Sometimes wishes really did come true. My mum would never believe this. Neither would Harry. Frankly, right now, neither did I.

CHAPTER TWO

From the outside, the office block looked like any other building in this mundane suburb of Colchester. Grey. Nondescript. Neither clean enough nor dirty enough to provoke comment. In fact, the façade offered about as much interest as a tooth faery talking about the perils of toffee. It was designed to discourage anyone from looking twice, in case the repel spells surrounding it failed and a human decided to wander inside. As soon as you stepped over the threshold, however, you could feel the frisson in the air. This was where the magic happened.

Even with my best suit and my brightest blouse covering most of my body, I could feel the delicious goosebumps rippling across my skin. It seemed unreal. Adeline Motus had only interviewed me on Friday and here I was, less than three days later, about to actually start my new job. I'd wanted this my entire life but I'd never really expected that it would happen. I knew how things worked and I knew that I would never be top of the godmothers' recruitment list. And yet I was here. Years of hard work with the dope faeries and I'd actually proven I was worthy. I drew in a deep breath, allowing myself to savour the fragrant scent of honeysuckle, before striding up to the desk with my heels clicking.

'Hi.' I presented the receptionist with my most enthusiastic smile. 'I'm Saffron Sawyer. I'm here for ...'

'Take a seat.' She didn't lift her head from her magazine.

I tilted up my chin and hardened my voice ever so slightly. As of this moment, I was someone important. Someone to be reckoned with. I was no longer the person who permitted herself to be delegated to the uncomfortable chairs set out for visitors. 'I said,' I repeated, 'I'm Saffron Sawyer. I'm the new faery godmother.' Then, because it seemed important to say it, 'it's my first day. The Director is expecting me.'

For a moment, the receptionist didn't move. I was half tempted to cough impatiently and start drumming my fingernails on the marble counter, even though my mother had insisted on phoning before I left home this morning to remind me to be polite and courteous to everyone, regardless of who they were. Then, however, the receptionist slowly raised her head and stared at me. She wasn't smiling. In fact, she looked as if she'd swallowed a sour plum.

'I know who you are.'

She didn't say anything else. I supposed she didn't need to. Perhaps her job entailed an enforced paucity of words. I had a brief memory of one of my old teachers telling me a story about how particularly garrulous fairies used to be chastised to the point where they were given enforced word limits for each day. Speak more than a thousand words in any twenty-four period and receive a pig's snout instead of the cute button nose that was indicative of our kind. At the time I'd assumed it was merely a teacher's ploy designed to make me shut up. I could have been wrong, however. You could never be entirely sure where faeries were concerned. In any case, I swallowed my tart reply and nodded minutely. Then I meekly turned and made my way to the nearest chair. It was more uncomfortable than it looked.

I wiggled and shifted, causing the chair to creak loudly. The receptionist's head snapped towards me. I didn't apologise. I'd be polite. But I wouldn't be weak. I gave her another sunny smile to suggest that being forced into a warped posture that was already making my back ache was exactly what I'd expected when I got up this morning. She just sniffed and looked away again.

The front door opened and three people piled in, chattering and giggling. To the untrained eye, they appeared to be normal office workers but I couldn't fail to notice the glimmer clinging to each of their dewy faces. I sat up that bit straighter.

'Darlings,' said the taller one of the three, whose shining blonde hair was so straight and so perfect I almost fancied I'd be able to see my reflection in it if I looked closely enough, 'enjoy it while you can. Now that the Director has opened the office up to any shite wee faery who thinks they possess the skills to be one of us, the canteen will be serving up fish finger sandwiches, and chips and cheese for the rest of our days. Watercress and pomegranate brioche delights will be an endangered species. Much like us.'

The only male in the group snorted. 'Alicia, you are *too* much. There's only one marsh faery joining the ranks. She'll learn her place quickly enough.'

'She'd better. In fact ...' Her voice trailed off as she caught sight of me. A slow grin spread across her face. 'In fact,' she repeated more loudly now, 'she'll probably run out of here with her tail between her legs as soon as she realises exactly what is required.' She sniffed. 'It's not all waving wands and granting sparkly wishes.'

The last of the trio, a raven haired woman with a cupid's

bow mouth highlighted by perfectly applied scarlet lipstick, opened her eyes wide. 'Do marsh faeries have tails?'

Alicia laughed. 'Quite possibly,' she said. 'I've never gotten close enough to one to find out.' She raised her voice in order to be absolutely assured that I heard her. 'They're certainly grotesque looking enough.'

The three of them glided up to the reception desk. I felt a twinge of angry irritation that, even with their barbed digs, I remained envious of their ability to appear so swan-like and graceful. There was a sensual fluidity to their every movement which I knew I could never hope to emulate. No doubt it was this which caused me to rise to my feet. Either that or it was the suggestion that fish finger sandwiches were somehow inferior to other food stuffs. I loved fish finger sandwiches.

'I'm not a marsh faery,' I said in a loud voice. My words bounced across the marble expanse with the faintest hint of reproach. Not that I had anything against marsh faeries. In actuality, I liked their dusky green skin and ability to meld into almost any natural background. 'Unfortunately, I cannot call them my kin,' I added. 'Much as I would like to.'

The raven haired woman tittered. 'Did something just speak?'

Cue another round of giggles.

'Yeah,' I said. 'I spoke.' I weighed up my options in my head. How tempting it was to snidely put down the glamorous trio. As a dope faery I'd probably have slapped them around until they apologised. I doubted that would be a good idea here. Creating lifelong enemies on my first day wasn't the best thing to do. Still, whether this pestilent trio wanted me here or not was moot. They needed me here. The very manner of my interview proved it. Besides, I'd been half expecting this sort of reception. And the most effective way to deal with poison was with a sugary antidote. After all, I couldn't let short term satisfaction get in the way of my own long term goals.

'I'm Saffron,' I said. I kept my voice light and pleasant. My sincerity, whether faked or otherwise, would be key. 'I'm looking forward to working with all of you. Perhaps I can learn how to speak like you so that you can hear me more clearly in the future. I've always aspired to a cut glass accent.' I curved my mouth into a small smile. 'Glottal stops are so under-rated.'

'What's a glottal stop?'

'Oh, do shut up, Figgy,' Alicia muttered.

My smile grew. 'It's the difference between 'flattery',' I said, carefully pronouncing the 'tt', 'and 'fla-ery'.' I widened my eyes ever so slightly. 'And may I say that I adore your lipstick. That shade is so dramatic and bold.'

Figgy fluttered her eyelashes in some sort of reflexive responsive to the compliment. 'You're too kind.' She glanced at the male faery by her side. 'I told you it was a good colour choice, Rupert.'

He rolled his eyes. But then he also inclined his head towards mine with a glimmer of brief approval. Go me. I'd avoided fisticuffs in my first hour. That had to count as a win. Then that glimmer altered slightly to something more like a leer. Perhaps I'd not won anything after all.

'The red makes you look pale and sickly,' Alicia snapped to the still smiling Figgy.

The receptionist, who had managed to peel her eyes away from her magazine, folded her arms and glared. A slight ripple of warmth ran through me. At least her unfriendliness was faery non-specific. 'Are you three planning to sign in for work at any point today,' she inquired, 'or are you going to stand around here and make my lobby look untidy until it's time to go home?'

Alicia opened her mouth. I waited, expecting a vicious retort. Instead, however, her response was soft. 'I do apologise,

Miranda.' She turned her back on me and reached for what I presumed was the log-in book. She pressed her thumb onto a pristine white page, tossed her head and then sauntered for the lift. Figgy and Rupert followed suit. Not one of them gave me so much as a backwards glance. I gazed at the receptionist, thoroughly impressed. This was someone who clearly wielded considerable power. I mentally thanked my mother for her admonishment to be polite. If this woman could bring the Alicias of this world into line, then she was someone I needed to get to know better.

'You,' she said, looking down her nose towards me, 'are either incredibly smart or incredibly stupid.'

'Well, Miranda,' I replied, 'I'm convinced it's the former. Naturally.'

She drew herself back with a sharp hiss. 'My name is Mrs Jardine and you will address me as such.' She slammed the flat of her palm onto the desk in front of her to add emphasis to her words. 'Now sit down. You look ridiculous flapping around like that.' And just like that, she returned her attention to her magazine. Fuck a puck. In three syllables I'd all but washed away any bonhomie I might have garnered myself. Nice work, Saffron. Nice bloody work.

Almost an hour later, I'd still not made it past the lobby. I'd counted all the bulbs in the twinkly chandelier dangling from the ceiling. I'd estimated the number of steps from the front door to the reception desk as thirty-eight. Twenty if I skipped. I'd even decided on the shade of paint I would choose to highlight the grand walls and soften the atmosphere once I was appointed Director (in around sixteen years if my plans came to fruition). In all that time, not another soul either entered or exited the building. And Mrs Miranda Jardine didn't once raise her head. Maybe this was a test. Dope faeries weren't known for their patience. Faery godmothers required it in abundance. In fact it was written all over the mission statement. *Achieving optimum wish fulfillment is a slow, laborious process with immense rewards. All our faeries exercise ultimate patience and decorum whilst waiting for results.* If I could show the powers that be that I could handle this sort of monotony then perhaps I'd prove myself worthy. Alas, that would have been far easier to manage if my arse wasn't quite so numb from sitting for so long in the uncomfortable chair.

Unfortunately, I wasn't quite as patient as I'd advertised myself at my interview. I was debating how I could rush the lift before Mrs Jardine stopped me – and I might well have done so - when there was a peculiar crackle in the air. Actually, crackle wasn't quite the right word because it wasn't a sound so much as a sensation. My skin prickled oddly in response.

I looked over at Mrs Jardine. She hadn't moved a muscle. I cleared my throat awkwardly but she didn't even blink. Biting my lip, I raised my hand tentatively in the air. 'Erm...'

She sighed. 'What now?'

Given that I'd sat silently for the last hour, I felt that both her tone and her remark were uncalled for. All the same, I ploughed ahead. There was an expanse of air a few metres to my right that was beginning to flicker with little sparks of red light. Maybe the entire building was about to spontaneously combust. If it did, at least sprinting for the door while screaming loudly would give me something to do. 'Is that supposed to happen?' I asked.

'Is what supposed to happen?' She finally looked up. When her eyes landed upon the dancing lights, she let out a tiny squeak of what sounded like terror. 'No,' she whispered. 'Oh no.'

Genuinely alarmed now, I stood up, ignoring the stiffness in my limbs. 'What?' I demanded. 'What is it?'

Mrs Jardine paid me no attention whatsoever. She reached for her phone with trembling fingers, lifting the receiver without taking her gaze from the ever increasing lights.

'It's me,' she whispered into the phone. 'He's coming. Again.'

She wasn't talking to me but I still couldn't help myself. 'Who?' I asked. 'Who's coming?'

Whether she'd have been willing to answer me or not, I'd never know. The lights coalesced, swirling together into a bright red glow. Then there was a sudden bang and the lobby filled with smoke. I coughed and spluttered. I flapped my arms in front of me, wondering whether to run out or if I dash upstairs and start screaming at people to get out of the building before it blew up. There was an unpleasant ringing in my ears. Of all the ways I'd imagined my first day would go, I'd not considered anything like this.

In the end, the building neither blew up nor set itself alight. As I continued to stare, the smoke dissipated quickly, leaving little more than a few curling wisps. I blinked. Then I blinked again. Standing smack bang in the middle of the lobby was a tall, broad-shouldered man. His hair was inky dark and he was wearing a suit which appeared to have been starched to within an inch of its life. He glanced towards me, revealing an aquiline nose, haughty features and piercing jade green eyes. The faint scent of musky cinnamon tickled my nostrils. I slowly sat back down in my chair. Uh oh. Okay, I knew exactly who this was. I just didn't know what he was doing here.

He dismissed me without a second glance and strode up to Mrs Jardine. 'Good morning.' His accent was even posher than Alicia's had been. 'I'm here to see the Director. I'm the …'

'Devil's Advocate,' I blurted out.

Oops. I hadn't actually meant to say that out loud. Fortunately, both he and Mrs Jardine ignored me so I could pretend that it hadn't happened. 'Of course,' she said briskly. 'Someone will be down momentarily to escort you up.'

He leaned in, towering over her. 'I do not require an escort,' he said. 'I am perfectly capable of finding my own way.'

'Certainly.' Her voice grew firmer as she repeated herself. 'Certainly.' She pointed to the side. 'The lift is over there.'

'In the same place as last week,' he said. 'And the week before that.'

Mrs Jardine's skin was curiously pale. I supposed I should be pleased that she was as shocked by the Devil's Advocate's sudden appearance as I was. In truth I actually felt sorry for her, especially given his sarcasm. I doubted she'd appreciate my sympathy. But I still felt it all the same. I provided a reassuring smile in her direction. Then I realised that the Devil's Advocate was looking at me again.

'You will join me,' he said.

I glanced round. Um ... was he talking to me?

'She will be delighted to,' Mrs Jardine said. She threw me a glance which was laden with meaning. Unfortunately, I couldn't tell what that meaning was.

As if on cue, the lift pinged open. The Devil's Advocate turned and walked towards it. Unlike the other three faeries who strolled in earlier, he didn't glide across the lobby. He massacred it with heavy, deliberate footsteps. Frankly, it was a surprise that he didn't leave a trail of blood behind him on the marble floor.

I didn't move. I wasn't sure that I could. Mrs Jardine waved at me frantically, however, gesturing that I should follow. Feet, Saffron. You have feet. Usually they worked. I straightened my shoulders, shook myself off and followed after him. Naturally, I neither glided nor massacred. I pootled. I wasn't trying to annoy the Devil's Advocate. Not deliberately anyway. I was just still a bit stunned by the turn of events. And my legs really were still quite stiff.

If he was irritated by the amount of time it took me to join him at his side in the lift, it didn't show on his face. I shuffled in round him, taking up refuge in the far corner. Then the doors closed and the lift jolted slightly as it began to rise.

The strains of jazzy muzak filled the air. I let out a nervous giggle. I clamped my hand over my mouth to prevent another from escaping but it didn't do much good.

The Devil's Advocate slowly turned. 'What is so amusing?' he inquired. His mouth didn't twitch and his eyes didn't crinkle. The man was not entertained in the slightest.

'Nothing.'

He stared at me uncomprehendingly. Oh. I removed my hand from my mouth and repeated myself.

'Nothing.' I hesitated. 'Sir.' Was that right? No-one had ever prepared me for this eventuality. Perhaps I should genuflect?

'If nothing was funny,' he said, 'then why were you laughing?'

I tried to put it into words. 'It's like when you're at a funeral and you can't stop giggling. You know?'

His frown deepened. 'No. I don't know.'

'It's a situation that creates a sort of uncontrollable hysteria,' I said, doing my best to explain but feeling like I was digging myself into a massive hole from which there would never be any escape. 'It's not that it's actually funny. It's that the anxiety and heightened emotion forces you into laughing.'

He leaned towards me. 'I make you anxious?'

I shrugged. He was the Devil's Advocate. Making people anxious was in his job description. He was in the very position that he was because he was considered the most powerful faery in the country. That was exactly why it was his job to keep everyone else in line. 'Yeah.' Duh.

His eyes darkened. 'And my presence heightens your emotions?' He gazed at me with a freakish intensity. 'Which emotions precisely?'

My cheeks began to flame red. Uh. Um. I twisted my hands as my brain continued to flounder. It was like that time when I was fourteen years old and I'd just been caught smoking a joint round the back of the school janitor's shed. On that occasion my path as a dope faery was carved out for me before I could so much as pretend I was holding the joint for a friend. The wrong answer now might send me back to where I'd come from. I flailed.

The Devil's Advocate pulled away. 'Sorry,' he said. 'I'm only teasing you.' Teasing? I gaped. Since when did the Devil's Advocate tease? He raised an eyebrow and I caught a slight gleam of humour in his expression. 'You're not a faery godmother, are you?'

I coughed and tried to recover my equilibrium. I raised my chin up and met his eyes square on. 'Actually,' I said, 'I am. It's my first day though.' Maybe that admission would encourage him to go easy on me. 'My name is Saffron Sawyer.'

Sudden interest sparked in his eyes. 'Ah,' he said. 'So you're the one.'

What? I swallowed. 'You've heard about me?'

The lift jerked as it reached its correct floor and came to a halt. 'Indeed I have.' He paused as the door opened. 'You're brave to come here,' he said quietly. 'Good luck.'

Brave? This was my dream job. I opened my mouth to say something in return but he'd already stepped out. A group of people were already there waiting. I wasn't so naïve as to think the welcoming committee was for me. I watched as the Devil's Advocate was hustled away into one of the offices beyond. I had no idea what to make of what he'd said. It seemed incomprehensible that he knew who I was. It was unusual for faeries to switch jobs like I had but it wasn't unheard of. I bit my lip and pondered it further. Then the lift doors began to close and I panicked. I threw myself out before I could be whisked back down to the lobby again. Enough already. Whatever the Devil's Advocate was doing here, I had other concerns. I'd never get another chance to make a first impression on my new employers.

CHAPTER THREE

'Your work station is here,' stated the squat, balding man who'd introduced himself as Billy. He pointed at a dusty corner in the open plan office. Although a surprisingly large number of the more well appointed desks were both empty and clean, as far as I could tell, this one had been used as a dumping ground for other people's crap. There were several filing boxes, each of which was bursting at the seams, and an array of crumpled wrappers from various snacks. Pinned to the wall was a yellowing poster with fire evacuation procedures and a scribbled advert for the staff Christmas party which, judging by the date, took place three years ago.

I beamed. 'It's wonderful! Thank you.'

Billy grunted. 'Are you mad?'

Possibly. I glanced at him.

'You don't have to be mad to work here,' he told me without cracking a smile. He paused for dramatic effect. 'But it helps.'

'Ha!' I nodded vigorously. 'Yes. I see. Good joke.'

He stared at me. 'I wasn't joking.' He sniffed and turned on his heel, walking away.

I shrugged to myself and pulled out the swivel chair next to my heaving desk. It jolted when I sat down on it, the seat slipping several inches downwards. I grimaced and stood back up to fiddle with the mechanism and return it to a more useable height. Unfortunately, the plastic knob was jammed. I gritted my teeth and twisted it as hard as I could. It was a fatal error. It creaked once and snapped off in my hand. Now the chair was stuck at dwarf height for the rest of eternity.

I'd admit it was a setback, albeit a minor one. I looked around. There had to be another free chair around somewhere. I eyed the desk next to me. The chair there seemed alright. I could swap them around. Then, however, an older woman appeared. Without paying me any attention whatsoever, she plonked down a cup of coffee, grabbed the chair and sat down. Her steel grey hair was set in rollers and she wore a set of pince nez spectacles. She actually looked like the sort of faery godmother you'd read about in a human child's book.

'Hello!' I peered round the partition wall. 'I'm Saffron.'

'Delilah.'

It was time to start making friends. I wouldn't give anyone else the opportunity to act like Alicia had. In order to do that, I had to set the tone. 'We're going to be office buddies!' I burbled. 'I know we'll get on wonderfully!'

Unfortunately, I used a tad too much enthusiasm. Delilah rolled her eyes and edged her chair away from me.

'Are there are any more chairs?' I asked, toning down the bounce in my voice to indicate that I too could be somber and serious as this job required. 'My one seems to be broken.'

'No.'

'It'll be difficult for me to get any work done because I'm not sure I'll be able to reach my desk if I sit on the chair I've got.'

Delilah used her middle finger to push her spectacles up her nose. 'Honey,' she said tiredly, 'no-one cares.' She reached for her computer mouse and began clicking. It appeared our conversation was over.

I pursed my lips. Despite the high regard the faery godmother office was held in, so far my new co-workers were most definitely not happy, contented people. I told myself that was only natural. This was high-paced, high stressed, vitally important work. Not to mention that I was a stranger. It was quite possible that my lack of a decent welcome so far was because everyone felt threatened by my arrival. The Devil's Advocate had heard of me. Alicia, Figgy and Rupert had all been concerned enough about my appearance to both gossip about me and attempt to bully me. They must all know that I was the highest achieving dope faery in more than twenty years. It stood to reason that they'd feel concerned I was here to throw shade. It was troubling but I remained reasonably confident. They'd all soon realise that I was the ultimate team player. In any case, no amount of snide remarks or unfriendly colleagues could dampen my enthusiasm. I looked around the busy office, breathing in the productive hum. This was going to be fabulous. *I* was going to be fabulous. Whether I could reach my desk or not.

'Ms Sawyer.'

I jumped at the sound of the voice behind me and whirled round. Adeline Motus, second in command to the Director himself, was standing there with her arms folded. I wasn't overly concerned by her stern expression. She'd looked exactly the same throughout my entire interview and she'd still given me the job. She was just a serious person in a serious position, that was all.

Adeline tapped her foot. 'Ms Sawyer,' she said again, 'I don't know what things were like in your previous office, but here we expect a certain level of tidiness. Whether this is your first day or not, you should keep your desk clean.'

I bit back my automatic apology. I wasn't a trouble-maker. I wasn't a doormat either though. 'All these things were already here when I arrived,' I said. 'I'm not sure what to do with them.'

'I can't abide excuses. Anyone who needs to make excuses for themselves is merely lazy.'

I scratched my neck, wishing away the hot flush that I could already feel rising up my skin. 'Should I throw them out?'

'I don't care what you do with them,' Adeline sniffed. 'All I care is that you keep your desk clean. Especially today. The Devil's Advocate is here.'

I nodded. 'Oh yeah, I know. We shared the lift up together.'

Adeline didn't blink. I felt myself pinned by her gaze. Even Delilah swiveled round in her chair to stare at me. 'You shared the lift?' Her voice dripped with disbelief, as if it were completely inconceivable that I could have been in the same space, breathing the same air as the scourge of the faery world. 'And he didn't mind?'

I coughed. 'He told me to come up with him.'

Adeline leaned forward. 'What did he say?' she demanded. 'Did you talk?'

Informing her that I'd spent most of the lift ride giggling hysterically probably wouldn't paint me in a very favourable light. 'He, uh, wished me good luck.'

She stared at me even harder. 'Did he indeed.' Her lips tightened. 'You'll need more than luck to do well around here.'

I straightened my shoulders. 'That's why I'm keen to get started right away.' I put on my best eager to please expression. Jacob had loved it when I did that and had often taken it as a measure of his own brilliance. I had the feeling, however, that Adeline would be a tougher nut to crack.

'It will be some time before we let you loose on the public,' she said. 'This is a complex job. You will need considerable training first.'

I smiled. 'I can't wait.'

She frowned at me, her expression clouding with suspicion. I wasn't being facetious though. I'd do all the training they wanted, regardless of what it was, just so long as I could stay here. 'You *can* wait,' she said. 'And you will. First of all, there are manuals to be read and papers to be signed. Not to mention sorting out your identification and your equipment.'

I couldn't prevent the gleeful grin from spreading across my face. 'Equipment?'

Adeline rolled her eyes. 'Here,' she said, thrusting a piece of paper in my face with a checklist on it. 'Do these things first. When you are done, come and talk to me.' She sniffed loudly and stalked off.

'Wow,' I said to Delilah, 'she takes no prisoners, huh?'

Delilah didn't hear me. 'Tell me what he was like,' she breathed.

I scratched my head. 'Who?' Then I realised. 'Oh, the Devil's Advocate.' I shrugged. 'He seemed nice enough. A bit stern perhaps but he was alright. What's he doing here?'

Delilah glanced around, checking that no-one was listening in. 'Pre-inspection,' she whispered. 'He's setting the tone before he comes in to do his full audit.'

I started. 'The Faery Godmothers are being audited?' That was almost unheard of. This office was usually held in such high esteem that they were left to get on with things themselves. *We* were left to get on with things *ourselves,* I reminded myself. I was part of this office now.

Delilah looked down. 'Yes, well, everyone gets audited sooner or later,' she said. 'It must have happened all the time with the dope faeries.'

Apparently, my reputation really did precede me. 'Not while I was there,' I told her. Then, unnecessarily, I added, 'We did our jobs well.'

'It can't be hard though, can it?' she said. 'I mean, all you're doing is creating trippy dreams for zoned out drug addicts. It's not ...,' her lip curled, 'honorable.'

That depended on your point of view. Despite my moans to Harry, I was proud that I'd managed to bring sixty-three people into rehab through the dreams that I'd granted them through their drug induced hazes. I knew instinctively that Delilah would never understand that the care dope faeries gave their clients could often steer them away from a destructive path, however. I thought briefly of the two deaths that had occurred on my watch. I might have been unable to bring them back to the light but my work had ensured that those people had slipped away without fear or horror. Perhaps it wasn't honorable work. Perhaps I'd been finding it unsatisfying towards the end. But, for all their faults, I'd liked my clients and done my best by them.

'We all have our roles to play,' I murmured.

Her eyes narrowed slightly. 'You might find this one more challenging.' She looked at me expectantly. 'Did you ever have anyone famous? I'd love to see inside the head of one of those Hollywood stars.'

Data protection was as important with dope faeries as with faery godmothers. 'The thing about those Hollywood stars,' I said, 'is that they tend to be in Hollywood. Not rainy Britain.'

Delilah tossed her head. 'So that's a no then.' She turned back to her computer, indicating that our conversation was over. I debated conjuring up a juicy titbit about the Devil's Advocate, as it was clear that gossip was the way to Delilah's heart. I wasn't going to get drawn into those kind of office politics though. That's not what I was here for.

I returned my attention to the piece of paper which Adeline had given me. Top of the list was arranging for my godmother

ID. I beamed to myself. It would make my new job title official. I was more than ready for my close-up.

THERE WASN'T A SPECIALLY DESIGNATED studio area. There wasn't a professional photographer. It was just me and a bored looking teenager in a corner of the main office. As far as I could tell he was on work experience.

'I have to take your photo,' he said, 'then I'll print it onto the laminated card along with your thumb print. Once you have that, you can gain access to all areas of the building.'

I patted my hair self-consciously. 'Do you have a mirror?' I asked.

He fiddled with his camera and didn't look up. 'You look fine. Say cheese.'

I blinked. 'What?'

The camera flashed. 'Done,' he said.

'Wait! I wasn't ready!' I wasn't sure I'd been looking at the camera.

'The photo is fine. What's your name?'

'Saffron Sawyer. Let me see the photo in case we need to take another one.' I wasn't vain but if I had to have this ID displayed for the entirety of my tenure here, I wanted it to at least look like me.

'There's no time.' He picked at a scab on his chin. 'You've got to go to HR now.' He picked up the camera and walked off, with the shuffling gait of someone who actually had all the time in the world.

I stared after him. It was only a photo. How bad could it be anyway? I gave myself a nod of vague reassurance that it would be fine then twisted round. Where was HR anyway?

Spotting a closed door not too far away, I headed in that

direction. It was worth a try. When I opened the door, however, all I was confronted with was a mop and a few buckets.

'Planning on doing some cleaning?' a voice inquired.

I glanced round and spotted Rupert, the male faery I'd met down in the lobby. Hoping that I wasn't in for another round of pointed digs as I really did have better things to do, I gave him a small smile. 'I'm looking for HR,' I said. 'I could do with a map. This place is a maze.'

'It's over there.' He gestured towards the other side of the room. 'You can tell it's HR because the closer you get to them the more joy is sucked from your soul.'

I looked at him. He grinned. 'You'll find your way around soon enough.' He hesitated. 'Sorry about earlier. You know, downstairs. It's been a long time since we had anyone new come into the office. Normally the new starts are already known to us. Faery godmothers tend to keep it in the family. I'm sure you know that though.'

I proceeded carefully. 'You're a faery god ... father?' It used to be that godmothers were only ever female. Male faeries had petitioned for decades to be allowed access and given the same opportunities as us women. They'd finally gained admittance but old habits were hard to break. Blame Francis Ford Coppola if you like but, let's face it, faery godmother had a better ring to it than faery godfather.

For his part, Rupert appeared unbothered by the terminology. 'Technically I am. Around here we stick to godmother though. It makes it simpler. I don't actually go out in the field much these days. I spend most of my time setting assignments.' He patted my arm. 'I'll make sure you get some good ones. You'll find it hard here to begin with but it's very rewarding. The others will come around soon enough.'

Despite his current friendly attitude towards me, I didn't trust Rupert even a tiny bit. Not yet. Not after the encounter downstairs. All the same, I smiled serenely. 'I know.' I pointed off towards HR. 'I'd better go. Thanks for your help.'

He swept into a mock bow. 'You're welcome.'

I wended my way around various pieces of office furniture, feeling Rupert's eyes on my back the entire time. I straightened my posture. A ramrod straight back might make walking somewhat more complicated but I knew I had to project confidence.

'You can do this, Saffron,' I muttered under my breath as the HR door opened. 'You are more than capable.'

The Devil's Advocate appeared in the doorway and raised an eyebrow in my direction. 'Talking to yourself already, Ms Sawyer?'

'Pep talk,' I told him.

'I suppose it's better than hysteria.'

'It is.' I nodded vigorously. 'You should try it.' I deepened my voice in an effort to mimic his. 'All you have to do, Devil's Advocate, is terrify everyone into the entire building. Make their knees knock and their lips tremble. Then whip them into shape.' I gave him an encouraging smile and returned my voice to normal. 'Like that.'

He leaned towards me. 'I left my whip at home. I usually find that a well written report is more than enough to suffice.'

I couldn't stop myself from grinning. The man had more of a sense of humour than I'd ever heard him be credited with. 'I've always been a fan of cutting comments myself.'

A strange expression crossed his face. 'Then,' he said, 'you'll fit right in here.' He looked me up and down. 'I like your blouse,' he said. 'The bright colour suits you. Is it yellow because of your name?'

'No.' Truthfully, I'd only worn yellow because I knew it would make me stand out. I wanted to be both noticed and remembered and every other faery godmother I'd ever met only wore muted, dull colours. 'This is dandelion yellow, not saffron yellow. And dandelions are my favourite flower.'

The Devil's Advocate looked skeptical. 'Dandelions are weeds.'

'They're the colour of sunshine. They'll grow in the toughest of soils and they can incredibly difficult to get rid of. Even when you think you've eradicated them, dandelions will still come back. They don't like to be beaten.'

'Hmm.' He rubbed his chin. 'They're edible as well, right?'

I grinned and waggled my eyebrows. 'Indeed. And they're very, very tasty.'

'I'll take your word for that,' he murmured, as the Director strode into view and a tremor of excitement ran through me at the sight of the ultimate faery godmother herself. He nodded towards her and walked off in her direction. She glanced at me. A sweet, indulgent smile lit her face then she focused on the Devil's Advocate.

I watched the pair of them as they walked off and thought about what the Devil's Advocate had said about fitting in here because I liked cutting comments. What was that supposed to mean? He'd changed the subject quickly enough and I could hardly run after him and ask him to clarify himself. Not unless I wanted to make myself look completely crazy in front of the Director anyway. I might have already made myself look nuts as it was by flirting slightly with the Devil's Advocate. Tasty dandelions? I sucked on my bottom lip. As if. I shrugged – anyway it didn't matter. Nothing would dent my enthusiasm. Not him. Not my daft runaway mouth. Not even HR.

CHAPTER FOUR

The atmosphere in the Human Resources office was remarkably subdued. The dope faeries' HR office was located in a temporary cabin in one of those building sites where no work was ever completed but which was permanently cordoned off. Despite its desolate air from the outside, once you were in, the team there always did their best to make you feel comfortable. Their fruit scones were legendary. By contrast, this HR office looked spick, span and stylish – and gave off the sort of vibe that could create severe depression in even the healthiest faery. Rupert's comment about its soul sucking nature had been spot on.

I stood at the front, hoping that sooner or later someone would approach me. When no-one did, I shrugged to myself and made a beeline for the closest desk, occupied by a tired looking man whose skin didn't seem to have seen the sun for at least the last decade.

'No,' he said, without looking up. 'I haven't heard anything new on any of the disappearances.'

I blinked. 'Disappearances?'

He finally raised his head. Something indefinable flickered in his eyes. 'You're the new one.'

'I am.' I smiled prettily. 'Bright-eyed, bushy tailed and ready to work.'

He snorted. Then he seemed to think better of it and looked around in case any one else other than me had heard his derision. 'You need to go and see Angela,' he told me. 'She's got all the paperwork you need to fill out. Once you've done all that, come back to me and I'll sign you off. Then you'll get your first list of assignments from Adeline.'

'Where will I find Angela?' I inquired.

He gazed me as if I had marshmallow for brains. 'Third desk on the right.'

'Thanks.' I turned to go. A moment later, however, I glanced back. 'Who's been disappearing?'

The man didn't answer. In fact, he was intent on pretending he hadn't heard me. My eyes narrowed slightly. That was okay though. I'd find out what was really going on by other means.

Angela was clearly the sort of faery who couldn't let a good – or bad – ornament pass her by. When I located her desk, I could barely see her behind her collection of fripperies. There was a snow globe of Disney's Cinderella castle, which I supposed was some sort of ironic homage given where Angela actually worked; an impressive collection of fuzzy gonks with googly eyes that followed me around, even when I attempted to shift out of their gaze; several tiny glass figurines, and at least three Lucky Cats of varying sizes and colours. Angela herself was slumped over a sheet of paper, a stub of a pencil in her mouth.

'No,' she muttered. 'No. Yes.' She retrieved the pencil, ignoring the trail of saliva which dangled from its tip, and made a small mark. 'No. No. No. Maybe.'

'Hi. I'm Saffron!'

She peered up through her half moon glasses. 'Ah, yes.' She spoke with a vaguely Irish lilt. 'We've been expecting you.' She scrunched up her face and leaned to one side, opening up a drawer and heaving out a vast tome. It landed on her desk with a thud, causing the glass figures to judder in response. I squinted at the title. *Rules and Regulations for Faery Godmothers and Fathers. Edition 119.* It was a good five inches thick.

'You need to read that by the end of the week,' she said, her tone implying that if I didn't then hellfire and brimstone would await me.

'I love reading!' I blurted out. My enthusiasm was still getting the better of me.

Angela stared at me. 'Great,' she said flatly. She pushed another piece of paper in my direction. This is your renumeration package. You will be paid monthly. There may be a raise once your probationary period is over but that will depend upon your performance.'

I looked at the figure. No, I wasn't here for the money but this was less than half of what I earned as a dope faery. It was also below the normal starting salary for a faery godmother. For *any* faery godmother. I had rent. And bills. I swallowed. 'And how long is the probationary period?' I asked.

'That is at our discretion.' She gave me a steely eyed glare. 'If it's a problem, I'm sure your previous employer will be happy to have you back.'

I thought about the empty desks out in the main office space. And the other HR worker's comment about disappearances. Not to mention the Devil's Advocate. Did I dare? I'd probably work here for free if it came down to it. I suspected, however, that this was as much of a test about my future here as the interview had been.

'Yeah,' I said slowly. 'I think you're right. They will be happy to have me back.' I lifted up my chin. 'Thank the Director for the opportunity. I'm sorry that it didn't work out. And if you happen to see the Devil's Advocate again, do tell him that I'll be more than happy to chat to him some more about his written reports.' I nodded at Angela and started to move away.

My heart was hammering against my chest and my brain was screaming at me. What had I done? I was a bloody fool. I ...

'Very well, Ms Sawyer,' Angela called out. 'We can perhaps negotiate your salary somewhat.'

I breathed out. Then I straightened my shoulders and returned.

'I don't want to negotiate,' I said, feeling somewhat emboldened. I grabbed a pen from Angela's desk, bent over and scribbled out the derisory number on the original salary offer before writing down my own version. 'That's what I was earning as a dope faery less ten per cent because of my lack of faery godmother specific skills.' I shrugged, pretending I didn't care either way. 'Either give me that or I walk.' I paused deliberately. 'If you require time to discuss it with the Director, I'm willing to wait.'

Fortunately for me, Angela knew when she was beaten. Her jaw tightened. 'That won't be necessary,' she muttered. She signed at the bottom of the paper and passed it to me to do the same. So this had been a shake down then. Angela had no doubt reckoned that she could persuade me to take whatever I was given, regardless of whether the Director sanctioned it or not. If I'd been greeted with a friendlier atmosphere over the last hour or two, I might have accepted it. I allowed myself a congratulatory smile for not being a complete pushover. Then I signed on the dotted line.

'You still have to read the manual,' Angela told me with a sniff.

I picked it up off her desk. It weighed a ton. 'No problem.' I gave her a nod. 'Like I said, I enjoy reading.' I hefted it under my arm before reaching my free hand down to lightly caress the head of one of the gonks. Angela bristled visibly. 'Cute.' I met her eyes. 'Very cute.' I smiled again. 'Thanks for all your help. I'll be sure to mention what a great asset you are when I speak to Adeline again later.'

Angela forced her own mouth to curve upwards. 'How nice of you.'

I stayed where I was.

'Is there something else?' she asked, her voice sugar sweet.

'Now you mention it, there is. I believe I have some equipment to collect as well.'

Angela twitched. 'Go down the hall to your right. Billy will sort you out.'

'Fabulous.' I still didn't move.

She sighed. 'Go on. What else?'

'There should also be some training,' I prompted.

This time, Angela's smile was genuine. 'Oh yes. Once you've finished up with Billy, get him to direct you to the conference room. I'll make sure everything you need is ready and meet you there.' She picked up the snow globe and shook it. 'Training.' She smiled again. 'Your wish is my command, Ms Sawyer.'

Uh oh. All of a sudden, I had a very bad feeling about this.

'You have to sign for everything you take,' Billy said. 'If you lose anything, or it gets damaged, you have to replace it.'

I bobbed my head. 'Fine. No problem.'

He handed me a pile of pink material. I stared down at it, then at him, then back at the material again. 'What's this?'

'Your uniform. What else would it be?'

I shook the material out and gave it a dubious frown. I'd seen the odd faery godmother in action before. I'd never seen any of them wearing this shite. 'I'm afraid I'm still unclear as to what it actually is.'

Billy took it from me. 'I'll show you.' He snapped his wrists and, with a deft flourish, swung the material round him. This was obviously not his first time.

'Oh, it's a cloak! Now I see.'

He pulled up the hood and tied the ribbon at the neck into a perfect bow. 'It needs to be freshly laundered every day. It's best if you use a good fabric conditioner too.'

'Pink is definitely your colour, Billy,' I told him.

His cheeks went the same shade as the cloak. 'I helped to choose it. It's one of the new initiatives. You know, so that all the humans believe you're a faery godmother.' He lowered his voice and leaned towards me. 'There are a lot of sceptics out there.'

'Mmm.' I gave him a serious nod. 'I can see how the cloak will help then.'

He picked the hem up and thrust it in my face. 'It has sparkly bits. See?'

'I do see. Thank you for the demonstration.'

'It's waterproof,' he said earnestly. 'And fireproof.'

It didn't matter what proof it was. I was still going to look like a pink blancmange. I couldn't complain about it, however. Dope faeries tended to wear dirty jeans and holey t-shirts with the names of various grunge bands written across the front. They didn't have real uniforms. Maybe the pink monstrosity would make me feel like I belonged here, especially if all the others wore them when they were out on the streets.

'Everyone wears these?' I asked, wanting to double check that this wasn't some sort of hazing ritual.

Billy's eyes went wide. 'Oh yes. Miss Adeline said every godmother has to wear their pink cloak whenever they are with clients. The godfathers have to wear blue, of course.'

I grimaced. 'Of course.'

He clocked my expression. 'If you don't identify as male or female,' he said, his eyes dropping momentarily to my breasts in a manner which was less lascivious and more cursory, as if he had to double check my gender, 'then you wear yellow. And we have to call you a godperson. There was an email about it,' he added. 'Equality in the workplace is important.'

Mmmhmm. There was nothing like forcing people into different colours to make them feel equal.

'Rule number one,' Billy told me, 'the boss is always right. Rule number two, when the boss is wrong, see rule number one.'

I gave him a distracted nod. It stood to reason that the faery godmothers were old-fashioned. It was the longest standing faery job role, after all. It was steeped in tradition. And at least they were trying to join in with the times. 'I was told that everyone pretty much used godmother, not matter what gender they identify with.'

Melodramatic alarm flitted across his face. 'But they shouldn't!' he said in a shrill voice. 'They really shouldn't! It was in the email!'

I decided that I was beginning to understand him. 'Rules are rules. I am a faery godmother and I will wear pink.'

He gave me a long look. 'Well,' he said finally, 'that's okay then.' He undid the bow at this neck and handed the cloak back to me. I made a vague attempt at folding it up into a neat square again before deciding to drape it over my arm instead. Folding had never been my forte.

Billy turned away towards a battered steel cupboard, opening it up and pulling out a clunky looking laptop covered in brightly coloured stickers, no doubt from a previous owner. 'The password is 'faeriesdoitbetter',' he said. 'No spaces or capital letters. You should change it first thing. You're already configured for email and stuff. If you have any problems with it, contact IT support.'

'Got it.'

He tapped the laptop sternly. 'Check the calendar daily. You don't want to miss any meetings. Sometimes they're set without much notice and you'll get into trouble if you're late.'

There was something about the way he said that which gave me pause. 'How many meetings are there usually?'

Billy's face darkened. 'Lots. Lots and lots and lots.'

I shrugged to myself. I wasn't a fan of meetings. Who was? But this was the Office of Faery Godmothers. Meetings were a necessary evil. 'Is that everything?' I asked.

For the very first time, Billy smiled. It transformed his face, making him look both younger and more relaxed. He held up his index finger and shook his whole body. To begin with, I wondered if he was having some sort of mild seizure. Then I realised it was pure giddy delight. 'There's one more thing,' he said. He waggled his eyebrows. 'You know what it is.'

I placed my palms together as if in prayer. I didn't want to get my hopes up unnecessarily but I was beginning to tremble myself. 'Is it...' I bit my lip, almost unwilling to say the word out loud, 'Is it my new wand?'

He cocked his finger and thumb towards me. 'You betcha.'

CHAPTER FIVE

I turned the wand over and over in my hands. It was far sparklier than the one I'd had in my previous job. When I swished it through the air there was also a pleasing whooshing sound. Wands like this one enhanced our natural skills and made it possible for us to fulfill our tasks properly. Not to mention that, given the nature of this particular job, using it added a certain flourish which helped clients believe that we were all above board. Or so I'd been told anyway. Naturally, it had come with all sorts of dire warnings about misuse and Billy had made sure that I signed in triplicate that I understood what would befall me if I were to lose it or damage it. It was a rather plain looking thing, made of dull, unvarnished wood. I made a mental note to customize it, possibly with a sparkly tassel, as soon as possible. I wouldn't go too over the top, however. I wanted everyone to know I meant serious business.

Resisting the temptation to start waving it around like a complete numpty, in case anyone was watching me through the glass walls which separated the conference room along two sides from the rest of the office, I leaned back in my chair and gazed at the various posters which adorned the brick wall to my left.

If You Are Not Willing To Learn, No-one Can Help You. A photo of a cute kitten was super imposed beneath the words but, rather unfortunately, the comic sans font somewhat distracted from the message.

You Are Not Here To Be Average. Hmmm. I scratched my head. Someone had to be average though. Someone had to be below average. Otherwise average didn't exist.

Look In The Mirror – That's Your Competition. Not going by the welcome I'd had from the other faery godmothers. I was already beginning to sense that this place was as cut-throat as you could get.

Craning my neck, I read the other posters dotted along the wall before allowing myself a small snort of disappointment. For some reason, I'd expected more from this office than trite phrases. Perhaps Billy had pinned them up when no-one was looking and leaving them in place was simply the path of least resistance. I stared at the smiling, heavily Photo-shopped picture of a young beaming faery holding up her wand and tried to wheel my chair out of her fixed line of sight. Alas, I could swear her eyes were following me around the room.

'What are you doing?'

I jumped. Angela was standing in the doorway and frowning at me. Someone should put a bell around her damn neck.

'Uh, I was just ...'

'Those chairs aren't toys. They're expensive, ergonomically designed pieces of architecture. Not racing machines.'

Ah. No doubt at some point that was indeed what they had been used for. I had sudden visions of various faeries scooting themselves from one end of the office to the other. My money was on Rupert as the instigator. He had that sort of air about him.

'I was moving round so I could see the posters more clearly,' I said, lying through my teeth.

Angela gave me a suspicious look. 'I put those up. It's important to keep up morale in order to boost productivity. There's been a three percent increase in workflow since those posters were put on display.'

'I'm not surprised.' I grinned enthusiastically. 'They're fabulous.'

Slightly mollified, her shoulders dropped a fraction. 'I know,' she sniffed. There was a faint blush to her cheeks. My compliment had pleased her far more than she was letting on. I suddenly felt a wave of sympathy for her. Given the egos of the other godmothers I'd met so far, her job couldn't be easy. Then I frowned to myself. If I was going to fit in, I needed an ego to match to theirs. 'I'm an excellent judge,' I told her, in an overly loud and imperious tone. 'If I say they are fabulous, then they truly are.'

Angela yanked her proud gaze away from the dubious artwork, looking at me as if was making fun of her. 'Indeed,' she sniffed. She set her jaw and turned away, seemingly deciding that further chitchat with me was pointless. Reaching for a small remote control which had been sitting forlornly in the middle of the table, she clicked it and there was a loud rumbling sound. From the ceiling, a projector screen began to unfurl. I was impressed. The most the dope faeries had was a grubby whiteboard and a television set so old that it had to be wheeled in on a trolley rather than affixed to the wall.

'Cool,' I said, as the screen came to a juddering halt about halfway down.

A spasm of annoyance crossed Angela's face. She stalked over and took hold of the corner, yanking it down the rest of the way. I kept my expression as straight as possible. So much for technology then.

'There are three training videos which you are required to watch,' she said. 'Each one has been made at great expense and with excellent production values. You will find the information contained within them very useful.' She smirked. 'Make sure you take notes.'

It was already clear from earlier that the videos were going to be interminable. I sat up a bit straighter in my chair. No matter how dull they were, I told myself, I would sit up straight, keep my eyes open and pay rapt attention. Anything less and I knew it would picked up. I could cope with a little boredom in exchange for the wonders this job would bring. It would be a small price to pay.

Angela clicked on the remote again and the projector behind me began to whirr. Flickering images appeared on the screen, coalescing into the familiar image of the Director. As Angela walked out, without saying so much as another word, I drew in a breath and prepared myself. I was actually hoping I might learn something useful. You never knew.

'Welcome to the Office for Faery Godmothers,' the Director intoned from the screen. 'You are entering an institution which is not only steeped in tradition and has an esteemed reputation amongst faeries all around the world, but also one which has the highest possible standards. To be a faery godmother is to be a part of excellence. We only accept faeries of the highest possible quality. We do not only require intelligence. To be a successful faery godmother, you require wits, the ability to think on your feet and...' Her image froze, her mouth hanging open in mid-sentence.

I stayed where I was for a moment or two but the video didn't re-start. I got up and moved round the table, reaching for the remote control. Then I jabbed the play button.

'Welcome to the Office for Faery Godmothers. You are entering an institution which is not only steeped in tradition and has an esteemed repu...'

It froze again. Fuck a puck. I pressed the play button once more. This time, however, the image of the Director didn't flicker. I pressed another button. Then another. Nothing happened. The video was kaput.

I glanced around. Out in the main office, everyone seemed to be busy, with their heads down over their computers. It didn't look like I'd get any help from out there. I'd have to go and find Angela and get her help again. It didn't take a genius to know that she'd automatically blame me for the video's failure. I didn't think I had much choice, however.

Sighing heavily, I pushed back my chair and stood up, walking to the conference room and pushing it open. I paused for a moment, watching the office. This was the perfect vantage point to see everything and everyone. Alicia sashayed her way from one end of the room to the other, pausing to lower her head and murmur something to Figgy along the way. Delilah was still at her desk, her lips moving as she spoke to herself. Adeline was tapping a clipboard and looking serious, and various others were doing everything they could to avoid eye contact with her. There was no sign of the Director or the Devil's Advocate but there was still a definite tension in the air which indicated that they remained in the building. I chewed on my lip and eyed the various empty desks once again. Was it faery godmothers who'd been disappearing? Was that why the Devil's Advocate was about to perform an audit? I nibbled on my bottom lip and shrugged to myself. I supposed I'd find out what was going on sooner or later.

I stepped out of the conference room, just as the lift pinged and a delivery faery wearing lurid cycling shorts which were tighter than tight and left very little to the imagination, walked out. He spotted me watching him and raised a hand.

'I'm looking for the Director,' he said. He waved a small brown box in my direction. 'I have to give this to her.'

I tried not to grin too widely. Here was someone who immediately accepted that I was a faery godmother like everyone else. He wasn't questioning my presence and he expected that I would know where the Director happened to be. I could feel my chest puffing up with pride.

'I can pass it to her,' I said, as if the Director and I were very close and spent lots of time together rather than the reality which was that she'd given me a brisk good morning on the day I'd arrived for my interview and that had been that.

The faery's mouth down-turned. 'I'm supposed to get her to sign for it personally.' He checked his watch. Clearly he was on a tight schedule.

'I think she's in an important meeting,' I said, thinking of the Devil's Advocate. I nodded at the parcel. 'I'll place it directly into her own hands,' I promised.

Indecision warred across his face but, in the end, my earnestness convinced him. He handed me the package. 'Thanks.'

'No problem. I'm a faery godmother,' I said importantly. 'Nothing is not a problem.' My brow creased. Did that make any sense? 'I mean nothing is a problem.' Somehow that didn't make any sense either. Damn it. Faery godmothers used correct grammar at all times, I told myself. So far I merely babbled.

The delivery faery gazed at me implacably. 'Yeah,' he said. 'Okay then.' He turned on his heel and stepped back into the lift.

I sighed and promised myself I'd do better next time. Then I looked at the box. It wasn't particularly heavy. Neither was it particularly remarkable. Whatever it was, I hoped it was important enough to warrant me interrupting the Director's busy day to give it to her. It was fortuitous that the delivery faery had appeared at that moment. It would give me the perfect chance to introduce myself properly to the Director. What would I say to her? I ran through various possibilities in my head. I'd aim for polite but not obsequious. Confident but not bolshy. Intelligent but not geeky.

I was pondering the merits of using a casual 'hello' over a more formal 'good morning' when I heard the murmur of voices and looked up to see the Director walk out of a room with the Devil's Advocate by her side. I jerked forward. This was my chance. Unfortunately, however, as I began to move, my toe caught on the edge of an expensive rug, laid out across the floor. The upper half of my body continued to propel forward while my legs were yanked back. I threw my arms out in a desperate bid to steady myself, flailing them around in order to keep my balance. The box flew out of my hands and went sailing across the room just as I managed to grab hold of the corner of the nearest desk and steady myself. If it weren't for the lightning speed reactions of the Devil's Advocate, thrusting his arm out in time to block it, the box would have hit the Director smack bang in the centre of her forehead. It tumbled to the ground while I straightened up and wished that the same ground would open up and swallow me whole. Every single head in the office swiveled towards me.

'I ... uh ... I ...' I stammered.

Alicia, who'd appraised the situation with astonishing speed, sprang towards the Director. 'I can't believe she almost hit you in the face with that thing! You could have broken your nose! It's awful, simply awful. I'll retrieve it for you straightaway.' She knelt down to pick the box up. She never got that far, however. Her fingers hadn't even touched it when her eyes widened and she began to scream. This time she wasn't putting on a show. Her inarticulate cry was filled with nothing but pure terror.

CHAPTER SIX

Five of us were in the Director's office. Despite the sun streaming in through the large windows, and the warm tones of the well appointed furniture which I reckoned Louis XIV would have been proud to call his own, a deep chill had settled into my bones. Alicia had wrapped her arms around herself and was still visibly trembling. I supposed I should be glad that there existed something in the world which unsettled her. The trouble was that it deeply unsettled me too.

'Go through it again,' the Devil's Advocate said, his expression set into harsh lines. 'What actually happened?'

I swallowed, wishing my mouth weren't quite so dry. 'I was in the conference room. I stepped out to find someone to help me with the training video because it had frozen. A delivery faery came out of the lift at the same time.'

'How do you know he was a delivery faery?' the Director asked, her dark eyes fixed on mine. Her voice remained pleasant and her expression was benign. There was nothing benign about this situation, however.

It was a good question. I licked my lips. 'I assumed he was.

He was definitely a faery and he was wearing cycling shorts. I didn't see any ID but he seemed to know what he was doing.'

Next to me, Mrs Jardine coughed uncomfortably. 'He showed me his ID downstairs. His name was Joe.'

'Surname?' the Director barked.

She twitched. 'He signed it in the book but it's illegible.' She held up the same book which I'd seen Alicia and the others use. There was a thumbprint next to the name Joe, followed by what could only be described as a squiggle.

'You didn't take his full name?'

Mrs Jardine shook her head. She had the grace to look shame-faced. 'I did not.'

'Have you seen him before? Has he made other deliveries here in the past?'

'A few times.'

A muscle jerked in the Devil's Advocate's cheek. 'I will contact the delivery faeries and find out what else they can tell us about him. Assuming he's genuine and actually does work for them, then perhaps he can enlighten us more on where the … box came from.'

We all stared down at the box in question. It still looked innocuous enough on the outside but the contents were clearly anything but. Nestled in some carefully arranged tissue paper was a single bloody ear. It was only just starting to shrivel up at the edges, indicating that it had been severed from its owner in the very recent past. A single pearl drop earring hung from the lifeless lobe.

'Do you know who it belongs to?' the Devil's Advocate asked quietly.

Alicia raised her head. 'Lydia,' she whispered, her answer barely audible.

The Director pressed her fingertips against her temples. 'Lydia DuChamps,' she said.

'She disappeared last month?' he probed.

She nodded. 'Yes.'

I stared from her to him and back again. 'She was a faery godmother?' I asked.

'She *is* a faery godmother,' the Director snapped.

I recoiled slightly at the tone of her voice even though I instinctively knew it was the stress of the situation rather than my word choice which had caused it. Almost immediately, the Director also seemed to regret it and softened her expression towards me once again. I couldn't help thinking that she was on a mission to play nice towards me. Something about it didn't sit quite right. There more important things to worry about anyway. At the same time as the Director relaxed, the Devil's Advocate gave me a long look. 'You don't know,' he said. 'You haven't been told what's going on here.' It wasn't a question.

'You may go now, Saffron,' the Director said.

I started. 'But ...'

'You've had a trying time. Get yourself a cup of tea and have a break.' She paused. 'Now.'

If this weren't my first day, I'd have stood my ground and demanded to know what was happening and who Lydia DuChamp really was. All this was too new and too baffling to cope with right now, however. Considering I would now be forever synonymous in the Director's mind with throwing a severed ear at her face, I decided that I should do as I told. I was going to find out what was going on here, however. I already knew who to ask as well. I inclined my head just once like the good girl I was attempting to present myself to be and walked out. As soon as the door was closed I could hear the raised voices behind me, although the words themselves were too indistinct to properly make out. Rather than lingering and trying to eavesdrop, I walked slowly back to my desk, aware that every single eye was watching my every step.

Despite her earlier unfriendliness, I'd only just sat myself down on my broken chair when Delilah began. That was what I'd been banking on.

'Oh. My. God.' Her eyes were saucer wide. 'That was an actual ear. Did it smell? Was there blood on it?' She looked me up and down, her expression suggesting that she was half expecting to see blood splatters.

'There was a bit of blood,' I admitted. I had to give her something in order to get her to talk. 'But I didn't actually touch the thing.'

The gleam of morbid delight in her expression made me feel nauseous all over again. 'Do you know who it belonged to?' she asked, leaning in towards me.

I followed her lead and moved closer to her. My chair squeaked alarmingly as I wheeled it the short distance over but it held steady. My arse didn't end up on the floor anyway, which I'd count as a win. 'They said it was someone called Lydia.'

'No!'

'Yes.' I nodded.

'Was the ear, you know, fresh?'

'I think so.' I blinked at her in earnest confusion. 'Lydia disappeared, didn't she? Last month?'

Delilah glanced round. There were still several people watching me but Delilah's glare was enough to make them drop their heads and return to their work. 'We weren't supposed to talk about it with you. The notice came down from on high. But,' she shrugged as if it were now out of her hands, 'you obviously already know about it.'

'Mmmm.'

'It's terribly shocking.'

I bobbed my head in agreement. 'Horrifying. Especially because she's not been the only one.'

'I know, right?' Delilah clasped her hands tightly together in her lap. 'Five faery godmothers in three months. And nobody knows where they've gone.'

Five? I swallowed down my shock. It was a miracle that the entire faery world wasn't abuzz with that news. 'Do you know much about what happened?'

She was clearly delighted to have someone new to discuss it with. 'Well,' she whispered, 'we all know they were out on jobs when they went missing. The clients have been investigated and there's nothing to suggest they were involved. The whole office has been on high alert though and there have been a lot of … questions. They seem to think that someone in the office is responsible for the disappearances.' She rolled her eyes at the suggestion but there was a still a dubious note to her voice. 'There's nothing tying any of the disappearances together as far as anyone can tell. Apart from the fact they all worked out of this office anyway.' She ticked off her fingers. 'Lydia, Alistair, Boris, Edwina and Jane. They weren't friends. They didn't work in the same team. They didn't have the same clients.' She paused for dramatic effect. 'But now they're all missing. You didn't hear this from me but I'm convinced that it's a disgruntled client who's taken them. There will be a ransom note before long, mark my words. I reckon whoever it is who's done this wants their own lifelong link to the faery godmothers. Just imagine what you could do with unlimited wishes. You could become anyone. You could do anything.'

'But clients don't remember us in between visits,' I pointed out. 'They certainly don't remember us once their wishes have been granted. Their memories are all but wiped clean.'

Delilah pursed her lips as if she'd not thought of this. Before she could say anything else, however, the door to the Director's office opened and the Devil's Advocate appeared. He cast a long look in my direction, his face dark. For a brief moment, I thought he was going to walk over towards me.

Instead, however, he turned and headed for the lift. I watched him go. No wonder he'd been brought in to do an audit. Every faery godmother in this place was running scared. And, I thought sourly to myself, no wonder I'd been brought in. It wasn't my excellence as a dope faery that had brought about this new job. It was because the godmothers were short-staffed and barely coping. I'd merely ended up here by default.

As soon as the lift doors had closed in front of the Devil's Advocate and the office was once again free from his brooding presence, Adeline stood up from her desk at the front of the room and stalked towards me. She thrust a piece of paper in front of my face. 'Here,' she said. 'Your first clients.'

I stared at the list of names. So much for that break and a cup of tea then. There were eight full names on the list. I reckoned it would take an experienced faery godmother a fortnight to get through them all and ensure their needs were adequately met.

'We're starting you off slowly,' Adeline told me, 'because you're new. But don't expect to always have it this easy. All the same, don't expect special treatment. These clients must be signed off by the end of week.'

Er, what? 'I've not completed my considerable training yet,' I said, using her own words against her. Hell, I'd not actually started my training yet. Beyond what little I'd managed to glean about how the faery godmothers operated from seeing them around the streets, I had no idea how they went about completing tasks.

'As I'm sure you've heard,' Adeline said briskly, with a side look at Delilah, 'we are no longer running at full capacity. You'll have to learn on the job.' Her eyes were flinty. 'It's the best way. I'm sure you'll pick up all the important details before too long.' Then, before I could say anything or ask a single question, she whirled away, tossing a single reminder over her shoulder. 'And make sure you clean up that sorry excuse for a desk!'

Delilah raised an eyebrow in my direction. Now that we'd shared some real gossip together, she'd warmed up considerably. 'You'll be fine,' she said. 'Besides, all those training videos are so boring your brain would turn to mush watching them.'

I gave her a small smile and wished my insides weren't trembling quite so much. Adeline's remarkably fast turn around on the subject of letting me loose on clients was very strange. Suspiciously so. Not to mention that now I knew why I'd really been posted here, I had even more to prove. And for the first time, I wasn't sure that I'd manage it. I looked down at my client list, and the case numbers next to each name. I had no idea where to begin. Coffee, I decided. I needed something stronger than tea and I did deserve a brief break. Unfortunately vodka was currently out of the question. I nodded to myself. Yes. First of all, I'd have to get myself some coffee.

In a final burst of helpfulness, Delilah pointed me towards the small galley kitchen towards the back of the office. I grabbed myself a large mug with a cartoon drawing of a multi-coloured unicorn on it which might at least raise my spirits and made a cup of instant. The granules smelled cheap and the only milk I could find was that crap powdered stuff. By this point in time, that hardly mattered. As long as it was vaguely hot, contained caffeine and was strong enough to numb my tastebuds, it would do the job. There was a small fridge but it was packed full of labeled Tupperware dishes and various cartons, each one stating categorically that terrible things would happen to anyone who so much as munched on a slice of limp cucumber that didn't belong to them. At least I knew that there was also a staff canteen where I could get food, even if I didn't yet know where it was located. After the ear debacle, I didn't think I could eat anything anyway.

As I wended my way to my desk, Billy reappeared. When he saw me, his expression darkened and he stomped over. 'What are you doing?'

I should have thought that was obvious. I smiled at him and didn't answer. In this scenario whatever response I gave would obviously elicit a minor explosion. It would be better to let him get on with it so I could start work sooner.

'You,' he said, wagging his finger in my face, 'cannot walk around here with a hot drink like that! What happens if you spill it onto someone and they end up with third degree burns?'

Considering the water from the urn was more lukewarm than piping hot, I reckoned the chance of anyone being burnt by the liquid in my unicorn mug was incredibly unlikely. 'It won't happen again,' I said. Of course I was lying.

He gave me a narrow-eyed, suspicious glare.

'Bill,' Rupert drawled, his head appearing from round a nearby partition, 'give the girl a break. It's her first day and it's already been a traumatic one.' He flashed me an open-mouthed grin. 'How are you coping, Saffron? Are you feeling alright?' He stretched his arms behind his head, his tanned biceps bulging as he did so. I suddenly had the distinct feeling that was a practised move designed to show his body off to the best effect. Ah. Okay then.

I fluttered my eyelashes and thought about that time that I'd gone on a snail trail holiday to New York, travelling by plane rather than magical Metafora, and had ended up in the longest queue for customs and immigration in the world. I'd had a dodgy stomach the entire flight over but I hadn't quite realised how bad it was until I was stood in a crowd of people with no toilets on hand and had released what I'd thought was merely a gassy fart. My cheeks flamed red at the memory and Rupert's grin grew. There was nothing quite like having the new girl blush in front of you on her first day to make you feel good about yourself. I might not trust him but that didn't mean I wasn't beneath manipulating the faery dust out of him.

'I'm doing fine,' I mumbled. 'Thanks.'

Billy looked disgusted. That was okay; I'd deal with him later. I ducked my head down and made the remainder of the journey to my dusty corner. Given how many clients I had to see before Friday, I'd have to put my concerns about my new work colleagues, the strange disappearances, and the severed ear, away for now. I placed my mug onto the one clear spot on my desk and hefted the cobweb strewn filing boxes into a haphazard pile underneath. I strongly suspected that if I simply threw them out without checking the contents, I'd then be held responsible for losing several vital pieces of paper. I'd go through them later before I consigned them to the dump. I sneezed as motes of dust swirled round me in the air and gave Delilah a brief apology. She waved at me as if were no matter but I could tell from the look in her eye that she was none too impressed. I paid her no more attention and instead wheeled my broken chair to one of the empty desks, swapping it for the one that already sat there. Whether it belonged to poor Lydia, Alistair, Boris, Edwina or Jane, neither of them would be needing it any time soon. My new chair's wheels were wonky, making it difficult to steer back to my desk. It was still an improvement on the other one though. I battled with it, managing to drag it to my little cubicle with some effort. I ignored the side glances of spitting hatred which I received for my actions, and settled myself down. Whatever. No matter what else was going on, I was still going to be the most awesome faery godmother the world had ever seen.

CHAPTER SEVEN

There was little to compare between my new clients. They each lived in different parts of the country and each were different ages, different genders and had different professions. I supposed it would be good to start with such a diverse range. I'd learn more that way.

The first name on my list was Luke Wells, a nineteen year old student reading Philosophy, Politics and Economics at Oxford University. I typed the case number into my laptop, ignoring the continuous whirring sound it made as its fan struggled to work, and scanned the sparse details. There was very little to go by – name, date of birth and basic family circumstances. His parents, Mr and Mrs Wells, lived in London in a small terraced house although Luke himself had actually been born in Oxford. There were no other details about his parents. Not even first names. Luke had no brothers or sisters and there was no indication of a criminal record on his part. Any further information I'd have to research on my own. It was just as well I'd worked with plenty of university students in my time as a dope faery. A number of them had come from prestigious universities, like Oxford. I knew the type. Privately educated, pots of money, and egos to match. This kid, however, was from a working class background. From what I could glean by hacking into the university records, his studies were going well and he was excelling in his tutorials. That could only mean that his problems were social.

'You don't feel like you fit in, do you?' I said to the screen. 'You're surrounded by Ruperts and Alicias and Figgys all of whom have important family names and country estates and the ability to perform dressage. You're feeling left out.' I rubbed my palms together. My first case was one I could get my teeth into. This would be fantastic.

I'd already clocked the silver door with its sparkly M located next to the lift. It was identical to the one the dope faeries used. I drained my cup and stood up. Lunch was fast approaching and my stomach was already beginning to rumble. If I could make contact with Luke before I got myself some food though, I'd prove to everyone watching me that I had a strong work ethic, even if I didn't really know much about the finer aspects of my job.

I grabbed my bag, the ridiculous pink cloak and my wand, before waving to Delilah and heading off, passing Alicia along the way. I hadn't seen her leave the Director's office. If I had, I'd have taken the time to check on her. Despite her earlier unfriendliness, she had been shaken badly by Lydia's ear. In any case, there was no point talking to her now. A crowd of other godmothers, including Figgy, were crowded round her, patting her shoulder and offering murmurs of deep sympathy. The vast majority of my sympathy was with ear-less Lydia if I were being frank. Even I knew better than to say that out loud, however. I doubted that Alicia would welcome my concern anyway. I kept my head down until I reached the Metafora door, when I shifted my bag, straightened my shoulders and pressed down on the door handle. The delicious undercurrent of magic reverberated through my skin.

'Wait!' A thin, reedy voice squeaked behind me. 'If you're going out, you need this!'

I removed my hand from the door handle and turned round. Standing in front of me was the teenager who'd taken my photo earlier. He was thrusting out a lanyard in my direction. 'You have to take this if you're going out. If you don't have it, the Metafora won't work.'

Well, that was going to be annoying. I cursed to myself before smoothing my features over. It wasn't the work experience kid's fault that the faery godmothers stuck to such rigid rules. 'Thank you for this,' I said. 'I appreciate that you did it so quickly.'

He looked startled. 'You're welcome.' He backed away and all but ran off in the opposite direction. I wondered if it was me in particular who was making him nervous or the Metafora room itself. Then I glanced down at the photo on my new ID and understood what the problem was. My eyes were half closed, making me look like I was on drugs, and my hair appeared to have escaped from the tight bun I'd drawn it into this morning. Curls were springing out in all directions. It looked less like I'd been pulled through a hedge backwards and more like I'd taken styling tips from Albert Einstein before being struck by lightning, hauled through a hurricane and then pulled through the hedge. To add insult to injury, my name underneath the photo was spelt Savlon. I grimaced and looked up but the kid had sensibly vanished. It didn't look as if I'd be getting a second ID card any time soon.

Sighing, I yanked out my hair clips and threw them into the nearest bin before shaking my hair out. If I looked a mess then I might as well own it and go the whole hog. Out of the corner of my eye, I spotted two other faery godmothers smirking at me. I did the only thing I could do and smirked back. And then, finally, I entered the Metafora room.

It was small but perfectly formed. No bigger than the lift next door, the white marble walls sparkled, light bouncing off them despite the lack of windows. I carefully stepped forward until my toes were touching the tiny X marking the floor. I fumbled with my cloak, eventually managing to swing it round my shoulders so that it at least looked vaguely cloak like, and tied the ribbon at my neck. I tugged at it so it didn't dig too much into the bare skin around my neck. It felt incredibly cumbersome and heavy. I wrinkled my nose. I supposed I'd get used to it sooner or later. At least I looked the part of faery godmother if nothing else. I adjusted my stance, then I pulled back my shoulders and recited the case number in a clear voice before closing my eyes. There was a familiar faint whoosh. A moment later, I found myself standing in front of a plain wooden door.

I glanced around. Stacks of shelves were behind me, each one crammed full of books. A library then. I nodded to myself. So far so expected. Luke Wells was no doubt in the study carrel in front of me, poring over complicated texts with a pen in his mouth and ink staining his fingers. I smiled to myself. This was it; this was what I'd dreamed of for all these years. I was about to grant him his wish and change his life for the better.

I rapped sharply on the door and entered, without waiting to be admitted. The client in question wasn't frowning over a book or taking copious notes, however. He was slumped across the desk, his arm covering his eyes, and a gentle snore was emitting from his nose. There was also the definite reek of stale alcohol. My brow furrowed. Perhaps the carrel's previous occupant had enjoyed a heavy night on the town. Luke Wells – *my* Luke Wells – would only have been up all night to study. I looked around. There were no books in evidence. All I could see were some scraps of paper with scrawled doodles on them. I peered at one of them. Actually, instead of the dick scribble I'd been expecting, it was an elaborate design of some sort of insignia. Maybe Luke here was a frustrated artist.

I cleared my throat. 'Hello!'

The only response I received was another snore. I drew out my wand and poked his shoulder.

Luke let out an unappealing nasal harrumph and groaned. I poked him again. This time, he started, throwing himself backwards in the process and almost knocking me off my feet.

'Who the fuck are you? This carrel is booked out for the morning. Go find your own corner.'

I must have interrupted a very good snooze. 'I'm here for you, Luke,' I said. 'I'm in the right place.'

He ran a hand through mussed brown hair and squinted. 'I don't know you.' He hesitated. 'Do I?' He looked me up and down. 'Did we shag last weekend after the Byers' party? Darling, as fun as that was, if you're looking for a re-run, then you're going to be disappointed. I make a point of never sleeping with the same person twice.' He peered into my face. 'I can't actually believe I slept you with once to be honest. You're a bit older than my usual.'

I blinked. This was far from what I'd expected. 'You're mistaking me for someone else,' I said stiffly.

'Then who are you?' He reached and touched my pink cloak. 'Is this some sort of prank?' He glanced round at the bare walls. 'Am I being filmed right now?'

'I can assure you that isn't the case.' I raised my chin. 'I am Saffron,' I said importantly. 'I'm your faery godmother.'

Luke stared at me for one long moment. Then he burst out laughing. 'Yeah, alright. And I'm Cinderella.' He leaned into my face, exhaling a noxious cloud of bad breath as he did so. 'Fuck off now. I've got important sleep to catch up on.'

I stayed where I was. Okay, perhaps he wasn't quite the righteously deserving client I'd been expecting but I could adapt. I'd dealt with plenty worse than him. I'd been a damned dope faery after all. 'I understand it's hard for you to believe,' I said softly. 'But it's true. I'm your faery godmother and I'm here to make all your dreams come true.' I paused. 'Well, one dream anyway. I don't have time for all of them.' I waved my wand around to prove the veracity of my words.

Luke rocked back on his heels. 'Right,' he said. 'I can see why holding a stick and wearing a pink sheet would make you think you look magical. What you don't realise is that you look like a prized fool. Whatever game you're playing or whatever you're selling, I'm not interested.' He nodded behind me. 'There's the door.' He turned round, heaved himself into his chair and slumped down over the desk once again.

I chewed on my bottom lip. Why would he believe me? He lived in a normal world where magic didn't exist. I'd given him no cause to think that I was telling the truth. This had never been an issue with my previous clients. Their drug filled heads had rarely required me to introduce myself. This was a whole new ball game for me. No doubt one of the training videos which I hadn't managed to see had covered this eventuality. Perhaps it was also in the heavy manual which I'd not yet read. It was too late now though. I'd simply have to wing it.

I thought about it for a second and then waved my wand. Almost instantly, the smell of bacon overtook the reek of old alcohol. Luke raised his head once again and stared at the bacon roll now sitting on the desk.

'Where did that come from?' he asked suspiciously.

'I conjured it from thin air,' I told him. 'It'll help with your hangover.' I took a step towards him. 'I need you to concentrate, Luke. You don't want to mess up your one and only chance with me. You only get one faery godmother wish. A clear head will help.'

He was still staring at the roll. I wasn't sure he'd heard anything I'd said. 'You brought that in with you,' he said. 'You know, food isn't allowed in the library.'

From what little I'd learned about him so far, somehow I didn't think that was a rule he particularly cared about. 'I didn't bring it in with me,' I said cheerfully. 'I magicked it up. If I'd come in that door with it, you'd have smelled it before now.'

He swiveled round in his chair and gave me another long look. His eyes were incredibly red-rimmed. 'I'd rather have a coffee,' he said.

I waved my wand again. There, right next to the bacon roll, was now a large cup of Brazil's finest. I even included a sachet of brown sugar.

'There,' I said, satisfied. 'Drink up. I'd like to get this out of the way before lunch.'

Luke reached for the cup, sniffing it cautiously before raising it to his mouth. Then he seemed to think better of it and placed it back down again. 'You've poisoned it,' he accused.

I frowned. 'I can assure you that I have not.'

'Listen, lady,' he said. 'I don't know who you are or what you're after but I don't need this shit. Fuck off out of here.'

'Luke,' I began, before deciding that perhaps being more formal would be the way to go. 'Mr Wells, if you just...'

I didn't get the chance to finish. He staggered up to his feet, reached behind me for the door, opening it with one hand and shoving me hand with a hard nudge with the other.

'Wait!' I protested.

The door slammed shut. I gritted my teeth. This was ridiculous. I would go back in there and do whatever it took in order to get him to believe that I really was his faery godmother. I glared at the closed door. Before I could reach for the door handle again, however, my surroundings began to blur and I heard the quiet whoosh indicating I was being transported to the office. Somewhat belatedly it occurred to me that I'd made a fatal error. Clients only received one wish. I'd given Luke Wells the coffee he'd asked for and the magic had decided that his needs had been satisfied. Fuck a puck.

'I'm not finished!' I yelled. A shadow flickered at the edges of my vision and I turned towards it in the vague hope that it was something I could cling on to. I couldn't leave yet; I'd not accomplished anything. Coffee didn't fucking count, whether I'd remember to include sugar or not. Unfortunately for me, however, it was already too late to even see who or what the shadow was. Within mere moments I was back in the shiny brilliance of the Metafora room. My shoulders fell. I'd not had lunch yet and I'd already failed miserably. Great.

CHAPTER
EIGHT

I was too miserable to want to talk to anyone. Through a stumbling process of trial and error, not to mention my sense of smell, which was amazingly still working despite the best efforts of Luke Wells' breath and body odour to send all my olfactory skills into extinction, I located the staff canteen on the floor below the main office. Quite a large number of other faery godmothers were present. Alicia was there, still surrounded by a crowd of well-wishers worried about her state of mind. I clenched my jaw and turned away. Not a single person had inquired after my mental health and I'd been the faery who had actually handled the severed ear box in the first place. But then I was a failure. Why would they care about me? Then I thought about how I had no damn right to complain about anything when five faery godmothers had been abducted and possibly murdered and felt horrifically guilty. I was far too mired in my own misery when far worse things were happening around me.

I caught Angela's eye in the corner, sitting with a few other faces I recognized from the HR office. She watched me for a moment and then bent her head to the person next to her, her lips moving. A second later there was a burst of uproarious laughter and her colleague glanced in my direction with unchecked amusement. I resisted the urge to stick out my tongue at them, feeling more dejected. This was far from the triumphant first day I'd envisaged for myself.

Ignoring the salad bar and tantalizing selection of different breads and cheeses, I instead walked straight up to the rosy cheeked woman standing behind the counter.

'I want a fish finger sandwich,' I declared in a loud voice. 'With salad cream.'

'I'm not sure we have that,' she began, before taking note of my expression. She offered me a sympathetic glance which was somehow worse than the snarky looks from everyone else. 'I'll see what I can rustle up,' she said. 'Take a seat.'

I shuffled over to the nearest empty table and sat down with a heavy thump. What I wanted to do was to lay my head in my arms and have a good cry. I wouldn't give my new co-workers the satisfaction of seeing me like that though. I looked down, picking at a small bubble in the dappled formica. No shiny marble here, I thought sourly.

'Just because the Devil's Advocate has left the building,' a voice said over me, 'doesn't mean you shouldn't maintain good posture. Faery godmothers are supposed to look proud, official and straight-backed at all times. You don't want to have to end up in Occupational Health. It'll count against you if you do.'

I squinted up at Billy. 'It'll count against me if I become sick? How's that fair?'

He gave me a blank look in return. 'What does fair have to do with it?' He began to shuffle away.

'Hang on,' I muttered. 'You can sit here if you like. There's plenty of room. You can tell me more about all the rules.'

Billy sniffed loudly. 'If you insist. I know them all. You'd do well to pay attention to what I say.' He twisted back and took the chair opposite me, its legs groaning as they took his weight. He dropped a bag in front of him and opened it up, pulling out a cellophane wrapped sandwich and a shiny apple. Before he'd even unwrapped the sandwich, I could tell that it was egg mayonnaise.

Bully pointed to a sign on the wall. 'If you've got a problem with what I'm eating,' he said through a mouthful, 'then it's rotten eggs for you.'

I glanced round and read the sign: *Any Complaints About Other Employees' Food Choices Are To Be Withheld.* I raised an eyebrow. 'Your doing, I presume?'

I caught the faintest answering twinkle in his eyes. 'There's nothing wrong with egg mayonnaise,' he said. 'S'good protein.'

I nodded. I liked a good egg sandwich myself. 'Indeed.'

The dinner lady appeared at my shoulder, laying a plate in front of me. She gave me a smile before walking off again. Billy gestured at it. 'What's that?'

'Fish finger sandwich,' I said. I picked the first half up and bit into it. It might not be the canteen's normal fair but it tasted damn good. 'With extra salad cream.'

Billy grunted. 'Good stuff.'

I chewed for a few moments and then leaned forward. 'Why do you do it?' I asked.

'Do what?'

'Act like the world's most annoying jobsworth,' I said. 'It obviously doesn't gain you any friends, otherwise you wouldn't be sitting here with me. Doesn't it get tiring keeping up that pretense of believing in every daft rule and regulation in this place? You're not the person you're pretending to be. Either you're some kind of bizarre masochist or there's something else going on.'

Billy stared at me. He slowly laid his half eaten sandwich down and dropped his head a fraction. Was he mortally offended or simply stunned? He remained unmoving for so long that I waved a hand in front of his eyes to check that he was still conscious. He blinked and shook himself. 'Well, well, well,' he said. 'Saffron Sawyer is smarter than she looks.'

I grinned. 'I knew it.'

'Six years.' He tapped his fingers on the table top. 'Six years I've been here and no-one has ever called me out. The Director suspects but she would never be sure enough to accuse me anything. You've been here six hours.' His mouth tightened. 'Is this a lucky guess or did I do something to give the game away?'

I shrugged. 'Your lack of self-awareness is too stubborn to be anything other than faked.' I gave him a curious look. 'Why do it?'

Various emotions flitted across his face. Clearly, he was trying to decide whether he could trust me or not. I'd leave it up to him to decide. Eventually, he offered me a rueful smile of admiration and raised his shoulders in a semi shrug. 'No-one is indispensable. I don't have the magic skills to be a faery godmother and, honestly, I don't really want to be one either. I don't like other people all that much.' He hesitated and then inhaled deeply. 'Do you know what it's like for someone like me though? A faery who's not on the front line or who doesn't come from an established family? If any of that lot over there took a disliking to me, I could be out on my ear before you could say employment tribunal. I'm not important like they are. Or like you are.' His eyes took on a distant look. 'I can be dismissed in a heartbeat. But I believe in the work that is done here, regardless of how it's conducted. And I need the money. I made the decision when I first stepped into this building that either I live every day knowing I'm on borrowed time or I could turn myself into the sort of person who everyone else is afraid to cross.'

I was beginning to understand. 'You can't fire the person who knows all the rules and knows who's breaking them.'

Billy grinned. 'I have a little black book. I make notes in it all the time.' He jerked his head at the other tables, filled with other faeries. 'It keeps them on their toes.'

'Doesn't it get tiring putting on an act all the time?'

He chuckled. 'We all put on an act. Mine is just more dramatic than everyone else's.' He winked. 'And surprisingly more fun too.' His fingers twitched and his expression sobered. 'Are you going to give me away?'

'No.'

Billy watched me thoughtfully for a moment. 'You were very bouncy and bubbly this morning. A few minutes ago you looked like you wanted to top yourself. I know about what happened with Lydia's ear. But I saw your face right after that happened and you look far more depressed now than then. What's happened since? Is it to do with Rupert?' He frowned. 'He's not the sort of faery you want to get involved with. He has a rather unsavoury reputation, you know.'

'I figured that already,' I told him. 'I was pandering to his ego this morning. It seemed a wise thing to do.' I gave him a pointed look. 'Not unlike what you yourself do with everyone around here.'

'So this isn't about him, then what is it?' he probed. I sighed and looked away. Billy reached across and took my hand, squeezing it. 'You already know my secret,' he said simply. 'I'll keep yours.'

I bit my lip. I could do with a friendly ear – not to mention someone who knew all about the nuts and bolts of this place. I wouldn't get much help from any other quarter. I shrugged to myself. Then I told him what had happened with Luke. 'I was so sure I would be brilliant at this,' I said. 'I was a fucking great dope faery. I thought I was going to be great at this as well. I know I can't expect to be amazing right from the get go but I didn't expect to fail quite so spectacularly. I can cope with faeries like Alicia or with daft rules and dafter uniforms. I can't cope with my own work being crap too.'

Billy interrupted. 'No-one actually wears that cloak when they're out working.'

I rolled my eyes. 'No shit. It's incredibly uncomfortable.'

'And it looks stupid,' he added matter-of-factly.

I let out a burst of laughter. 'Yeah,' I agreed. 'That too.' I sighed again. 'Even if I had to wear it every day though, I'd manage. What I can't manage is failing at this. I want to be the best. But I'm not. I'm just rubbish.'

Billy picked up his sandwich again and began chewing thoughtfully. 'Have they told you yet why you're really here?' he asked through a mouthful.

I stiffened. 'No. But given the ear I all but threw at the Director, it doesn't take a genius to work out that I'm here to make up the numbers because the office is starting look dangerously empty. I'm also well aware there's still more going on that I don't know about. The Devil's Advocate would have told me more but the Director shoved me out of the room before he could say anything.' I raised an eyebrow in his direction. 'I'd hazard a guess,' I said, 'that my presence here has got more to do with those disappearances than the office being short-staffed. I can't believe that five damn faeries have gone missing and outside of this office no-one knows about it.'

'Yeah.' He sighed. 'We 're not supposed to talk to you about it either.'

'And you're a stickler for the rules.'

That elicited a faint smile from him. 'In theory.'

'I've already heard a fair amount,' I told him. 'My desk buddy likes to gossip.'

Billy laughed slightly. 'I'd have been disappointed if you'd worked me out and not done the same with Delilah. You can't keep anything secret while she's about. I imagine she's also one of the reasons why we've not been given the full story about the disappearances. Despite the interrogations.'

More intrigued now than merely miserable, I leaned forward. 'Interrogations?'

'Everyone in the office has been interviewed,' he told me. 'Every single person. The Devil's Advocate spoke to us all and,' he gave a delicate shudder, 'it wasn't pleasant. They clearly think that the disappearances are some sort of inside job.'

Delilah had also suggested that was the case. 'Why?' I asked, grimly fascinated.

'Every godmother who disappeared was supposedly out on a job when they vanished. Only someone in this office would know their whereabouts.'

I felt sick. 'Oh, man.' Just what sort of place was this?

'There was also a staff meeting last week,' Billy continued, 'where all was supposedly revealed. The disappearances and the subsequent questioning have everyone on edge, you understand. All the godmothers are looking around at each other and wondering who will be next and who is responsible. Adeline and the Director presented a united front and pretended that we weren't all under suspicion. Then they told us that they would recruit more godmothers from outside the usual ranks. First of all, because we were already short-staffed even before those five vanished. Second of all, because the current crop are deemed to be less 'street-wise',' he drew quotation marks in the air, 'than some of the other faeries in other departments.'

'Like me,' I said.

'Yep.' He swallowed another mouthful. 'I should add that streetwise was their word, not mine. The faeries around here might come across as privileged little fucks but you'd be surprised at their abundance of experience in different arenas. They're not all naïve little angels.'

'That much I also worked out,' I murmured. I lifted my chin. 'So as an ex-dope faery, I'm considered more capable of defending myself against a potential abduction than others might be.' I could feel my spirits sink further. I really hadn't made it here as a result of my own merits then.

'Do you think it's true?' Billy asked, genuinely curious. 'Are you tougher?'

I shrugged. 'Potentially. I suppose it remains to be seen.' I scrunched up my nose. 'You know, you're not cheering me up very much.'

'The point I was making,' he said, 'was that nobody actually expects you to rock being a faery godmother. They're all expecting you to be shit. HR are pissed off that they have to spend time training you. The other faery godmothers won't take anything you say or do seriously. Some probably think you're a spy sent to find out which one of us is abducting our colleagues.'

I curled my hands tightly together. 'When in truth I'm here to make up numbers and put my fists up in a fight if it comes to it.'

He nodded. 'That's the official line.'

'So,' I asked quietly, 'what's the unofficial line?'

He gazed at me with a somber air. 'Are you sure you want to know this?'

My answer was firm and instantaneous. 'Yes.'

'This is only conjecture, you understand. Admittedly, my conjecture based on what little whispers I've managed to pick up from around the place but it doesn't have any concrete underpinnings. If I'm right, the powers that be won't want anyone in the office to know the truth.'

I didn't look away. 'Spit it out. Spit out this truth.'

'You're bait.' Billy said it with an air of depressing finality.

'Bait?'

'You don't come from an important faery family. If you go missing like the others, there will be less ... ruckus caused as a result.'

I clenched my fists together, forgetting that I had part of my fish finger sandwich in my left hand. It crumbled into fishy bits which scattered across the table top. 'I'm expendable.'

He at least looked faintly embarrassed. 'Not entirely. But you're less,' he hesitated slightly, 'vital than others. In some faeries' eyes,' he added hastily. 'Rupert normally does most of the client assignments but he's not done your ones, no matter what else he might say. Your list has come down from on high. It's no smoking gun but when you take that little fact along with everything else...'

'I'm being dangled out there in particularly visible spots in the hopes that the kidnapper will make another move.'

'That's what I believe. You'll probably be followed every time you head out to meet a client. Discreetly of course. They won't want to give the game away.'

I thought about the flickering shadow just as I'd been yanked away from Luke Wells. Everything was suddenly starting to make more sense. 'They'll be pissed off if I'm not the next one to go missing then,' I said. I was trying very hard to remain seated. What I wanted was to stand up and start throwing things around the room. Heavy things. For reasons I couldn't fully articulate, I was particularly annoyed that the Devil's Advocate was clearly in on this plan. I'd thought he'd seemed like a decent bloke. Instead, he was treating me like I was nothing more than a tasty worm dangling on the end of a faery fishing line.

Billy gave me a sympathetic look. 'Don't take it personally.'

'It's pretty hard not to.'

He pursed his lips. 'You've been chosen because they think you can take care of yourself. You've not been chosen because they think you have untapped talents for wish fulfillment.'

'So what you're saying is that I shouldn't beat myself up for being shit.' I took a deep breath. 'I should wait instead for the boogeyman to come along so he can beat me up and slice off my ears in the process.' I said the last part flippantly but my own choice of words gave me pause.

'What is it?' Billy asked. 'You look like you've thought of something.'

'It's been known to happen,' I said. Not that most people around here would think I was capable of sentient thought.

'It might not be true, you know,' he reminded me. 'You might not be here as bait at all.'

I smiled. I didn't need a mirror to know that it didn't reach my eyes. I pulled my shoulders back and raised my chin. I certainly didn't feel happy but there was a flicker of renewed self interest and purpose deep in the pit of my stomach. That had to count for something. 'Well,' I said, 'I'd better try and find out for sure then.'

CHAPTER
NINE

The office was considerably emptier after lunch, with the vast majority of godmothers making use of the Metafora room to head out and meet clients. I still couldn't prevent myself from looking round at everyone and wondering if one of my new colleagues was behind the abductions. Then I shook myself. No wonder everyone was on edge and unhappy. Everyone was suspicious of everyone else. Whether I knew any of them or not, the more I thought about it, the more unlikely it seemed that another faery godmother was behind all this. It was too ... pat. I sighed loudly then busied myself moving the various boxes from my desk to satisfy Adeline's need for cleanliness until the opportunity I was waiting for presented itself. The very moment I spotted Rupert heading into the galley kitchen to make himself a coffee, I grabbed my own mug and strode in after him. I acted as if I were caught up in my own thoughts, only glancing towards him when he said hello.

'Oh hey.' I smiled, acting surprised. I even managed another little blush.

'How's your first day going?' he asked.

I did my best to put on a troubled expression. It wasn't hard. 'Not great,' I admitted. I bit my lip. 'I had my first client meeting. It didn't go well.'

Rupert's sympathetic murmur was so fake I struggled to maintain my own act. 'That's terrible,' he murmured. 'Can I help at all?'

I put my mug down. 'I'm just not sure why he was assigned to me. In fact, I'm not sure why he's a client of ours at all. The only thing he asked for was a coffee.'

'Well,' Rupert drawled, 'did you get him a coffee?'

I nodded.

He smiled at me. 'Then you've achieved your goal and his. Move onto your next client and forget about that one.'

As if. I withheld my snort and gazed at him with wide eyes. 'A coffee can't be his only wish.'

Rupert moved in closer. I resisted the urge to take a step back. 'Perhaps not,' he said, 'but for the purposes of your list, he's had a wish fulfilled. His name will have already been ticked off. You can move onto someone else.'

I shook my head in disbelief. 'How would his name have ended up on the list in the first place?' I asked.

'Did no-one show you the Adventus?'

'What's the Adventus?' I breathed, as if I were a complete ignoramus. Everyone knew the Adventus, no matter what kind of faery they were.

Rupert hooked my arm round his and took hold of my hand, stroking the back of my palm in a most bizarre fashion. 'I'll show you,' he husked.

Maybe he wasn't cut out to be a faery godmother. Maybe he'd missed his calling as a throaty phone sex operator. 'Aren't you busy?'

'I'll find the time for you, Saffron.' He stroked my hand some more. 'You're more than worth it.'

Unbelievable. Did this guff work on anyone? 'You're so kind, Rupert.'

He dipped his head further down. 'I know.'

I managed a girlish giggle. From across the other side of the room, Billy caught my eye. I winked at him before hastily re-focusing on Rupert before another case of the giggles overtook me. One occasion of hysteria a day was more than enough. Somehow I didn't think Rupert's reaction to it would be as mild as the Devil's Advocate had been.

'Access to the Adventus is strictly controlled,' he said, as he led me out of the main office area and to a set of stairs. 'Even most faery godmothers aren't allowed inside.' He flashed me a white toothed grin. 'But you'll be fine with me. Because I'm responsible for assignments, I can enter whenever I want to.'

'You're so lucky!' I tittered. I was actually starting to annoy myself.

'I know.' He nodded towards a brick red door at the top of the stairs. 'There it is.'

We walked up together. I stayed back, giving the magic a chance to acknowledge Rupert and permit him entrance to the room itself. Then he held the door for me. I stepped in after him, my mouth dropping open when I saw what was inside. This time I was being genuine. It was one thing to know of the Adventus. It was quite another to experience it first hand.

For some reason, I'd thought the room would be small, akin to another Metafora room. Instead, however, this place was vast. Perhaps it was trick of architecture but it seemed far larger than the entire building's blueprint could possibly be. Then again, the Adventus was as magic as magic could get so I shouldn't have been surprised.

'Along that wall,' Rupert told me, with a flick of his wrist, 'are all the wishes that have already been attended to. Those which where granted and those which were refused.'

'Ever? Across the whole of time?'

He seemed amused. 'Oh yes.' He tugged me over. For as far as my eyes could see, in all directions, were hundreds and thousands of little wooden drawers. Little symbols were inscribed on the front of each one. I recognised them as magicarna, a similar written system to the hieroglyphics which the Egyptians had once adopted. I'd never been able to read more than a few dozen of the symbols, however, even when I'd been particularly studious and trying to learn them. 'Choose one,' Rupert told me. 'Any one.'

I sucked on my bottom lip and then briefly touched one of the drawers with my fingertips. The wood was warm. Not just that – it seemed that it were actually pulsating with a heartbeat all of its own. That was ... unexpected.

Rupert reached across, his own hand brushing against mine as he did so. It was a hopelessly deliberate movement but, rather than draw away, I allowed it to happen. Frankly, that made me about as shameless as he was. I had more honorable underlying intentions though.

He slid the drawer open. It was filled with little cards, much the same as you would have found in an old-fashioned library. He ran his finger along the top of them before randomly plucking one out. He held it up, pinching it by his forefinger and thumb so that I could read the beautifully calligraphy inscribed upon it.

'Thomas Haldon. June 1st, 1973,' I read aloud. 'Assigned faery – J. Walsh. Request – Parental agreement for marriage. Wish granted.' I gazed at in awe. Very little information was given away but those words inscribed there had changed Thomas Haldon's life. And quite possibly that of his wife to be and his parents. It was incredible.

'Cool, huh? Every drawer relates to a different faery godmother. You'll have one of your own up at the front.' He chuckled. 'Of course it will be empty at the moment but I'm sure you'll fill it up soon enough.'

I could only nod in response.

Rupert carefully returned the card to its original spot and turned around. I followed his gaze. Suspended high above our heads was what looked like a vast silver cauldron. 'Humans might not realise it,' he said, 'but as long as they keep their wishes secret from others, magic will transport each and every one of their names into the receptacle above whenever they wish for something. Sometimes their names end up there because the wisher has blown out the candles on their birthday cake. Sometimes they've thrown a penny into a well. Sometimes their wish is placed on a shooting star. There are all sorts of methods. Their names are then assigned to different faery godmothers who will do their best to grant their wishes.'

'There must be millions of wishes to get through,' I said.

'Billions,' Rupert told me. 'The worst thing is that even when you visit them, the clients are rarely clear or specific about what they want. We have their names but we have no idea what their actual wishes are. To have a wish granted, each human has got to be visited by a godmother who will investigate and find out what they're really after.' He gave me a knowing look. 'You didn't know what that coffee guy this morning wanted before you met him, did you?'

I shook my head. 'Not a clue.' I still didn't know. Maybe Luke Wells' heart's desire really was for a cappuccino. I didn't want to think about him right now. Slowly turning, I took in the vastness of the cauldron. 'There's no way every single wish can be granted.'

He chuckled. 'Certainly not. There aren't enough faery godmothers for one thing. Even if every single faery in the world became a godmother, we'd only get through a tiny fraction of the wishes. As it is, we only manage to grant a miniscule amount. The wishes which receive attention are selected at random. It's not a perfect system but it's the best we can do. Besides, wishes are supposed to be special. If every single one was granted then they would stop being whispers of awe and wonder and become simply mundane. Only the lucky ones get attended to. Of course, that's also without mentioning,' he added darkly, 'blood wishes.'

I glanced at him. 'Blood wishes? What are those?'

Rupert looked morbidly delighted that I'd asked. 'Not everyone has wholesome, positive wishes. A considerable amount are downright evil.'

Yeah, yeah. I'd been a dope faery. I knew better than most what depravities the human race was capable of. All the same, I pasted on a shocked expression. I'd do whatever I could to keep Rupert sweet. For now. 'Evil wishes?' I gasped. 'Like what?'

I was sure that I'd overdone my melodrama but Rupert was too wrapped up in his own magnificence to notice. 'People might wish for their husband to end up brutally murdered. Or for their next door neighbour to meet a grisly end. Sometimes, those blood wishes are granted. After all, there are occasions when the world would be a better place if certain people were put out of action.'

I wasn't convinced that it was our place to make those sorts of decisions. Regardless of my own misgivings, however, I nodded encouragingly at him. 'But?'

'But sometimes the wisher is being petty or mean or they're just simply nasty.' He pointed over at the other side of the room, where several large red boxes sat silently. The ominous colour and something about the way they were all lined up and waiting gave me the shivers. 'Once it's been identified by the initial faery godmother, every blood wish is automatically filtered into there,' Rupert continued. 'There's a separate team of faeries dedicated to weeding any worthy wishes out and visiting the clients in question again if they need to.'

I glanced around, half expecting to see some sign of this team. Rupert caught me looking. 'They're part timers,' he said. 'Only work Fridays.'

Huh. That was a cushy gig if ever I heard one. Then it occurred to me that if I had to work through the worst that humanity could possibly wish for, I might need six days off a week as well.

Mistaking my expression for curiosity, or perhaps some sort of disgusting eagerness, he lolloped over to the nearest red box before reaching and plucking out a card. He waved it in my direction. 'This is a good one,' he told me.

'You don't have to read it out,' I began. It was too late, however. He'd already started.

'Andrea Covea, 9th May 2019. Assigned faery – not yet known. Request – turn the eyeballs of the British Prime Minister inside out then chop off her toes and feed them to her Cabinet.' He looked up at me and grinned. 'What do you think? Will this one make it through the censors?'

I laughed weakly. Rupert tossed the card back into the box and reached in for another one. Okay. Enough already. 'So,' I said, making my tone as casual as possible, 'what about those faery godmothers who have disappeared? Were they working on blood wishes? Is that why they were abducted?'

Rupert paused, his brow furrowing. 'Not as far as I know.' I could tell from the faint twitch above his eyebrow that he was intrigued at the suggestion.

'It would be interesting to find out, wouldn't it? It would even make a sort of sense. Someone could be kidnapping for revenge for terrible things their wishes have done.' I shrugged. 'It's a shame we can't check.'

He yanked his arm out of the red box and straightened his

shoulders. 'I told you,' he said importantly, 'I have power here. I can check.'

I blinked rapidly. 'Oh, but you'll get into trouble. I'm sure someone has already been through all that anyway.'

'This is my domain.' His bottom lip jutted out ever so slightly. 'I won't get into trouble.' He flicked his eyes around, even though we were completely alone. 'And maybe no-one has checked their past assignments yet.' His expression took on a distant sheen. No doubt he was imagining himself heroically solving the disappearances with snap of his fingers. Idiot. Checking the recent work of all the vanished faeries would have been the first port of call for the most obtuse of investigators.

Rupert shook himself and then began striding down to his right. I followed, staying on his heels all the way. He scanned up and down the different drawers before exhaling when he found the one he wanted. 'Here we go,' he said. He tapped the drawer with his fingertip. 'The last wishes which Boris granted are all in here.' With more drama than was necessary, he pulled the drawer open and peered inside. Every card was white. 'Oh.' Rupert's chest deflated. 'No blood wishes here.'

'What about the others?' I asked. 'There's no harm in checking. Just to be sure.'

He nodded half to himself and spun round, heading for another drawer. As soon as his back was turned, I reached into Boris's one and took out the final five cards, shoving them into my back pocket before Rupert thought to turn around. Then I skipped off after him.

'Lydia's,' Rupert muttered to himself. He slid the drawer open. This time there actually was a red blood wish inside but it was some distance from the front. He carefully picked it out. 'This one is from almost six years ago.' He peered at it, reading the wish out. 'Request – for father with dementia and stage four bone cancer to die quickly.' He rolled his eyes. 'Pffft. This can't be anything important.' He grimaced. 'Neither Boris nor Lydia disappeared because of any blood wishes they might have granted.'

I reckoned I could have pressed him to continue, and check at least one of the other missing faeries' drawers. I didn't want to push my luck unnecessarily, however. Two out of five would serve my purposes. 'You're right,' I told him. Then I snapped my head to the side. 'Did you hear that?' I whispered suddenly.

More than determined to continue his act of brave investigator, Rupert marched forward to the site of the imaginary noise. I reached into Lydia's drawer, taking the last five cards just as I had with Boris. I closed the drawer behind me and followed Rupert yet again.

'Nothing's here,' he said, swinging his head this way and that.

I frowned. 'Maybe I was hearing things.'

'Yes. You must have.' He scowled, clearly annoyed. The expression made quite a twisted impact on his handsome face. Perhaps he was suddenly remembering that I was to be viewed as little more than a disgusting interloper rather than a potential one night stand. 'We should go,' he announced. 'We've lingered here long enough.'

I touched his arm. 'Thank you so much for showing me the Adventus, Rupert. You've explained the entire wish process so clearly. I think I understand it all a great deal better now.' I smiled up at him. 'You help set the wish assignments and I see what you've done now. You've made sure that I get some easy ones to start off with. That's why my first client only wished for coffee. It was really very nice of you to do that.'

Rupert's answering cough and the awkward twist of his fingers confirmed that he'd had nothing at all to do with my assignments. 'No problem,' he said. 'I always try to look out for the newbies. I know you didn't have the best of starts this morning but I hope you're feeling better about it all now.'

'Only thanks to you,' I told him. 'You're wonderful.'

His features relaxed and he grinned once more, completely believing his own hype. 'Any time, doll face.' He began walking to the exit. Behind him, I rolled my eyes. I also patted my back pocket where the precious wish cards I'd borrowed lay hidden. Soon I'd have some more answers.

CHAPTER TEN

Unfortunately for me, there was no chance to look through my purloined cards. By the time I returned to my desk, Delilah was back. Unable to flick through the wishes without being noticed, I instead attempted to busy myself by removing all but one of the dusty files to the back of the office where the recycling bins were located, finally confident that only the remaining box contained papers which might be important. I stowed that box under my desk and then spent the rest of my time researching the rest of my clients. I wasn't going to be caught out again by the sort of attitude I'd had from Luke Wells. I might make mistakes but I didn't make them twice. Concentrating hard, I made copious notes on all of the names remaining on my list. I'd try to forget the misery of this morning and hit the ground running first thing tomorrow. First impressions counted for nothing, I told myself. Second impressions were far more important. Maybe if I said that often to myself I'd even start believing it. Then again, if Billy's suspicions were correct, I could find myself abducted with my body parts hacked off before the week was out. In that eventuality, none of this would matter at all.

Harry's enthusiasm when I met him in the Stagger Inn on the way home was considerably greater than mine. 'How did it go?' he beamed. 'You have to tell me every single little detail. I want to know who you met, what they were like, whether you have any new clients yet, what the office looks like, what the Director said to you, what wishes you've granted so far, how many...' His voice faltered in mid-sentence when he saw I wasn't jumping up and down for joy like he was. 'Saffron,' he said slowly. 'What's wrong? What happened?'

I took a deep breath. 'My co-workers are mostly bullies, apart from one sleazy guy who seems to think he can smile at me and I'll drop my knickers over the photocopier and one rather nice guy who pretends to be the worst kind of nerdy jobsworth so that he doesn't get sacked. I haven't been employed because I was a wonderful dope faery but instead because various faery godmother abductions mean that the office is virtually on its knees. Current thinking is that one of my fellow faery godmothers is responsible for those abductions. I threw a severed ear from one of those abducted godmothers at the Director herself. It was all crusty with dried blood,' I added, as Harry's face grew whiter and whiter. I reached into my back pocket and pulled out the wish cards which I'd stolen. 'I'm also about to discover if I'm about to be used as bait to catch the abductor in question. So it looks like my days are numbered and so are my own ears.' I paused. 'Let me think. What else?' I tapped my mouth thoughtfully. 'I met the Devil's Advocate and giggled hysterically in his face. I also met my first client and screwed everything up, failing to give him any sort of decent wish whatsoever. In fact, all I gave him was a cup of coffee. He was lucky enough to have his name pulled from all the billions who have made wishes and all he got to show for it was a fucking coffee. I've had no training or guidance about what I'm supposed to do or how I'm supposed to do it and I have a list of clients who I've got to attend to and sign off before the end of week. So, yeah,' I nodded, 'all in all, it was a really shitty first day.'

Harry stared at me for one very long moment. 'You're not joking about any of this, are you?'

'Nope.' I pointed at my pint. 'I don't need beer. I need tequila. And lots of it.' I raised my head to indicate to the barman and get his attention. Harry, however, grabbed me instead.

'Whoa there. Before you getting yourself the mother of all hangovers, let's back track. This is your dream job, Saffron. If you feel like this at the end of your first day then you make damned sure that your second day is more of a success. Go back to the beginning. This time,' he said, 'I want every single detail. Especially about those abductions.'

I sighed. Then I started again, without leaving anything out. Although Harry remained stony faced, he listened without comment until I'd completely finished.

'So,' he said, when I finally stopped talking and began to swiftly drink instead, 'you've nicked those wish cards because ...'

'... because,' I said, wiping my mouth with the back of my hand, 'I want to see if the places or the people here match up to anyone on my client list. If I'm being sent to the same places as those faery godmothers who've vanished then Billy's theory that I've been hired to be nothing more than bait will be correct.' I gave him a side long look. 'Remember what the trolls used to say. It's not paranoia if they're really after you.'

'The trolls all died in a freak accident,' he murmured, 'as you well know from all those modern history lessons at school. No-one was after them. And nobody knows what the trolls used to say either because they always avoided faeries like the plague.'

I shrugged. 'So we've been told. My grandfather met one once. He said that he was actually a nice chap.'

'Yeah, yeah.' He picked up the first card. 'Let's focus on the living instead, shall we?' He scanned through the card's details. 'Boris here was sent to someone called Alice Fairworthy who lives in the Lake District.' He raised a questioning eyebrow in my direction.

'Nope.' I shook my head. 'None of my clients live there and the name doesn't ring a bell.'

He placed the card face down. 'Next. Spencer Goldberg. Notting Hill, London.'

I hissed through my teeth. I'd already memorized the list Adeline had given me. I knew without looking that my third client was Rachel Goldberg. Also Notting Hill, London. They were probably related.

Harry noted my expression and began a new pile. Then he took another card. 'Denzel Forrest. Birmingham.'

'No.' I breathed out.

He nodded and put the card down. 'Mick Jones. Aberystwyth.'

Shit. 'Yes. One of my clients lives there too.'

He cycled through the rest of the cards. There were four distinct names which I had that matched with those clients who both Boris and Lydia had worked with before they'd disappeared. Then Harry picked up the final card. 'Luke Wells,' he said. 'Ox...'

I interrupted him. 'Oxford University.'

Harry very deliberately put the card down in the match pile. 'Yes.'

I reached across him and picked the card up again, reading the rest of the details. Request – Unknown. Lydia DuChamp had never even managed to find out what Luke wanted. She must have been abducted before she'd properly investigated him.

Harry looked at me questioningly and I sighed. 'He's the client I had today. The fact that Lydia also had him as a client right before she was abducted pretty much says it all.' My mouth tightened into a thin line and I wrapped my arms around myself. 'It's true then,' I said distantly. 'They really are sending me out to the same places as those other faeries. I really am bait.' It was bad enough when I thought I'd only been brought in to make up the numbers. Now that I knew I was being dangled out there in order for the faery kidnapper to make a move on me, I felt physically sick. Not to mention incandescently angry. This was my dream – and it was already becoming a nightmare.

'It certainly looks that way.' Harry's voice was heavy. 'Fucking hell, Saffron. And they didn't have the decency to tell you that your life might be in danger.'

'I'm not one of them, am I? I'm expendable.'

He drew himself back and glared. 'You are not expendable. You are Saffron Sawyer. You're the best dope faery that department has ever seen. You will not let these faery godmother fuckers get the better of you. You *will* show them that you have the ability to be the very best.' He punched my arm. 'Got that?'

'Ow.' I rubbed the spot where he'd hit me. 'That hurt.'

He punched me again. 'Got that?' he repeated.

'Jeez. Yes, I've got that. Anything to stop you beating me up.'

'Stop complaining. You're the toughest person I know, Saffron. We're going to put our heads together and work out a way out of this. But you're right. First of all, what we need is tequila.'

'Amen,' I muttered.

We de-camped to a quiet table at the back of the pub where we wouldn't be disturbed, bottle and shot glasses in hand.

'You've done a better job so far than you've given yourself credit for,' Harry told me, after the first bone juddering shot. 'You've got this Billy guy on your side, not to mention Rupert as well.'

'Rupert will lose interest as soon as it's clear I'm not about to jump his bones in the office toilets,' I said.

Harry made a face. 'Yuck. Don't do that.'

I half smiled. 'Don't worry.'

'In any case, it's not just those two. You've been polite and smiley to everyone else. On the face of it, you've given not one person in that office any cause to despise you.'

'Apart from,' I reminded him, 'the Director herself.' Who'd been surprisingly nicey nice to me so far. But then that was suspicious in itself.

'Lydia Thingy's ear didn't actually strike the Director in the face and you didn't even know that it was her ear until the Mean Faery began screaming. It was an accident.' He shrugged. 'Don't dwell on it. You've got bigger problems.'

True that. 'So you're saying that I should continue being Miss Happy?' I asked.

'And then some. When they go low, you go high. Don't let them beat you down. No matter what anyone else says to you, remind yourself that you want to be a faery godmother. You're thrilled to be there.'

I nodded. 'Thrilled. Yep. Got it.'

'Maybe if you can get to know all your co-workers better, you'll find your inside man and solve the case. Keep chatting to that Delilah woman. As annoying and gossipy as she might be, you can wrap her round your little finger in no time. I reckon this receptionist woman will be an easy nut to crack too.'

'I just have to remember to call her Mrs Jardine.'

'That's not hard. You can do that.'

I nodded again. 'I can.'

'Next, training or no training, do your job and do it well. Go back to this Luke kid and sort out a proper wish for him.'

I wrinkled my nose. 'I got pulled away though. I'm not sure I'll be able to go back.'

Harry's expression was stern. 'Try. Rupert told you that faery godmothers have to investigate to get to the root of clients' wishes. That has to take more than one visit.'

'I suppose.'

'Find out what he wants. And give it to him.' He poured himself another shot and raised it to his mouth. Then he thought better of it and put it down on the table again. 'When people make a wish, they say the wish. They don't blow on an eyelash and merely say *I wish*.'

I frowned. 'Yeah. So?'

'So why don't the details of their wishes show up on the wish cards along with their names? Wouldn't it make life a lot easier?'

I thought about it. 'Maybe wishes change over time so it's easier for the magic to add the client's name to the Adventus cauldron rather than the wish.'

'Uh huh.' He bobbed his head but he didn't look convinced.

I gazed at him. The tequila on my empty stomach was already dulling my tired, misery-laden brain. It was clear, however, that Harry had thought of something which hadn't yet occurred to me. I scrunched up my face and thought harder. 'Last week,' I said slowly, 'if I could have had one wish granted, it would be to receive my dream job as a faery godmother. Today,' I continued, 'I'm on the verge of running to Jacob and begging him to take me back as a dope faery.'

Harry grinned approvingly. 'Be careful what you wish for.'

I sat up straighter. 'We have to investigate and find out

what the clients' wishes are,' I said. I snapped my fingers. 'But what if *they* don't know what their wishes are themselves?'

'Indeed.' Harry picked up his glass again, this time swallowing the contents in one go. 'Becky might wish for a pair of shoes. But what she wants isn't a pair of shoes. It's the financial security to not have to worry about money and to be able to buy shoes whenever she wants them.'

'Or,' I said, warming to the topic, 'Becky wants a new pair of shoes because what she's really wishing for is for the new guy next door to notice her. She wants to be loved.'

'Maybe she's got arthritis and she has wished for new shoes because her body aches so much.'

'So what she wants is to feel normal and pain free again.' I gave him an enthusiastic nod. 'In fact her underlying desire could be anything. Shoes have nothing to do with it.'

'You can't take anything at face value,' Harry said. 'If you want to be an effective faery godmother, you have to forget about what your client says they wish for and instead be a therapist, a private detective, and *then* Santa Claus all rolled into one. Remember that and it doesn't matter what else happens. You'll be incredible at your job.' He patted my arm. 'You were always going to be incredible at your job. You just needed a bit of support with it. If those godmothers won't support you, it doesn't matter. I'll always be here.'

I sniffed. I was starting to feel quite teary and emotional which was most unlike me. 'Everyone should have a friend like you, Harry.'

He wagged a warning finger in my face. 'No crying. Saffron Sawyer does not do crying. Not today anyway. Cry tomorrow if you need to. Today we are too busy.' He reached into his pocket and passed me over a handkerchief. I blew my nose into it.

'Fanks.'

'No problem.' He rested his chin on his hands. 'Now that

we've solved the easy part, let's think about the hard part. There's a faery kidnapper on the loose who's clearly not afraid to use violence. The godmothers are lining you up next in his sights. How do we make sure you keep both your ears? Not to mention that my complexion doesn't suit black, Saffron, as you well know. If you die I won't go to your funeral.'

'You're all heart.'

He threw me a worried look. 'Seriously though. Maybe I should take some holiday time and hang around you. Be a bodyguard or something.'

'You've got rainbows to make and faery twins to usurp,' I said sternly. 'Besides, defense won't win the day here. This is about attack.'

He scratched his head. 'What do you mean?'

'If I want to stay safe, keep my pretty shell-like ears attached to my head, make a name for myself as a brilliant faery godmother, and generally remain utterly amazing, then what I need to do is to find whoever is behind the disappearances. I have to solve the crime. There's no other choice.'

'Easier said than done.'

'I'm Saffron the Superb,' I slurred. 'You know, I don't think this can be an inside job at all. As unfriendly as most of my co-workers are, I don't think any of them is daft enough to actually kidnap five faery godmothers. Even if they wanted to do it, it would be far too easy. My gut is telling me that despite what the evidence is saying, someone else is behind all this.' I set my jaw. 'I will find out who. And I've already got an idea about where to begin. I will take him down before he takes me down and I become the hero in the process.'

Harry grinned. 'I'll drink to that.' He poured us another two shots and we clinked glasses. 'Bottoms up.' He leaned forward and pointed at my ID card which I'd forgotten to remove when I'd left the office. 'Now tell me two things. First of all, what on earth is that thing around your neck? Is that supposed to be you?'

I made a face.

'Secondly,' Harry said, 'And most important of all, is the Devil's Advocate really as dark and scary as everyone says?'

CHAPTER ELEVEN

My alarm went off at 4am. It wasn't the worst thing that could have happened but, at that moment in time, it kind of felt like it. Then I remembered that I was a) a genuine, honest-to-goodness faery godmother who needed to make her mark and b) my life was being threatened. With those thoughts in my head, I sprang up and propelled myself into the shower.

Less than twenty minutes later, I was out on the streets. I no longer had the same Metafora access to my dope faery clients as I used to but that didn't mean I didn't think I could still find them, especially at this time in the morning. Even without the presence of hard drugs in his system, Duncan didn't sleep well. He'd already be up, waiting in his tiny bedsit for dawn to break. I didn't need my case files to check his address; I'd committed it to heart long ago. I was particularly fortunate that he also lived near by to me. I couldn't afford the time it would take to travel halfway across the country when I didn't have magic to aid me. I still had to get myself to the faery godmother offices by 8.30am. No matter what else had occurred yesterday, I wasn't about to show up late on only my second day.

Surprisingly, the building where Duncan's room was situated was in a remarkably well-heeled part of town. No doubt the residents in the expensive houses nearby were none too impressed that there was a charity-led house of multiple occupancy right on their doorstep. People always laid far too much emphasis on the social status of their neighbours, when they should be concerning themselves with whether they were nice enough to pass over a cup of sugar when required and respectful enough to keep the noise levels to a minimum. In truth, the only thing I could hear around here was the muted twitterings as the birds began to grow restless for the start of a new day.

I walked up to the heavy blue front door and located the buzzer for Duncan's room. Due to the fact that I was here unofficially, I couldn't afford to leave any magical trace behind me. It wasn't so much that I'd get into trouble for checking up on an old client and more that it wasn't de rigeur to interfere with another faery's caseload. I didn't know who was now responsible for Duncan's drug-filled dreams and I didn't want to rouse any suspicions or ruffle any feathers.

As I'd suspected, it didn't take long for Duncan's tinny voice to answer me. He didn't sound sleepy in the slightest, although his voice was laden with suspicion. That was only natural; it was still ridiculous o'clock.

'Who is it? What do you want?'

I kept my own tone soft and pleasant. 'It's me, Duncan. I've got what you asked for.'

There was a pause. 'Me who?'

It was quite possible that his subconscious would recognise me. His actual surface memory, however, wouldn't manage to dredge up any specific instances of our meetings. It was just the way the memory magic surrounding faeries worked. It didn't matter whether we were dope faeries or faery godmothers or tooth faeries. Any humans we'd encountered during a job would automatically forget all about us as soon as we left them. Of course, memory magic didn't kick in when we weren't working so that we could still have social lives that involved humans. It would get rather tiresome to have to keep introducing yourself to the same people when you weren't on the job. I'd never paid much attention to the specifics of how it worked. I'd never needed to. In any case, memory magic protected us as well as humans, even if it was annoying sometimes. Duncan wouldn't consciously remember me, despite the fact that we had met many times. The only way my little subterfuge would work would be if I could persuade Duncan that he really did know me.

'It's Saffron, of course,' I replied into the grubby speaker, injecting the faintest hint of hurt to add credence to our supposed relationship.

There was yet another beat of silence. I crossed my fingers tightly, hoping that he wouldn't just tell me to piss off. I was in luck; a moment later the door buzzed. I pushed it open and exhaled loudly. I'd passed the threshold now; there was no turning back from this point.

I walked up the stairs to the third floor, rounding the corner towards Duncan's room. The lingering smell of last night's curry clung to the walls and carpet. Hell, it could have been last month's curry for all I knew – this place always smelled the same. I pretended to my grumbling stomach that I wasn't hungry and presented myself at Duncan's own front door. It was already open and he was standing there waiting, frowning at me as I stepped up.

'Duncan!' I beamed. 'I won't hug you. I know you don't like that sort of thing. It's great to see you though.'

His brown eyes shifted. I could see that he was straining to remember who I was. I had to throw him another titbit to convince him that he did.

I glanced past him into his small but incredibly neat bedsit. 'You're alone?' I questioned. 'No green monsters hanging around?'

He drew back. 'How do you know about that?'

I blinked in obvious surprise. 'You told me, silly.'

'Did I?' He rubbed his eyes.

'Yeah!' I smiled again, the very picture of non-threatening friendliness. 'Anyway, I know it's super early but I did promise you I'd come by. I've got the early shift at work so it was now or never. How about that cup of tea you promised me?'

'You're …'

'Saffron,' I reminded him helpfully.

'Oh yeah.' He nodded. 'I remember.' He clearly didn't. It didn't matter now; he stepped back and, just in case he suddenly changed his mind, I walked past him and headed directly for the straight-backed chair sitting in the corner. Duncan closed the door and turned round.

'You said you'd got what I asked for,' he mumbled.

I grinned and reached into my pocket, pulling out a plastic bag containing a few wrinkled mushrooms. They were far from hallucinogenic. They'd been sitting in the bottom of my fridge for goodness knows how long. Perhaps they'd provide some sort of placebo effect or perhaps Duncan would be sorely disappointed later on when he tried them. Either way, I could hardly give him the real thing. That hadn't been in job description even when I'd been a dope faery at the top of my game. Such an action was severely frowned upon and old habits died very hard.

'They'll make you fly,' I told him, lying through my teeth.

Duncan edged towards me and took the bag. The plastic

rustled as he peered inside. 'They look like button mushrooms,' he said doubtfully.

Duncan was many things. Stupid wasn't one of them. 'I know, right?' I said. 'They're legit though. I already told you. If you don't want them, that's okay. I'm happy to keep them for myself.'

He pulled the bag towards his chest, on the off-chance that I was about to reach out and take it from him. As doubtful as he was about the mushrooms' providence, he wasn't about to look a gift horse in the mouth. 'Thank you.'

I waved a hand in the air. 'I'd say that there's more where they came from but they're the last of my supplies. I hope you enjoy them.' I leaned back and crossed my legs. 'So how have you been since I saw you last?'

'Fine.'

He was considerably less verbose when he was stone cold sober. I'd thought that hard part would be getting in here. It appeared that getting Duncan to talk was going to be the toughest thing. 'How about that tea then?' I prompted.

With obvious reluctance, he shuffled over to the tiny stove, still clutching the plastic bag. Using one hand, he re-filled the kettle at the sink and then placed it onto the hob before turning to me. 'Where did you say we met?'

'Out by the train station.' I hesitated, then added in a small voice, 'Don't you remember?'

He was too kind to be honest. 'I remember.'

I smiled to make him think I was relieved. 'Oh good. You were so nice to me and you made such a difference to my day that I'd feel terrible if I'd not had the same impact on you. All that time we spent talking about the boogeyman!'

Duncan stiffened. 'Who?' he whispered, his eyes going wide.

I pretended I hadn't heard him. 'You might say that

monsters don't scare you but the boogeyman would certainly scare me.' I glanced around as if the boogeyman in question was about to jump out from the rose patterned wallpaper. 'I hope I don't bump into him too.'

'Steer clear of St Clements Park then,' he grunted.

Bingo. 'Oh don't worry,' I said with fervent promise, 'I will.' I fiddled with my cuffs and took a deep breath, casting my net a little further in a bid to get more information that might help. The boogeyman Duncan had mentioned might not have a single thing to do with whoever was disappearing faeries. He might not exist at all, much like my own conjuration of the green skinned monster. But Duncan's ominous mention of him the other night was too much of a coincidence for me to ignore – especially given my lack of other leads. 'The way you described him,' I said with a shudder. 'The way he looked with his ...' my voice trailed off hopefully. With any luck, Duncan would fill in the blanks for me.

'His hair?'

I nodded enthusiastically. 'Yes! His hair.'

He dropped the bag containing the mushrooms at his feet. 'You should leave.'

Uh oh. 'Pardon?'

'I don't know who you are or what you're after but you have to go. I don't want you here. I didn't see anything and I don't know what you're talking about.' He raised his arm, extending his trembling index finger at his door. 'Leave.'

'Wait, Duncan, I ...'

He lunged towards me. I squeaked in fear, suddenly afraid of what he'd do. He didn't hurt me though. He just grabbed my shoulder with one hand and opened the door with his other. I considered standing my ground and putting up a fight. It wouldn't have been hard. I suspected, however, that such a display of strength would cause more problems than it would solve. Besides, I'd already gotten what I'd come for. I relaxed my body and allowed Duncan to shove me ceremoniously out. He slammed the door shut and I could hear the jangle of the lock as it was slid into place.

'I didn't mean you any harm, Duncan,' I called back, unsure if he could hear me. 'I'm sorry if I bothered you.' I sighed. 'You look after yourself.' I waited for a moment but he didn't answer. I'd done all that I could. I shoved my hands into my pockets and then left him in peace.

I DESPERATELY WANTED to head directly to St Clements Park and see what – or who – was there. Duncan had been genuinely scared and even if his boogeyman was innocent of anything to do with any missing faery godmothers, I liked my old client more than enough to want to put a definite end to his fear. If I were being honest with myself, it was more than likely that this shadowy monster was some sort of human drug dealer trying to get Duncan to sink himself lower into that world. A nasty monster indeed but not the sort that I was actually looking for. Still, in that scenario, I was well placed to do some good – which given the last twenty four hours was more than I could ask for.

Unfortunately, time was already working against me. I'd definitely be late for work if I took a detour to the park and Duncan's problems weren't my only problems. I shouldered my bag, checked the sky and drew out my umbrella, then instead headed towards the office. It would be far better to be early rather than late. Now that I actually had ID, at least I could be sure that Mrs Jardine would let me in.

It might have only been my second day but already the sheen of stepping into the building had worn off. Now I was already starting to sense some of the despair from the floors above leaking down to the glitter of reception. As instructed by Harry, however, I wouldn't let it put me off. Yet again, I put on my very best smile and walked up to the front desk.

'Good morning, Mrs Jardine! How are you on this most glorious of days?'

She gazed at me, owl-like. 'It's raining.'

'I know!' I grinned happily. 'It's not even just drizzle. It's proper rain. There are some rainbow faeries out there who will be delirious.'

Something altered in her expression, although I couldn't have said exactly what. 'Hmmph.' She adjusted her spectacles. 'You'll have to take a seat over there and wait,' she told me, pointing at the same uncomfortable chairs that I'd been forced into yesterday morning.

'There's no need,' I chirped. I held up my lanyard. 'Now I'm official.'

She looked from it to me and back again. 'I can't possibly accept that. It looks nothing like you.'

She had got to be kidding me. 'Of course it's me. The photo was only taken yesterday!'

Mrs Jardine sniffed. 'Even more reason for it to resemble your actual face then. She shook her head. 'No. With the trouble yesterday when that delivery faery didn't properly identify himself, I can't be too careful. I need this job.'

Somehow I didn't think Mrs Jardine would ever be sacked. I reckoned that the Director herself would be terrified of her. The Devil's Advocate had put her in her place but he was special. I thought about that for a moment and leaned forward. 'I understand,' I said. 'You have to be very careful. We can't have more severed ears being thrown around the office.'

She didn't twitch. 'From what I heard, it was you doing the throwing.'

Yeah. I did that when I was up in the office. The office I belonged in just like every other damn faery godmother. I bit my tongue back from saying that, however, and played more strategically instead. 'Mm. I'll wait in that chair as you wish,' I told her. 'If I'm lucky, the Devil's Advocate will show up again and we can share a lift together once more. He's such an interesting man, don't you think? We got on very well together. Not many faeries get the chance to have a proper tete-a-tete with him. I did though.' I allowed myself a tiny smile. Then I added a conspiratorial wink for good measure. 'I think the two of us had a special connection, you know. He was most surprised that I'd been left cooling my heels for so long down here but I assured him that I didn't mind. I think he believed me,' I added, tapping my mouth thoughtfully. I met Mrs Jardine's eyes. 'When is the actual audit taking place?'

She didn't immediately respond. When she did, her voice was icy cold. 'You really do seem to think you're very smart, don't you? I don't take to threats very well, Ms Sawyer.'

'I'm not the enemy, Mrs Jardine. And I'm not threatening you.' Not exactly anyway. I smiled pleasantly. 'All I want is to get upstairs so that I can do my job to the very best of my ability. I'll admit that based on yesterday's evidence that's not a very great ability but I still want to try. I deserve the chance to try. I understand that you might take great joy out of teasing new starts like me and, under other circumstances, I'd probably find it entertaining as well. But there's serious shit going on up there and with all those disappearances I don't think this is the best time for a sense of humour that involves either or pranks or hazing. This is the time for all of us to pull together as a real team.'

For a brief second, I thought I'd over done it and gone too far. Mrs Jardine stared at me long and hard before speaking again. 'You shouldn't be here,' she said quietly.

My smiling façade broke. 'I might not be from a high brow faery family but I have the right to be here as much as anyone else,' I snapped.

'Oh, you have the right. And you are stronger than the others. I do indeed act like this with every new godmother and godfather and you've reacted very well in return. You've been one of the better faeries to come through that door, even though I've been harsher to you than to others. But you still shouldn't be here.'

'Why the hell not?' I growled.

For the first time her expression softened. 'It's not safe for you here.'

I was so surprised that I took an involuntary step backwards. 'Because I'm here to lure the kidnapper in,' I whispered without thinking.

It was Mrs Jardine's turn to be surprised. 'They told you?' She shook her head and answered her own question. 'No. They wouldn't do that. Someone else whispered in your ear.'

Billy took that very moment to push open the door and walk in. A knowing flicker lit Mrs Jardine's eyes and she nodded to herself. Apparently I wasn't the only one who saw through Billy's act then. 'Thumbprint here,' she said to me, in a sudden brisk and business like fashion.

I reached for the book and pressed my thumb down in the appropriate space. Then I met her eyes once again. 'I'll be fine,' I told her as Billy came up behind me.

'You are not wearing regulation shoes,' he said to me with a frown. 'Those are patent leather and patent leather is prohibited.'

'I'm so sorry,' I said. 'It won't happen again.' I glanced at Mrs Jardine, whose face remained entirely expressionless. Was everyone in this building playing a role? 'Listen,' I said to her. 'My best friend is a rainbow faery. If you ever want a rainbow created for you for a special occasion then say the word and I'll see what I can do.'

Mrs Jardine's cheeks turned pink. Even Billy's mouth dropped open in shock. 'Thank you,' she murmured. 'I appreciate that.'

I bobbed my head once. Then I trotted off to the lift in my non-regulation shoes. What was the problem with patent leather anyway?

CHAPTER TWELVE

I already had a plan in my head. As I was a fraction early, Delilah wasn't yet at her desk. I'd wait until she arrived so that I could exchange pleasantries with her and continue to work on getting her onto my side, then I'd head off to sort out Luke Wells before moving onto my other clients. I could almost smell my own success in the air. Grabbing the unicorn mug from where I'd left it the day before, I walked towards the little kitchen, humming as I went. Frankly, if I could conquer Mrs Jardine, I felt like I could conquer anything.

I'd just finished making myself a strong coffee when Alicia strode in. She seemed intent on entirely ignoring my presence. That was until she caught sight of the mug. Her eyes fixed on it, widening to an alarming size.

'What,' she gasped with remarkably vicious horror that wasn't all that far from the way she'd reacted to poor Lydia's ear yesterday, 'do you think you're doing?'

'Having a coffee,' I said. And then, because there was no reason why I shouldn't try to get on her side as well as everyone else's, I added, 'would you like one?'

She ignored the offer. 'That is my mug. You've stolen *my* mug.'

Oh. I should have realised that the cardinal sin of working in any office held as true here as it would anywhere else. 'I didn't know,' I said, in an appropriately apologetic manner. 'I thought we could use any mug we wanted to.'

'Well, you can't! You can't go stealing other people's mugs! Everyone knows that the unicorn one is my one. I spent half an hour looking it for yesterday. I was desperate for a cup of tea after the trauma I had to undergo because of you throwing that ... that ... thing at me. That trauma was compounded because my mug was missing. Except it wasn't missing, was it? You stole it! I might have known that a marsh faery like you would be a dirty thief.'

I counted to ten in my head. It didn't help. 'Marsh faeries aren't thieves,' I said. 'They are honorable members of our race who deserve respect. They accomplish a great deal for our environment and we should thank them for it. Although I should add again that I am not a marsh faery. More's the pity. However, I am sorry I took your mug. I didn't steal it. I merely used it to put coffee in.' I opened the cupboard, pulled out another mug at random and poured the coffee from the unicorn mug into it. 'Now you can have your mug back.'

'I don't want it back until you've washed it thoroughly!' She glared at me, putting her hands on her hips.

'Well,' I said calmly, 'I will wash it now and then you can have it right back.' I paused. 'And if I could make just one minor point of criticism before I do that, I'd like to say that the hands on your hips thing is too much. I appreciate it's important to stay in role as the mean girl but the tone of your voice is more than enough.' I waved at her vaguely. 'The half baked flouncing detracts from your scariness.'

A strange flush began at the base of Alicia's neck and started to rise upwards. 'The what?' she stuttered. Her hand snapped out and she grabbed the mug from me. 'I'll wash it myself,' she hissed. 'I don't know who you think you are or why you think you can talk to me like that but I am a Beauchamp. Beauchamps have been the top performing faery godmothers for generations. I am someone around here. You are no-one. If I want to put my hands on my hips, then I will bloody well do so!' Her voice was rising. Somewhat belatedly, it occurred that I'd made yet another catastrophic error. Unlike Billy and Mrs Jardine, Alicia wasn't acting at all. She really was the person who she portrayed herself to be.

From behind her, Adeline suddenly appeared. 'Alicia,' she said, 'may I have a word in private?'

'Did you hear how this creature spoke to me?' she shrieked.

'Saffron, leave us.'

Gladly. I picked up my new mug and tried to slide out before Alicia's yells reached ceramic-shattering levels.

'Oh and Saffron?' Adeline murmured. 'That's my mug.'

Fuck a puck. I gave up on any sort of coffee whatsoever and handed it to her. Then I all but sprinted to the supposed safety of my own desk.

I'd have given up on the office entirely and escaped via the Metafora room as soon as I possibly could but for the fact that the Director appeared at the front and beckoned everyone forward.

'Here we go,' Delilah said to me, shrugging off her coat, 'it's pep talk time.'

'Pardon?'

She leaned towards me. 'It's dressed up as the morning

briefing. You missed it yesterday but it happens every morning. It's supposed to get us ready for the day. You know, raring to go and pumped full of enthusiasm and provided with all the information we need to be good little faery godmothers. It's by far the most depressing part of the entire day.' She smirked to herself. 'Although today I can't wait to hear how she will put a positive spin on what happened with Lydia's ear.'

I was beginning to warm to my gossipy neighbour. She was far more canny than initial appearances suggested. Following her lead, I got to my feet and walked to the front of the room. I had to admit that I was also curious about what the Director was about to say about yesterday's events – especially considering how much I'd been kept in the dark so far.

A group of godmothers towards the back of the small crowd were still chatting. The Director fixed them with a stern look but, amusingly, it took them some time to notice. She eventually had to resort to clearing her throat overly loudly in order to encourage them to fall silent.

'Good morning, everyone.'

There was a mumbled chorus in response. I added my own voice into the mix, a beat behind everyone else and considerably louder. It might have made me look vaguely idiotic but it did raise a faint smile from the Director in my direction. Anything was an improvement after yesterday's debacle.

'I know that many of you are feeling unsettled after what happened yesterday. We have no reason to believe that Lydia is not still alive, and I would like to assure you that we are very much engaged in investigating the disappearances of all our beloved colleagues. We will find the person responsible for this and they will be brought to justice.'

An older man standing a few feet away from me raised his voice. 'What about our safety? You can't guarantee that. We shouldn't be going out alone. Not any more. If we had a buddy system ...'

The Director's expression remained calm. 'That is one of the steps we are considering. However, we already have a backlog of clients to get through and I'm sure you're all with me when I say that we don't want our work to suffer. I've consulted with the Devil's Advocate at great length on the matter. Every godparent will be issued with a panic button by the end of the week. It will link directly back to here. We don't anticipate any further vanishings.'

She was making it sound as if we were discussing stain removal instead of brutal abductions. I nodded to myself. Yep. I could see why she was the Director.

Several hands shot up into the air but she ignored every single one of them. 'Now,' she smiled, 'moving on, we have some successes to report. Yesterday, Mark did an excellent job, fulfilling the needs of eight clients. That's almost a record. I must remind you that the godmother or godfather who grants the most wishes in this quarter will receive a fabulous and very well deserved bonus. There's still time to catch up to Mark's numbers so I want to see you all beavering away as much as you possibly can.'

By my side, Delilah nudged me. 'He's won that bonus every quarter for the last two years. Either he's granting crappy wishes that don't mean anything or he's shagging her. Or Adeline.' Her lips pursed. 'Maybe both of them.'

The Director was still talking. 'We do have some more complex clients on the horizon as well. A considerable number of older humans have been selected. It is an honour to grant wishes for those people who are in their twilight years and I expect that each and every one of those clients is given the same due diligence as everyone else.'

I glanced at Delilah. 'Why wouldn't they be treated the same?'

'Try granting wishes for someone with dementia,' Delilah whispered. 'Or someone who wants their life extended beyond what's possible. It's a nightmare.' Ah. I could see how that could be difficult.

'Finally,' the Director intoned, 'no matter who your clients are, please make sure you truly drill down into what their heart desires. You might have think outside of the box to give them what they want but never forget that only the sky is limit. We are faery godparents.' She raised her fist.

I blinked. Everyone around me copied her suit before chanting the same words back at her. 'We are faery godmothers!'

'Again!' roared the Director.

'We are faery godmothers! We are faery godmothers!'

I squinted. Was that supposed to mean something? Beyond the obvious, anyway?

'See?' Delilah said under her breath. 'It's like the Nuremberg rallies.'

The Director clapped her hands. 'To work, people!'

Almost immediately, the crowd dissipated. Everyone melted away to their own desks until I was the only person still standing. That had been … weird. I shrugged to myself, spotting Adeline striding for the Adventus room. I pulled my shoulders back and jogged after her.

'Excuse me,' I called.

She didn't hear me. I tried again.

'Adeline! Excuse me?'

She kept walking. I frowned slightly. Actually, I thought she had heard me and was just choosing to ignore me. Not gonna happen. I picked up speed until I was neck and neck with her. With a swift move and some particularly fancy footwork, I positioned myself directly in front of her. Now she wouldn't make it out of the office until I got out of the way.

'I want to apologise,' I said, 'for what happened earlier. I didn't mean to take your mug. I didn't mean to take Alicia's mug either. I'll bring my own one in tomorrow.'

'Good.' She gazed at me with icy eyes. 'Was there something else?'

'Is Alicia alright?'

'She's fine.' She tapped her foot. 'It might be wise to stay out of her way for the time being, however. Another incident like that and I might be forced to give you a verbal warning.'

I swallowed. Alicia had been the one to hopelessly overreact. She was the one with her feet under the table, however. I'd defer to her for now. 'Noted.'

Adeline's expression softened. 'I appreciate that you haven't had the smoothest of starts. We are all under a great deal of pressure at the moment. Things here are usually far calmer and happier and I am confident they will return to that before too long.'

'I'll look forward to it,' I murmured.

She pressed her lips together. 'Mmm.' She began to side step. 'Now I have to make a move...'

'Wait, before you go, I need some help. I saw my first client yesterday and it didn't go quite as I'd planned. I need to go and visit him again.'

'That's fine. You may visit as often as you like before granting his wish.' She paused. 'As long as you don't take too long over it, however. You heard the Director. There's quite a backlog of clients to get through. The audit is starting next month and the last thing we want is for the Devil's Advocate to think we're all slackers. You need to get through that list of yours by the end of the week remember. We're already granting you considerable leeway as you're new.'

That didn't bode well. I nodded obediently all the same. 'Yes. I'll be as fast as I can. The thing is that I might have already granted him a wish. He asked for a coffee so I conjured up a coffee. That's won't be a problem, will it?'

'If he wished for something, Saffron, and you gave it to him, then that case is closed. Move on to the next one.'

'He didn't get what he wanted though.' I corrected myself. 'I didn't give him what he wanted. I need to try again.'

She crossed her arms. 'It's incredibly difficult to re-open a closed case. There are forms to be filled out. In triplicate.'

I pleaded to her better nature. 'He's my first client. I want to do a good job with him. I was only with him in that study carrel for a few minutes. There wasn't really any chance to do much at all.' There wasn't even any chance for any would-be kidnapper to make a move on me. Hopefully, that would register with Adeline and she'd be more inclined to help me return to Luke. 'The sky is the limit,' I added, repeating the Director's own words. 'Right?'

'It's not going to be viable. Re-opening a case is...' She stopped and gave me a closer look. 'Study carrel? What's your client's name?'

'Luke Wells,' I said instantly. 'At Oxford University.' And, I added silently to myself, he was the very last client the now ear-less Lydia had before she went missing. I'd been given him as a client for a very deliberate reason. One that wouldn't end in my own abduction and dismemberment. Not if I had anything to say about it.

A strange expression crossed her face. For a fleeting moment, it actually looked like guilt. Maybe she was capable of some honest emotion after all. 'Very well,' she said eventually. 'I will see what I can do. This is a one-off, however. I won't do this sort of thing every time. You must up your game. After your interview, I expected you to be able to hit the ground running, Saffron.'

Yeah, I thought. Running from a mysterious kidnapper who wanted to chop off my body parts. I smiled sweetly. 'Thank you so very much.'

She sniffed and walked away. My smile turned more genuine. Baby steps. I was getting somewhere though.

CHAPTER
THIRTEEN

Adeline came through for me quicker than I'd thought she would. Less than forty-five minutes later, I was standing back in front of the Metafora room with her assurances that I'd be able to return to Luke Wells and attend to his real wish, whatever that might happen to be. No doubt she'd gone to the Director in order to hasten the process, regardless of her mumbles about the bureaucratic complications. They really were desperate for me to get myself kidnapped as quickly as possible. I shook off my renewed surge of fury. I wasn't going to let myself lose focus – and I *was* going to solve this. There was no other choice. I even took the horrific pink cloak with me. I wouldn't put it on yet but I'd bring it just in case. All or nothing, baby.

This time, I wasn't transported to the quiet, literary heaven of Oxford University's main Bodleian library. Instead, I arrived somewhere outside, my feet landing onto the grimy pavement of a squalid, rubbish strewn street. Interesting. I pulled into the nearest doorway, giving myself the best opportunity to scan my surroundings and work out what was going on. Then I glanced round, scanning every nearby nook and cranny for other mysterious shadows. I wanted to know exactly how long it would take my watchers to catch up to me. Whichever faeries were trailing me, they wouldn't want to leave me on my own for too long. After all, the bastard kidnapper could show up at any point. I wasn't sure how fast they'd be able to move once my signature triggered the Metafora room. Within minutes certainly. Frankly, I was hoping for a little faster than that. My life was quite possibly at stake.

Initially, there was no sign of either a knife wielding maniac or any flickering faery shadows. I was starting to think I was out here on my own. Then I spotted a woman pushing a pram on the other side of the road. Her head was turned away from me, her face concealed from my view. I didn't need to see her features, however. She didn't walk with the weariness of a tired mother. She *glided*. I sniffed to myself and I turned my gaze to the left. Further up the street, exiting a grubby looking newsagent's shop, there were two men. Both wore hooded tops, their faces equally indistinct. There was also a strange prickling at the back of my neck. Using my periphery vision, I caught a brief glimpse of another figure not too far behind me. That meant there were potentially four faeries trailing me in total. They weren't taking any chances. I supposed I should have been grateful for the attention. I knew they weren't interested in keeping me safe, however. They just wanted the ear-cutter to show up so they could deal with him and rescue the others. Clearly, I was to be considered collateral damage.

Taking a deep breath, I pretended that I hadn't spotted any of them and focused instead on my supposed target. Luke Wells had to be around here somewhere. I nibbled on my bottom lip, breathing out only when I saw him step from another doorway further up. Ah ha. I would be smarter this time and hang back, until I had a better idea about what he was up to as well as what he was like as a person. My own watchers could do whatever they wanted. I would still do right by Luke, no matter how much of a shit he really was.

He put his hands into his pockets and turned right, walking away from me. I immediately followed him, wondering what he was doing in this part of town. Given what I'd learned about my new client on my earlier visit, no doubt it was some sort of grubby transaction. It might be drugs, I mused. It would be amusing if I were to bump heads with one of my former dope faery colleagues while in pursuit of the same human. It was unlikely, however. Magic didn't usually allow for such occurrences. Besides, I couldn't recall any drug dealers who lived near here. I pursed my lips. I might have been distracted by my own followers but I was genuinely curious as to where Luke might be heading. He didn't live anywhere near here. I knew both from my earlier conversation with him and the file I had on him that he didn't have a girlfriend he might be visiting. He certainly didn't strike me as the type who simply went out for a walk from time to time to enjoy the fresh air.

In any case, while the other faeries followed me, I continued to follow Luke. Hopefully, I'd glean more about his lifestyle and his desires. I pretended that I was completely alone. As furious as I was about the entire set-up, I had to admit that being trailed by other faeries was the perfect opportunity for me to show what I was really capable of. I might as well kill several birds with one stone and prove to my watchers that my existence was as worthy as anyone else's. I could be an excellent faery godmother as well as evil bastard bait.

Although Luke's shoulders were hunched against the cold and he walked with the sort of sloping gait that seemed universal amongst undergraduates, I had the sense that he knew where he was going and he had a very specific destination in mind. At the next crossroads he didn't pause. He strode out into the road, narrowly avoiding being run over by a small car.

He ignored the driver's irritated honk and kept going. I picked up my own pace and hurried after him. I didn't think it was my imagination that he was walking faster than before.

I splashed through a dirty puddle and ignored the grey drizzle which had started up again. My hair was already about as frizzy as the laws of biology would allow for. It couldn't get much worse. Unfortunately, my faster pace and my fixed gaze on Luke's back meant that I didn't notice the shuffling man who stepped out from the small pub to my left to have a cigarette. I collided with him, my body jolting against his.

'Sorry!' I rubbed my forehead where it had banged into his bony shoulder. Damn, that hurt.

'Watch where you're bleeding going,' the man returned, before noisily hawking up a ball of phlegm and spitting it in the direction of my feet.

My hackles immediately bristled. 'Piss off,' I snapped.

If I'd banged into just about anyone else in the street, that would have been the end of matter. We'd both have stamped off in our separate directions. This guy, however, was having a bad day. Or perhaps he was nothing more than an antagonistic prick. Either way, he took extreme umbrage that I'd dared to mutter an expletive at him. He grabbed my arm with rough, painful intent.

'Nobody talks to me like that,' he hissed in my face, his breath a cloud of stale beer and smoke. In fact it was remarkably reminiscent of the reek in the study carrel where I'd first found Luke.

I wasn't in the mood to be pushed around. There was simply too much other shit going on in my life to allow this to pass. I puffed my chest out and glared at him. 'Oh yeah?' I said. 'Because I think I just did. What are you going to do about it?' My glare grew harder. 'Are you going to hit me?'

If I'd been a man, my bravado wouldn't have worked. In

fact, if there hadn't been other passersby, it wouldn't have worked either. The bully boy in front of me realised, however, that he wouldn't win himself any favours by smacking a woman half his size. He abruptly released me. 'I see you again,' he told me in a low voice, 'and you won't get off this easy.' He threw his cigarette butt down onto the pavement, barely half smoked, and turned back into the pub. Ha. I grinned to myself, immensely satisfied. That was until I spotted the fake mother with the pram watching me from across the street. She looked away as soon as I glanced at her. It didn't matter though. Rather than portraying myself as a cool, collected faery who de-escalated tension instead of creating it, I looked like some sort of maniac.

'Stress,' I muttered. 'I'm under a lot of stress.' Then I looked down the street. Fuck a puck. Luke Wells had completely disappeared.

Bitterly angry at myself, I took off. He couldn't have gone far. I ran down towards where I'd last seen him, checking every side street and glancing in the window of every shop. This was ridiculous. I'd never physically lost a client before. I slowed to a walk. I supposed I could return to the office and then use the Metafora room to transport myself to his exact location again. Somehow that felt like I'd be admitting defeat, however. I had too much pride to advertise myself as quite this stupid to the entire office. I didn't dare look in the direction of my followers either. No doubt they'd all be sniggering to themselves at my desperate incompetence. I'd gotten myself into this stupid situation. I'd get myself out of it.

I half closed my eyes. What did I know about my client? He liked to drink. Except he'd passed a pub and hadn't so much as glanced towards it so he wasn't looking for a beer. He slept around. But he liked to pretend he had standards so he wouldn't simply be trawling the streets in order to pick some random girl up. He was intelligent enough to get into Oxford University and to get good grades whilst he was there, despite all of the afore-mentioned character flaws. Perhaps he attended a secret study group somewhere around here. If I searched for some sort of flat that looked like it contained students then I might find him. There were several flat buildings up ahead. Maybe I could try those.

With no other solution, I began to march forward once again. A moment later I halted. There, on the opposite side of the street, was a tattoo parlour. It had barred windows and had the sort of despairing façade that would make any sane person run a mile before they'd wander inside to get their skin permanently inked. But there had been that doodle he'd fallen asleep over in the study carrel back in the library. That could easily have been some sort of tattoo. I felt a brief spark of hope and immediately crossed the street.

The door was stiff on its hinges and heavy to open. I ended up shoving it with my shoulder just so that I could create enough of a gap to squeeze through. It slammed shut behind me with a thud of finality. Even the vague lingering scent of patchouli in the air wasn't enough to lighten the tattoo shop's atmosphere. A single florescent strip hanging overhead lit the tiny space, which I supposed was necessary given that no natural light was able to enter. Every single scrap of space on the walls was taken up with examples of tattoo designs. None of them looked appealing. Not to mention that I could see three photo examples with badly misspelled words. *No Regerts* was emblazoned on the nearest one. Some poor sod actually that had tattooed across their arm. I shuddered. It had been a decent hunch to come in here but there was no chance that Luke Wells would get a tattoo from this place. He had far too much narcissistic pride.

I turned on my heel to leave as abruptly as I'd entered, just as there was the shuffling sound of footsteps.

'Help you?'

I turned. A large man, wearing a tank top which was at least two sizes too small and had probably been white once, was staring at me. My eyes involuntarily dropped to his hands. His fingers were pudgy and squat with the nails bitten down to the quick. They did not look like the hands of an artist.

'No,' I began. 'I was having a look but...'

From further inside the shop but hidden from view by an interior door marked ominously *This Is Where The Magic Happens*, an insistent – and familiar - voice proclaimed, 'I'll pay you whatever you want.' Luke Wells was here after all.

I coughed. '... but now I think I know which tattoo I'd like.' I jabbed randomly at the nearest picture. I supposed it could have been worse. I was pointing at a little cartoon cat. Admittedly, it was a misshapen cat which wouldn't have looked out of place in a horror film but it was still identifiably a cat. Barely.

The man raised his eyebrow. 'You want to book in?' he asked.

I shook my head. 'Nope. I'll lose my bottle if I don't do it now.' I grinned. 'Besides there's no time like the present, right?'

He shrugged at me as if he couldn't care less. He did, however, point me to the door in question. I wasted no more time and hastily stepped through. I had to find out what Luke was up to.

The back room was even more terrifying than the shop floor. There seemed to be three separate cubicles, although the thought that this place would have any customers, let alone three at one time, almost defied belief. Without waiting, I headed straight for the nearest cubicle – and the one which I knew was already occupied by Luke.

Fortunately for him, he didn't actually appear to be getting a tattoo done. He was on his feet, with his hooded top still on, and remonstrating with his hands at yet another burly bloke whose features were similar enough to the other man's that they had to be related.

'Just check your records,' Luke insisted, before turning to me and frowning. 'Who are you?'

I waved at him in apology and backed out.

'This one,' the first man said, jerking his head at the next cubicle. 'Where do you want the art done?'

I didn't want it done anywhere. I'd make up an excuse and get out of here before any needle got anywhere close to me. I needed to listen in to Luke's conversation first though.

'Uh, my arm,' I said. I pointed at a random spot a few inches below my shoulder.

He grunted. 'Payment up front.'

I nodded and reached into jacket for my wallet, leaning back at the same time so I could continue to eavesdrop.

'We don't keep records like that,' I heard the other man say.

There was a faint hint of desperation to Luke's voice. 'I don't believe you.'

I passed over a fifty pound note and stepped back, eager to get closer to the other cubicle and hear more. Whatever was going on here, it was clearly important. Unfortunately the other tattoo artist in front of me seemed determined to get on with his own job too. He shoved the money into his pocket and gave me a hard-eyed, suspicious stare. 'You need to take your jacket off.'

I managed a smile. 'Yes, of course. I'm just a bit nervous.' I shrugged it off my shoulders.

He continued to stare at me. 'And either take off your top or roll up your sleeve.'

I wasn't going to strip. I had limits, no matter how determined I was to make a success of this mission. I reached for my sleeve, slowly pulling it up and taking as much time as I possibly could.

'Look, mate,' came the other voice again, 'we won't hand over someone else's details. You could be anyone, innit?'

'I appreciate that,' Luke returned. 'But I can make it worth your while.'

A heavy hand placed itself on my shoulder, all but forcing me down into the leather chair next to me. Almost immediately, the tattoo artist picked up his machine and clicked it on. I'd have protested or at least found some way to stall him, but Luke was getting to the good stuff.

'Don't move,' the artist grunted.

It was becoming difficult to continue to eavesdrop over the sound of the machine. I leaned back to listen more closely.

'I said,' he repeated, 'don't move.'

'How much?' came the disembodied voice.

'How much do you want?' Luke asked. 'We can come to some sort of arrangement. I know he used to live in this area. I just don't have an address for him. I used to but all that sort of stuff was lost when my mum moved house. I'll pay you whatever you want.'

I let out an inadvertent yelp as the needle touched my skin. Fuck a puck, that hurt. 'Wait!' I squeaked. 'I need a few moments! I'm not sure I do want this any more...'

The artist chose not to hear me. I'd have yanked myself away as quickly as I possibly could if he wasn't holding me down in place, supposedly so that I didn't wriggle. Maybe he did that because he was used to customers running out of his shop and screaming. He continued to press the needle against my bare skin. I gritted my teeth. It would be worth it, I told myself. As soon as I'd heard enough, I'd leave this hell hole with at least most of skin still intact. I tried to re-focus on the conversation next door.

'I don't care how much you offer. I might need the money but I'm not telling you a thing. It wouldn't be right. Now get the fuck out of here.'

'This is important!' Luke protested. 'I've got lots of money. I swear I do! Just...'

'Get the fuck out.' There were sounds of a brief scuffle and then all went silent.

I swung my head towards the tattoo artist. 'Stop! I don't want it any more. You have to stop!'

He didn't look up. 'If I stop now, it'll look like shit. This is art, lady. I've started so I'll finish.'

'But...' I glanced down at my arm. Beads of blood were rising up across my skin where the needle had pierced through. And with only a vague outline completed, the tattoo thus far did look like shit. Bastards. Maybe it would look better when he was finished with it. My shoulders sagged. I was going to end up with a creepy cat on my skin whether I wanted it or not.

CHAPTER
FOURTEEN

My arm felt like it was on fire. I hadn't dared to take another look at the tattoo itself but the artist himself had completed it so quickly that I had a very bad feeling about what it was going to be like. I was an absolute idiot for not thinking of a way to eavesdrop on Luke. It was definitely all the stress, I told myself. It didn't seem like it would get any better either. The entire faery godmother office was filled with unhappy people who were under similar pressure. Unfortunately for me, several of them were continuing to take their frustrations out on me as the newbie. I'd barely made it back to my desk and double checked the information on Luke's file before I could hear the sneering begin.

'It's not fair when others get special treatment,' someone said in an overly loud voice from another part of the room. 'The rest of us only get one stab at our clients. We don't get re-dos if we mess up their wishes.'

My lip curled. The only reason I'd been granted another stab at Luke Wells was so that the evil kidnapper and cutter of ears could potentially also stab me. If I yelled that back and made it clear that I'd worked out why I was really here then it was quite possible the Director would turf me out before I had the chance to prove myself. She was probably banking on the theory that my ignorance would do even more to encourage the bastard to come at me. And I'd never get another shot at being a faery godmother. Despite the pounding in my head and the burning pain of my arm, I had to continue to play nice.

'I'm going out for lunch,' I announced brightly. 'Would anyone like anything while I'm out?'

'Yeah,' another nearby faery sniped. 'Some of your special treatment would be nice. Not to mention a hundred percent pay rise like the one you negotiated with HR before you'd even begun.'

Alright. Fuck playing nice. I whirled round, located the bully in question, and walked over. I didn't stomp. I *strolled*. I also kept the same picture perfect pretty smile on my face.

'Hi,' I said. 'I'm Saffron. I don't believe we've been formally introduced.'

The other faery smirked and pointed at my ID. 'Saffron? I think it's Savlon, actually.'

I looked down at her own ID. 'And you're Philippa Clear-worthy.' I didn't miss a beat. 'You think that I'm getting special treatment.'

She sniffed. 'I don't think. I know.'

'Tell me, Philippa,' I said, leaning towards her, 'was your mother a faery godmother?'

She straightened her back proudly. 'She was.'

'And your grandmother?'

'Of course.'

I folded my arms but kept my expression benign. 'I bet you could trace your entire family tree back as far it goes and you'll find faery godmothers at every point.'

'Yep.' She looked me up and down. 'Unlike you and your family.'

I nodded. 'Indeed. Definitely unlike me and my family. No-one in my family has ever been a faery godmother. I got here purely on my own merits.' That was an outright lie of course but I wasn't supposed to know that and neither was Philippa. 'I couldn't rely on the *special treatment* my own family name gives me. I had to get here without that sort of hereditary help.'

Out of the corner of my eye, I saw Alicia open her mouth as if to jump in and help Philippa out. Then she seemed to think better of it and closed her mouth again. That was probably a wise move.

'Well,' Philippa said, her cheeks beginning to colour, 'that's because your family are losers.'

I continued to smile. I was getting good at this. 'If you believe that to be true, then you have to believe that your family are winners. Ergo I had to work about a million times harder than you to get to this very point.' I cocked my head, pretending to be confused. 'So how am I the privileged, special one? Unless your family aren't winners at all. Perhaps they're just losers like mine.'

'My family aren't losers,' she spluttered.

'Ah.' I nodded wisely. 'So you're the one who's had the special treatment then. Not me. Thank you for clearing that up.' I hitched my bag onto my shoulder. 'So would you like me to fetch you anything while I'm out then?'

She sank down into her chair. 'No,' she muttered.

I grinned. 'Okay then.' I turned around and began heading for the lift. Behind me, I heard Billy's voice pipe up.

'Philippa!' he said, sounding utterly aghast. 'Are you typing your reports in *that* font? It gives the Director a migraine! And are you seriously eating crisps at your desk? That's the worst possible thing you can do around a keyboard. The germs that you're both spreading and picking up could cause an outbreak across the entire office!'

I permitted myself another smile and pressed the button to call the lift. Rupert walked up and winked at me. 'You have no idea,' he said, 'how turned on that made me.'

I reached into my bag and drew out a tissue, then dropped my eyes to his crotch. 'I guess you'll be needing this then.'

He blinked rapidly but, to give him a smidgen of credit, he recovered quickly. 'Ha! Yes, good one.' He took the tissue from me and made a show of folding it up and putting it into his breast pocket. 'Could you perhaps pick me up some dark chocolate when you're out? The canteen doesn't sell anything like that because it's not supposed to be healthy. But dark chocolate is different. Not to mention,' he added with yet another wink that made my stomach heave, 'it's an excellent aphrodisiac.'

Fortunately, the lift took that moment to arrive and I stepped in. 'Sure, Rupert. I'll get you some of that.' The doors closed on him, leaving me alone. I doubled over and breathed out. Man. Talking to Philippa that way had been unwise. But so much damn fun.

Mrs Jardine gave me a surprised look as I walked out past her desk, giving her a wave.

'I don't need the Metafora room right now,' I explained. 'I'm only going out for a spot of lunch.' Besides, if I triggered the Metafora room I'd also trigger my trackers. I wanted to be alone for this little venture.

She raised an eyebrow. 'You're already bored of the staff canteen?'

'I'm meeting someone,' I told her. Hopefully anyway. 'Don't worry though. I won't be late back.'

'I don't expect you will be,' she murmured.

I smiled and walked out. St Clements Park was, quite fortuitously, less than a fifteen minute's walk. I'd be there and back with the identity of one creepy boogeyman clutched in my sweaty little hand in no time. And if the gods were smiling on me, Duncan's boogeyman would match the faeries' one too.

Despite the lunchtime rush, as other office workers poured out of their offices in the search of a sandwich, I made it to the park without delay. Even with golden sunshine cascading down from the cloudless blue sky, it was a dreary place. Perhaps once upon a time it had been pretty, with orange and lemon trees dotted around to give weight to its name. Now, however, the grass was patchy, there was litter all over the place and the only tree appeared to be half dead. That was unfortunate. A flyer attached to the iron railings which fenced the park in proclaimed that the 'Friends of St Clements' were meeting in the park the following weekend to attempt to tidy things up. I made a mental note of the time. Some voluntary work might impress the Director. If that didn't work, it would also spruce up my CV. I might need it.

A few brave souls were sitting around the park on rickety wooden benches. Not one of them looked in my direction as I passed. In fact, it was quite the opposite. They kept their eyes resolutely away as if to suggest that meeting the eyes of anyone whilst in this place would immediately turn them into stone. I had the distinct feeling that if I approached any of them to inquire about suspicious strangers, I'd cause several strokes and at least one heart attack. I checked my watch. It was early yet. I still had plenty of time before I had to get back to the office.

I headed for one of the empty benches, brushing off the worst of what I hoped was merely dirt before I sat down. My stomach grumbled loudly and I wished I'd thought to actually bring some lunch with me. My arm seemed to be hurting more now, rather than less. I leaned back and pretended I was enjoying the view, whilst neither in any pain nor hungry in the slightest. If only wishing always made it so.

I stayed where I was for several minutes. A few people got up and left the park. A few people entered. The gentle hum of traffic from beyond continued unabated. A scruffy looking dog which was being dragged along on a lead by its owner cocked its leg against the only other empty bench, liberally spraying it with urine. I grimaced and leaned to one side, sniffing and wondering if I'd made a mistake by sitting down. That was when I saw him.

He was shifty as hell. Truthfully, he couldn't have looked more shifty if he tried. Despite the warm sunshine, he was wearing a filthy trenchcoat which had bulging pockets that no doubt contained all manner of dodgy objects. His eyes were sliding around the park, landing on everyone there with an assessing consideration. He was looking for new clients. I was sure of it.

When his gaze moved to me, I looked away, then looked back, then looked away again. My pink faery godmother cloak was still tucked away and I knew that in my office suit I might not look like one of his usual punters. If I'd learned anything in my time as a dope faery, however, it was that you should never ever judge someone's secret proclivities by the way that they dressed. I was hoping that this man, as unkempt as he was, would know that.

He ran a hand through his greasy grey hair, which was in dire need of a good wash and trim. Then he extended his pinky out towards me, gently beckoning me towards him with a questioning glance. Satisfaction settled in my stomach. My little nervous dramatics had been enough.

I looked around, as if checking the area for secret undercover police, then got to my feet and walked over to him. He was hovering beside an old rosebush which, surprisingly, had a few budding flowers. I stopped a foot or so away from him.

'Afternoon,' he muttered, in a perfect example of Essex accented English. Almost too perfect. It was like the dirty coat coat he'd shrugged on – all part of a very deliberate persona.

'Hi.' I rubbed my palms against my black skirt, indicating to him that I was still terrified.

'Can I help you with sumthin?'

This was where I had to be very careful. It was vital that I played my cards correctly if I were going to find out anything at all. It was possible indeed that this bloke was the boogeyman I was looking for. I was already starting to have my doubts, however.

'I don't know,' I hedged. 'I'm here to meet a ... friend of a friend.'

'Oh yeah?' He'd perfected the art of appearing disinterested. 'Who's that friend then?'

The last thing I wanted to do was to give up Duncan's name. I had no desire to get him in any deeper than he already was. From what I'd already gathered, he was terrified of this man. I deliberately misunderstood his question and licked my lips. 'I'm told he's the boogeyman,' I whispered.

For a brief second, he didn't react. Then he threw back his head and laughed uproariously. 'Yeah,' he said through a series of phlegmy snorts, 'I've been called that before. And worse too.'

I didn't doubt it. I opened my eyes wide. 'Why?' I asked. 'Why do they call you that?'

He grinned, showing me his crooked, tobacco stained teeth. 'Cos I'm scary as fuck.' He took a step towards me, his left hand drifting towards one of his pockets. I caught a glimpse of what could only be the handle of a large knife. It was interesting that he was making such a show of strength this early on in our 'relationship'. 'What do they call you?' he asked.

'Alicia.' I twisted my fingers together.

'Nice to meet you, Alicia.' He nodded at my bulging bag. 'Whatcha got there then?'

I reached in with one hand, keeping a close eye on his expression as I did so. I pulled out the pink cloak, shook it out and placed it awkwardly round my shoulders.

The boogeyman blinked. 'You going to a fancy dress party?'

'I'm a faery godmother,' I told him, taking a gamble. I wasn't officially working right now so the memory magic wouldn't work and the boogeyman here would remember me and everything I told him. I decided it didn't matter, however. He would either be the bastard I was looking for or I'd never see him again. This was the quickest way to divine the truth.

He laughed again. He didn't believe me for a second. 'Course you are. Well, I've got something that will truly make you fly.' He paused. 'If you're interested.'

My stomach clenched. Despite his attempts to be intimidating, he was nothing more than another run of the mill drug dealer. He didn't know anything about faery godmothers. He wasn't the fucker I was looking for. I'd known all along that it was a long shot but that didn't mean I hadn't still hoped this was my guy.

My disappointment must have shown on my face. 'It's not an upper you're after, then?' he inquired. 'It's a downer. I can do that, little faery. I can bring you right back down to earth.' His toothy smile grew. 'It won't cost you very much. Not this time.'

I pulled back my shoulders. 'Not today. Thanks though.'

He leered at me. 'Whatcha afraid of? I don't bite.'

I had the distinct sensation he was lying. I looked him up and down. Actually, now I could see why he'd earned the nickname of boogeyman. He did possess a particularly menacing air. It wouldn't be wise to get on his wrong side. I shrugged to myself. He might not be the villain I was looking for but he was someone's villain.

'Another time,' I said. I whirled away, marching to the park's exit as his laughter followed me. I dug out my phone on route and hastily pressed a few numbers. 'Hi,' I said in a low voice into the receiver. 'I'm in St Clements Park. There's a man in there who's wearing a trenchcoat. He just flashed a young kid. In broad daylight. I think he's got a knife too.'

'What's your name?' the operator asked.

'He's coming towards me!' I squeaked. 'I think he heard me talking to you! I have to go!'

'Wait, can you ...'

I hung up. With any luck that would be enough. I walked out of the park as my stomach grumbled again. Grimacing, I headed across the road and into a small café which faced the park.

The bell jangled as I entered and a man wearing an apron looked up from behind the counter. He seemed far too old to still be working, his wrinkled skin loose and flabby looking. Maybe his love of food was such that he couldn't bear to retire. Or maybe his beady dark eyes which were fixed sharply on me meant that he actually had extraordinarily poor vision and I'd end up with yoghurt on my sandwich instead of mayonnaise.

'Can I help you?' he asked.

'I'd like a sandwich to take away please,' I said.

'Ah, yes. You must work nearby.'

'Mm.' I pointed vaguely behind us. 'Over there. It's my first week so I'm just getting to know the area. This looks like a good place for a quick lunch though.'

He smiled, showing off a set of surprisingly sharp yellow teeth. Ex-smoker, I decided. 'Oh, it is that. Are you enjoying your new job?'

I wasn't in the mood for small talk. 'It's alright,' I said in a non-committal manner. I glanced at the ready made sandwiches he had on offer. Nothing looked very appealing but I selected one at random anyway. I'd never get through the afternoon if I didn't get some sustenance. Even if it was a flaccid cheese sandwich.

'Good choice.'

Judging from the sandwich's appearance, I doubted it. At least I could eat it in peace without any side looks and mutterings though. Every cloud had a silver lining.

CHAPTER
FIFTEEN

When I walked back out onto the street again, there was already a police car parked on the pavement, its flashing blue lights creating a little dance across the grey stones. Beyond, in the park, three police officers had pinned down the boogeyman and were cuffing him. I smiled to myself. It hadn't been an entirely wasted half hour. I began to turn right, in order to head to the office. I had plenty of time left before I had to be back so I didn't have to rush. I'd enjoy the sights and bustle of the city and ponder over what my next move could be. I wasn't about to give up on looking for the kidnapper. Not a chance.

Just as I started to move, something else caught my eye. I froze before quickly drawing into the door of the coffee shop. Striding along the other side of the road, and making a determined beeline right for the park, was the Devil's Advocate.

For one fearful second, I thought that he was here for me. That I'd committed some sort of cardinal sin by coming here and speaking to the supposed boogeyman myself. I briefly touched my bag, where my godmother cloak had yet again been stuffed. Then I told myself that I was being stupid. I'd not done anything wrong. I'd only chatted to a dodgy man and gotten him arrested. Yes, he'd remember me because I wasn't here on official business, and I'd stated quite categorically that I was a faery godmother. I'd done so in the interests of good, however, and he hadn't believed me anyway. Why would he? I squared my shoulders. If the Devil's Advocate was going to admonish me for taking some initiative then I'd give him a piece of my own mind in return. I was still in that sort of mood.

Despite the expression of grim intent etched onto the Devil's Advocate's face, he didn't once glance over in my direction. His head tilted towards the supposed boogeyman as he was unceremoniously dragged towards the waiting police car, then he politely stepped out of the way to give the police officers more room. He watched the proceedings with little more vague curiosity, turning his back as soon as the path in front of him was clear enough that he could proceed. I scratched my head and watched him more closely. Maybe it was because he was dressed all in black but he had far more of a threatening air about him than the boogeyman himself had enjoyed. The question was, however, if he wasn't here for me then what was he actually up to?

At first, it appeared that he was heading to the bench I'd previously vacated. Then he swerved past it. Every time he passed one of the other seated people, each of whom had clearly been enjoying the show of the boogeyman's arrest, they got up to their feet and immediately left the entire park. The Devil's Advocate didn't say anything and I couldn't spot any surreptitious magical hand signals. He was definitely doing something to cause them to walk out, however. He wanted the place to himself – and I wanted to know why.

I hurriedly crossed the road again to get closer, just as the Devil's Advocate reached the lone tree towards the back of the park. He circled round it, his head tilted upwards. He appeared to be examining it closely, but for what I couldn't say. Then he disappeared out of view, crouching down behind the skeletal trunk. I chewed on my bottom lip before sidling back in and skirting round the park's fringes to stay out of his line of sight.

I was very careful. I edged round while keeping an eye on the sun so that my own shadow didn't give me away. I kept to the balls of my feet and avoided the fallen twigs in order to stay silent. I avoided looking at him directly so that his subconscious wouldn't feel the force of my gaze and cause him to turn towards me. It worked. The Devil's Advocate was entirely intent on scrabbling around in the dirt at the foot of the tree. If he'd also been snorting, I'd have imagined he was questing for truffles. He was completely silent, however.

After a minute or two, he got up to his feet and began walking round the tree again, moving further and further out in ever increasing circles. His gaze remained fixed to the ground. He was clearly searching for something and he was taking his time over it. I moved round with him, remaining behind him at all times so that he didn't notice me. I might not have bothered. The Devils Advocate was completely focused on his own task.

Eventually he stopped what he was doing, stepping back, putting his hands into his pockets and frowning. The man didn't crack a smile very often. Without giving anything else away, he abruptly strode off again, obviously in the direction of the park's exit.

I waited until I was sure he was far enough away. Then I too walked over to the tree. There was a pile of loose dirt by the patch of ground where he'd been crouching. I knelt down and looked at it. Something was there. Something ... dark. I reached down and brushed my fingertips against it. They came up sticky. I raised them to my nose and sniffed. I was no forensic expert but that smelled like blood to me. There wasn't a lot of it and I'd never have noticed it if the Devil's Advocate hadn't paused here for so long. I swallowed and stared at it, feeling nauseous. Then I scrambled to my feet and took after the Devil's Advocate. He was onto something. I had to know what it was and where he was going now.

I was worried about the time – after all, I still didn't want to be late getting back to work. I was also slightly worried that he might notice I was following him. I shouldn't have been concerned. It didn't take to long to work out exactly where he was going. Fortunately, it was the exact same place as me. I began to relax. It wouldn't matter if he spotted me now. I was simply returning to work after my lunch hour. That was a perfectly normal thing to be doing.

Thirty seconds after he entered the Faery Godmothers' building, I strolled in after him. I smiled cheerily at Mrs Jardine. She managed a tiny smile in return even though it was clear that the Devil's Advocate's return was unsettling her. I signed back in and scooted round her desk towards the lift, where the Devil's Advocate was also waiting, drumming his long fingers against his thigh.

'Good afternoon,' I chirped.

He merely inclined his head in response. That was a bit rude, I decided, given that we'd shared a lame joke or two yesterday. I shrugged to myself and instead cast an appraising eye up and down his body. I wanted to see if there was evidence of any more clues. Alas, I couldn't see even so much as any dirt on his shoes from his park explorations. I couldn't say the same about my own footwear. Billy wouldn't be able to complain about the patent leather now. You could barely tell that my shoes were black given the layer of dirt and dust that now covered them.

The lift arrived and both the Devil's Advocate and myself stepped in. He still smelled of cinnamon, which I had to admit was a pleasant change from the other people I'd been spending time with recently. I stepped into the corner and eyed his straight back. What are you really up to? I wondered at him. What took you to St Clements Park?

The lift doors slid shut and the same tinny muzak filled the air. Without turning round, the Devil's Advocate murmured, 'Are you about to begin giggling again, Ms Sawyer?'

'I wouldn't say I'm in the giggling mood today,' I replied.

There was a beat of silence before he spoke again. 'That's a shame.'

All of a sudden, the lift jolted. Instinctively, I put my hand out against the wall to brace myself. I was still knocked forward, however, colliding against the Devil's Advocate before jumping back.

'Sorry!' I held my hands up.

He tutted at me. Then he stepped over to the control panel and jabbed a few buttons. 'We've stopped,' he said.

Even I'd worked that out. 'I'm sure we'll start moving again in a moment.'

'Mmm.' He didn't sound convinced. He pressed a few more buttons. Nothing happened. Expelling an irritated sigh, he hit the intercom. 'This is the Devil's Advocate,' he said. 'I'm in the lift with Saffron Sawyer and it appears to be stuck.'

I winced internally. I could imagine the expression on Mrs Jardine's face right now. A moment later, her voice filled the air. 'I'm calling an engineer straight away,' she said. 'My sincerest apologies. We will have you moving again in no time. Are you both alright?'

His response was clipped and to the point. 'We are fine.'

'I'll keep you updated,' she promised, 'this won't take long.' The intercom clicked off.

'You know,' I said conversationally, 'Mrs Jardine is a scary woman. She's also a very intelligent one. She sees everything that goes on in this building and knows everyone. She's also incredibly intimidated by you. It wouldn't hurt to be a bit … nicer towards her.'

The Devil's Advocate slowly turned round, as if unable to believe that I'd dared to give him advice. 'She intimidates other people,' he said, with a pointed look to me. 'She should be able to handle being intimidated herself.'

I wrinkled my nose. 'She can handle it. She can probably handle everything. It's just … unnecessary for someone in your position to not be a bit kinder.'

He didn't move. He gazed down at me with dark, unfathomable eyes. 'I will take your comments on board,' he said with the sort of air that told me he wouldn't give them a second thought. He cocked his head. 'Why were you at the park, Ms Sawyer?'

I started. Fuck a puck. 'Er … pardon?'

A tiny smile played around his lips. 'Why were you at St Clements Park?' he repeated. 'You weren't following me. Not to begin with anyway, because you were there before me.' He tilted forward, using his size to loom over me. It was quite unnecessary. I was already feeling claustrophobic and trapped enough in the lift as it was. 'So why,' he said softly, 'were you there at all?'

'I was getting some fresh air,' I replied, panic forcing me into a daft, unnecessary lie. 'It's a pretty park and it's not too far away from here.'

'You don't really expect me to believe that, do you?' His eyes glittered.

Feeling crowded, I crossed my arms. He got the message and stepped away slightly, although his expression didn't change. 'Why were *you* there?' I shot back. 'Maybe *you* were following *me*.'

The Devil's Advocate appeared amused by the suggestion. 'Why would I do that?'

Something snapped. Perhaps it was his humour at my situation. Perhaps it was simply that I'd had enough of this entire thing. Either way, the words came tumbling out of my mouth before I could stop them. 'Why wouldn't you? Everyone else is following me, after all. You probably can't wait until someone jumps out of the shadows and kidnaps me. It'll make your day.' I changed the pitch of my voice. Let the dope faery be the one to be kidnapped. Don't tell her that her life's in danger so she can prepare or protect herself though. She's not that important. She's expendable and she'll make excellent bait.'

Judging by the look in his eyes, I'd genuinely surprised the man. 'The Director told you why you're here?'

'No,' I half snarled. 'I worked it out for myself. With a little help from the one or two faeries who work here who aren't complete wankers anyway. In any case, I'm not as stupid as you all seem to think I am.'

He watched me carefully. 'I don't think you're stupid, Ms Sawyer.'

'Oh, I see,' I said with heavy sarcasm. 'You only think that my life is less important than anyone else's then. Thanks a lot. Good to know.'

He hissed under his breath. 'That is not what I think.' He muttered to himself before meeting my angry gaze. 'The plan was not my idea. I counseled against it. I would have forbidden it outright if it hadn't already been in motion before I visited yesterday. There are many things which occur in this office which are against both complicated regulations and simple morals. Why do you think I'm conducting an audit in the first place?'

'How the hell should I know? I assumed it might have something to do with the five missing faery godmothers.' I drew back my shoulders. I should have known he'd try to deny his involvement. Why would anyone admit to such a thing? 'I'm hardly the go-to person around here for information!'

'You should calm down, Ms Sawyer.'

Oh, he did not just go there. 'Calm down? Calm the fuck down? I'm being used as mushroom bait for some bastard who enjoys cutting pieces of faery godmothers and sending them through the post by special delivery and you're suggesting I calm down? You patronizing tosser.'

He blinked. I didn't suppose that anyone had ever dared to call the Devil's Advocate anything like that before. Now that I'd started, however, all my pent up emotions were bursting out like an uncontrollable steam train. There was no stopping them. My brakes had well and truly gone.

'Why aren't you out there trying to find the kidnapped faeries?' I demanded. 'Why isn't someone doing something about those poor sods instead of playing around with me? Is this the best you could come up with? Offering me up like some sacrificial lamb?'

'Ms Sawyer…' the Devil's Advocate said stiffly.

'I mean, no-one seems to care that Lydia DuChamp is now missing one ear. You're all too busy congratulating yourselves on your genius plan.'

'Ms Sawyer, if you would be quiet for one moment and let me speak…'

'What happens if he doesn't take the bait? What happens if he goes after some other faery godmother instead? Will I get the blame for not being a tempting enough victim? Because right now nothing you lot do would surprise me in the slightest.'

The Devil's Advocate shifted his weight. 'Saffron!'

I stilled. I continued to glare at him though. 'What?'

He pointed at the corner of the lift. 'Sit down and I will explain everything.'

I folded my arms, ready to refuse. That was until he sat

himself down in the opposite corner, stretching out his long legs and glancing at me askance. I sighed audibly and rolled my eyes. Then I sat down as well, leaning my back against the side of the lift.

'Go on then,' I said icily. 'Explain.'

His expression turned thoughtful. I could tell that he was considering how to begin. Somehow, despite my seething ire, something told me that it wasn't because he was planning to lie to me or manipulate me in some way. It was because he wanted to be absolutely clear in his explanations without leaving any detail out. A small part of the tension in my stomach uncoiled.

'The Office for Faery Godmothers has always been held in very high regard. For a long time this was because it deserved it. In recent years, however, and under various different Directorships, standards have been slipping. No-one has ever questioned what's been going on because,' he offered me a faint smile, 'they're Faery Godmothers. They've rested on their laurels for too long and used their reputation to skate by.' He held up his hands. 'That doesn't mean to say that their intentions aren't still good or that good work isn't being done. Just that things could be ... better.'

I snorted. That was hardly news to my ears. Not after my last couple of days.

'With that said, however, there have been attempts to improve matters. My predecessor discussed the chance that the office would be placed under special measures...'

My mouth dropped open. 'No! Really?' Only the very worst faery departments ended up like that. Special measures meant regular inspections, constant target setting and frozen funds until things improved. Unfortunately, the stress of being under special measures usually meant that things actually got a whole lot worse.

The Devil's Advocate nodded. 'Oh yes. Since then there has

been a marked improvement across the board. Next month's audit was already scheduled, however, when the shit truly hit the fan.' His mouth flattened into a grim line. 'The kidnappings have everyone reeling. No-one has ever experienced anything like this before. Not in generations. Every single faery godmother up there is dealing not only with the anxiety about what has happened to their colleagues but fear that they will be next.'

My rage sparked once more. 'That doesn't mean I should be next either!'

He remained calm. 'Let me finish. What I am trying to say is that the atmosphere and welcome you have experienced so far is not typical. Under different circumstances, things would be very different for you.' He didn't move his eyes from mine. 'Fear causes people to react strongly. Especially when those people are faeries who aren't used to being threatened. That's without the atmosphere of mutual suspicion which now clouds everything. I understand you might not be impressed with your new colleagues but you should cut them some slack. They have all been struggling. Far more than they are letting on.'

My lip curled. 'So I'm a convenient scapegoat.'

'Something like that.' He grimaced in sympathy. 'It doesn't excuse the way you're being treated but it does explain it.'

I sniffed. 'A few barbed comments is one thing. But...'

'Being bait is something else,' he finished. 'Yes, I appreciate that.' He brought his palms together as if in prayer, before resting his chin on the tips of his fingers. 'I recommended some time ago that the office diversified itself. Long before the abductions began, I gave the Director a list of names of faeries who might suitable godmothers and who would bring different skillsets. Your name was on that list.'

Part of me felt a warm glow at being recognised in this

manner. Part of me remained disgusted. 'So it *is* your fault that my life is now on the line.'

'The plan to use you as bait was not my idea and I counseled against it. The Director is desperate, however. With every new disappearance, there is more strain to find out what's going on.' He gave me a pointed look. 'I'm sure I don't need to remind you of how important the families of the godmothers are and how much pressure they are able to bring to bear upon the entire department.'

'That's still no excuse,' I said.

'No,' he answered quietly. 'It's not. I had initially been under the impression that you were aware of the plan and had agreed to it.' His jaw tightened. 'You should have been given that opportunity.'

'They didn't want to give me the chance to back out,' I said bitterly.

His gaze remained steady. 'I can tell you that every precaution has been taken to ensure that you will not be in any actual danger. Every time you trigger the Metafora, you are followed. Usually within minutes. There is an entire team of faeries who are watching you work on the off-chance that you are then targeted.'

I tilted up my chin. 'If that's supposed to make me feel better,' I said, 'it doesn't.'

The Devil's Advocate exhaled. 'No, I don't suppose it does. Look, until now, we have had no leads. There have been no clues and no way to tell who is behind all of this. Lydia DuChamp's ear has changed things.'

I sat up straighter. 'You got something from the delivery faery?'

'No. He was a dead end. He never met the person who sent the ear. But I've been able to use some old magic to link to her ear and trace Lydia's whereabouts. I can't tell where she currently is but I can tell where she was. Until we had that ear, such a thing wasn't even remotely possible. Believe me, Saffron, I'm doing everything I can to find the bastard who's behind this without going near you and your work.'

'The park,' I said. 'That's why you were at St Clements Park.'

He nodded. 'As far as I can tell, she was taken from there. It's not much but it's a start. I was coming back here to check the records and see if she was at that park for any specific reason. She might have been meeting a client there. Once I can find out who, then I've got more chance of finding more about her actual abduction.' His expression turned darkly earnest. 'I am trying to find the perpetrator before anyone else gets hurt.'

There was an odd whirring sound. Both the Devil's Advocate and I looked around, expecting the lift to start moving again. Unfortunately, it just juddered for a moment before the whirring stopped.

'Saffron,' he said, 'you know you can leave at any time. The dope faeries will have you back with open arms. Your old boss was most reluctant to let you go in the first place. No-one will reproach you for returning there.'

'But some other poor bugger will then be drafted into my place, right? Some other expendable faery will be used as bait.'

His gaze shifted. 'Probably,' he admitted.

'If I walk out that door,' I told him, 'I'll never be allowed back in. This is my one and only chance to be a real faery godmother. I've always dreamed of this. I'm won't allow one evil bastard or a bunch of conniving godmothers stop me from achieving my dream.'

The Devil's Advocate was silent for a moment before speaking. 'Good for you,' he said finally. He dropped his hands and leaned forward. 'So why were you there? What brought you to St Clements Park?'

I pushed back my hair. 'I thought that if I could solve the

kidnappings, I'd no longer be in danger.' I told him about Duncan and his drug-dealing boogeyman. 'It was always a long shot but it was worth checking out. Even if everyone else thinks the kidnappings are an inside job.'

He absorbed this. 'You're sure that this ... boogeyman has nothing to do with it?'

I shrugged. 'Pretty damn sure. He's scum but he doesn't know anything about faeries.' I twiddled with my cuffs. 'You know, Mr Devil's Advocate, that no-one does. The only people who know faery godmothers exist are faeries themselves. Whether it's someone from this actual office or not, it still has to be one of our own who's behind all this.'

'Yes,' he said heavily. 'I realise that.'

'Do you have any ideas as to motive?'

He shook his head. 'No. I can't imagine why a faery would want to do this to another faery. It beggars belief. It's clearly some sort of vendetta against the godmothers, however. No other department has been involved.'

'Apart from yours,' I pointed out. If you could call the one man band of the Devil's Advocate's office a 'department'.

He laughed slightly. 'Yes. Apart from mine.' He hesitated and looked at me. 'It's Jasper, by the way.'

I stared at him. 'Pardon?'

'My name is Jasper. After being stuck in a lift together for this long, the least you deserve is my real name.' He raised an eyebrow. 'And if you're serious about finding the bastard behind all of this, why don't we join forces? I'm sure you've got work to do this afternoon. Once I've checked out Lydia's records, I'm going to find out more about St Clements Park and then return there. Why don't you join me? Around five o'clock? I've been too close to all this shit for too long. A fresh perspective might help.'

I swallowed. Out of all the things I'd been expecting him to say, this hadn't been one of them. I could hardly say no, however. 'That depends on whether we both ever get out of this lift,' I reminded him.

His mouth crooked up. 'True.' He reached one hand out towards me. 'You have a few crumbs stuck to your chin,' he said. 'Stay still.' He gently brushed them away.

'You could have said something before now,' I accused.

He grinned. 'Where would be the fun in that?' He glanced down, his smooth brow furrowing. 'Why is your arm bleeding?'

I started. 'What?' I followed his gaze, then realised he was staring at the spot where I'd unfortunately gotten myself tattooed with a very ugly cat.

'It's nothing,' I said.

'It doesn't look like nothing. Did that drug dealer attack you?' His eyes glinted with a hard anger that reminded me of who he actually was.

'No. Don't worry about it.'

Jasper glared some more. 'Show me.'

'No.'

'Saffron, if you're hiding some sort of wound in order to make yourself look tough in front of me, then your intentions are very misguided.'

'It's not a wound.' I sighed then rolled up my sleeve. 'It's a tattoo.'

He did a double take. 'A tattoo?' He peered at my arm. 'Of what? Is that some sort of dog?' He squinted. 'A raccoon perhaps?'

'It's a cat,' I said stiffly. The last thing I wanted to do to tell him that it hadn't been an entirely deliberate choice. 'A stylized cat.'

'Are you sure? Because...'

I yanked my sleeve down. 'What I do with my own body is up to me.'

'Of course it is. I'm just ... surprised. That's all.' He fidgeted in a most uncharacteristic fashion. 'You know, Saffron,' he began, 'I ...'

'We've got it!' Mrs Jardine's tinny voice broke through the intercom. 'Any second now! I'm so sorry about all of this. It's never happened before.'

The Devil's Advocate – or rather Jasper – pulled back and immediately stood up. 'You should see to it that it doesn't happen again,' he said gruffly for Mrs Jardine's benefit.

There was a jolt and the lift began to move. I hastily got to my own feet and brushed myself down before the lift doors opened and the main office floor was revealed, along with the large group of wide-eyed faery godmothers who had clearly been panicking that the Devil's Advocate was stuck in the lift.

'Well, that was fun!' I declared loudly. I turned to Jasper and gave his cheek a kiss. 'We should spend more time in the lift together,' I told him, adding in a saucy wink for the benefit of everyone else.

His arm went briefly round my waist and his mouth found my ear. 'It wouldn't be the worst thing that could happen,' he murmured, before releasing me and striding off in the direction of the Director's office.

I swallowed hard. No. Surprisingly, it wouldn't be the worst thing at all.

CHAPTER
SIXTEEN

It turned out that all I had to do in order to gain myself some office 'friends' was to get stuck in a lift with the Devil's Advocate for half an hour. By the time I got back to my desk, I'd garnered myself all sorts of hangers-on.

'I always said,' sighed Figgy, blinking her enormous eyelashes in my direction, 'that if I was going to get myself stuck in a lift with anyone, it would be the Devil's Advocate.'

'You didn't snog him, did you?' Rupert asked me, with a dark edge. Clearly, sex was the only thing on his mind. Ever.

Alicia snorted in derision. 'He wouldn't kiss *her*.' She tossed her head and stomped off to her desk, muttering to herself about the important work she had to complete.

Billy wasted no time in getting himself involved. 'There is to be no crowding around cubicles!' he said in a high pitched complaint. 'It's a fire hazard!' He gave me a long look, apparently as curious to know what had happened as everyone else was.

Delilah ignored everyone and leaned across to me. 'You'll tell me all about it once everyone's gone,' she said, her tone suggesting a command rather than a mere request.

Not everyone was impressed. Adeline appeared, again as if out of nowhere. She put her hands on her hips and glowered at the small crowd. Almost immediately, they all melted away.

'I trust there are no ill side effects from your little misadventure, Saffron?' she inquired.

'No.' I shook my head. 'I'm fine.' I managed a fake smile. 'Thank you so much for asking though.'

She looked at me, seemingly convinced that I had ulterior motives and had engineered the lift's failure just so I could have some time alone with the Devil's Advocate. 'How are your clients coming along? How many have you completed?'

She seemed to have forgotten that this was still only my second day and that I'd had no training whatsoever.

'Er, none.'

Adeline stared at me, her foot beginning to tap the floor. 'How many have you visited?'

'One.'

She folded her arms. 'Luke Wells.' She arched her eyebrows. 'And you've not yet granted him another proper wish?'

'I haven't finished investigating him yet.'

Her expression grew more stony. 'I gave you eight clients to work through by the end of the week.'

I stood my ground. I'd had enough of being treated like dirt. 'I will do my best to get through them all,' I answered evenly. 'But I want to do my best by my clients as well. That takes time.'

She pointed at the Metafora door. 'Then get out there and do so! Go visit more of them!' She spun around and marched away.

I couldn't help thinking that she wanted me out on the streets and trying to do my job so that there was more chance I'd be kidnapped in the process. All the same, I snapped my heels together and saluted her in return. No matter what else had happened today, I meant what I said. I was still a faery godmother no matter what. And I would still prove that I could be fabulous at it. I reached for the nearest file on my desk, giving a Delilah a helpless shrug to indicate that I couldn't stay and gossip now. Then I headed back for the Metafora room. Perhaps my other clients would be less complicated than Luke Wells and I'd be able to tick through their names with ease.

I smirked to myself. As if. Nothing about this job was every going to be easy.

For no other reason than it would make Billy smile, I wore my pink cloak. In this part of London, no-one blinked an eye. I knocked on the door and waited for Rachel Goldberg, client number two, to answer.

It took longer than I thought for her to come to the door. When she did, she looked considerably wearier and more harassed than both her picture and her file had suggested. From somewhere further in the house a baby cried. Hmm. That was something else the file had failed to mention.

'Mrs Goldberg,' I began. 'I'm ...'

She motioned inside. 'Come in.' Her voice wavered and I had the sudden feeling she was about to start sobbing. 'I was expecting you half an hour ago.'

She was?

'I know you health visitors are busy,' she said, 'and you have lots of people to see. Thank you so much for coming at such short notice. I'm at the end of my tether.'

Ah. I nodded to myself and put on an apologetic smile. 'I'm so sorry I couldn't be here earlier.' I walked into her house as she closed the door.

'Would you like a cup of tea? I don't have any milk.' She sighed. 'Actually, I'm not sure I have any tea.'

I waved a hand at her. 'I'm fine.'

She bobbed her head distractedly and turned away. I followed her into the next room, where she picked the still crying baby up out of his crib and held him out to me. 'Here,' she said. 'You take him.'

I didn't feel I had much choice in the matter. I had next to no experience with children, let alone ones of this sort of age. I awkwardly took him from her arms and did my best to cradle him. His face was red and screwed up and, rather than calm down now that he was getting some attention, he simply squalled even louder.

'He doesn't need changing,' Rachel Goldberg said. 'He's just been fed. I've read him a story. I've picked him up. I've put him down. I've taken him for a walk. I've sung to him.' She raised her hands to her head and, for an alarming moment, I thought she was going to start hitting herself. 'I don't know what to do. Nothing works.' She looked at me with large, pleading eyes. 'You have to help me.'

'That's what I'm here for.' I began to rock the baby. He cried harder. 'What's he called?'

'Mikey.' She sank down into the nearest chair. 'Oh God. I don't know what I'm doing. I'm terrible at this. Do you know, this time last year, I was in Peru. I hiked along the Inca Trail. I traversed the Amazon. Now I can't traverse my own damn living room without wanting to give up.' Her head dropped. 'I don't want to do this any longer. I don't want to be a mother. I made a mistake.'

It wasn't much of a stretch to realise that this wasn't actually her wish. I could do it. I was certain I could wave my wand and disappear away baby Mikey. This wasn't what Rachel needed though. I supposed I could wave my wand and make him stop crying. Give Rachel a decent night's sleep from here on out. It would make her happy, no doubt about it. But I could do better than that.

'I'm a horrible person,' she whispered. 'I'm a horrible, horrible person.'

I barely heard her over Mikey's cries. 'You're not a horrible person, Rachel. You're a normal, tired person.'

She sprang up to her feet. 'Look at him! Listen to him! My child is screaming his head off! How unhappy must he be if he has to cry that loudly that often? And I. Don't. Care.'

'But,' I said equably, 'you do care. Otherwise you wouldn't have called me. You wouldn't be so upset now.' I smiled at her. 'You want Mikey to be happy, don't you? Because when he's happy, you'll be happy.'

She wiped her nose with the back of her sleeve. 'Yes.' She nodded. 'That's what I want. That's all I want.'

Whether I was going to be the best faery godmother in the world or not, I couldn't make Mikey happy for the rest of his life. Happiness didn't exist without unhappiness. If you didn't know what it meant to be sad, then you'd never know what it meant to be happy. Yin and yang. What I could do, however, would be to make Mikey *mostly* happy. And able to deal with life's inevitable hardships with a positive outlook. Such a wish would fulfill both Rachel and Mikey's needs right now – and also for years to come. A child was for life, after all.

'Rachel,' I said, wishing I could conjure up some sort drum roll or dramatic music to add wonderful emphasis to this moment, 'your wish is granted.'

She frowned. 'Huh?'

'Here,' I said. 'Take Mikey.'

A fearful expression crossed her face. 'Can't you keep him for a little bit longer?'

'Nope.' I beamed.

With obvious reluctance, she lifted him from my arms. Once I was free from my temporary burden, I reached into my sleeve and drew out my wand. With one sweeping swirl, I waved it around the pair of them. Mikey's sobs subsided. He let out a small hiccup and then looked round, clearly confused. He knew something had changed. He just didn't know what.

'I don't understand,' Rachel said. 'What did I do to make him stop?'

'You're his mum.' I leaned over and smiled at him, gently chucking him under the chin. His blue eyes, with the traces of tears still collecting in their corners, blinked up at me. 'Things will be better for you now,' I promised. I glanced up at Rachel who was staring at her son in frank astonishment. 'He'll still cry. It's how he communicates with you. But it should be easier now for you both.'

She didn't look up. She remained absorbed in the miracle that was her now quiet baby. 'Hey Mikey,' she cooed.

I grinned. 'I'll let myself out.'

'Mmm.'

I strolled out, pausing at an elaborate sculpture of a dancer. I gave her outstretched hand a high five. 'I did it,' I told her. 'I did this.' I winked at her and then all but skipped back out.

Although it was yet again beginning to rain outside, and I was standing in a puddle, I remained thrilled enough at my own achievement that I completed a full Wonder Woman spin. My entire body buzzed with adrenaline and delight. This was why this job was worth all the trouble. This was why I wanted to be a faery godmother. Then I caught sight of another faery on the other side of the road, hastily dipping out of view. Ah, piss off, I thought to myself. Even a stark reminder of my impending doom wasn't enough to ruin my current mood. I glanced around for signs of any evil kidnappers. But unless the rosy cheeked health visitor now bustling towards Rachel's house had a secret fetish for severed ears, I appeared to be safe. At least for now.

CHAPTER
SEVENTEEN

I'd have built on my success with Rachel and gone off to visit more clients but it took so long to navigate the report system and write up what had occurred that in the end I didn't have time. It didn't help that I lost my work twice when I clicked onto the next screen, even though I'd been sure that I'd pressed save. It took me three times as long as to write my report as it had to actually visit her and grant her wish. The joys of bureaucracy. I was only just finishing up when Jasper reappeared, his looming presence filling the entire office. I supposed I should be pleased that almost everyone else had already vanished, and only Billy remained to send me an arch look as I joined Jasper before we headed out together.

'Maybe we should take the stairs,' I said, eyeing the lift doubtfully.

'Lightning doesn't strike twice.'

I scratched my neck. 'You know that's not true.'

'We'll be fine.' He strode into the lift without any further hesitation. Then he beckoned towards me. 'Come on. I'll fill you in with what I discovered along the way. I should warn you though. There's not much to tell.'

I followed him in, pretending to myself that I wasn't holding my breath all the way down. Strange that I hadn't felt nervous when the lift had actually broken but that now the thought of it doing the same again made me anxious. Anticipation, I decided. It could either be the most delicious thing in the world or the most terrifying.

In any case, we made it down to the ground floor without incident. Mrs Jardine, who was in the process of packing her own stuff up, looked up as we exited. I thought I detected a glimmer of disapproval in her eyes but whether it was directed at Jasper or me, I couldn't have said.

'None of Lydia's recent clients,' Jasper told me, 'had anything to do with St Clements Park. None of them live even remotely in the vicinity. In fact, she's not had a client in this city for some time. There's no documented reason why she would have been there at all. But the blood I found there is definitely hers. I'm convinced it's where she was abducted from. If we can find out why she was in the park, then we might be able to discover who she was meeting and then who took her.'

'Maybe she went out there for lunch,' I said, thinking aloud. 'You know, to take in the fresh air and have a change of scene.'

Jasper shot me a wry glance. 'You did the see the same park I did, right? It's hardly a picturesque peaceful haven of nature.'

True. And I could also attest to the fact that the one and only sandwich shop in the vicinity was not worth travelling any distance for. My cheese and pickle had been repeating on me all afternoon as an unpleasant reminder that I should stick to the staff canteen.

'In any case,' Jasper continued, 'if Lydia DuChamp wasn't actually visiting a client when she was taken, then the memory magic wouldn't have worked. Anyone who witnessed her abduction would remember it. And there have been no reports made to the police, no remarks on social media. There's nothing to suggest she was ever there at all.'

'Apart from her blood.'

His mouth flattened. 'Apart from that.'

I considered his words. 'So,' I said, 'you reckon she was there at night time. She wandered into that dodgy park under cover of darkness and then she was kidnapped. Unless she was looking for illicit drugs from the boogeyman, someone else lured her there.' I breathed out. 'That means that you can stop pointing fingers at everyone in the faery godmothers' office. It's not an inside job after all.'

'That's highly likely. Whoever is behind all this wanted us to blame each other.' He continued to watch me. 'Until now, we believed that Lydia had vanished some time late afternoon while meeting a client in Oxford. We believed the same of the others who've gone missing. That they all disappeared when out working. But if that was part of the kidnapper's plan and each victim was lured out instead of being abducted while on the job then he also wanted to spread considerable dissension in the ranks. He wanted us to think that it had to be another faery godmother who was responsible.'

'Which is why I'm being followed whenever I go out to nearby locations,' I interrupted, unable to help myself. 'If the others were supposedly taken while they were working then the same will happen to me. If I'm actually targeted at all, that is.'

He gave me a curt nod. 'Regardless of what happened to the other faery godmothers, there's no trace of Lydia at the location of her last job and her client's wish wasn't granted.'

'Luke Wells, you mean.' At Jasper's glance, I raised my shoulders. 'He's one of my clients now too.'

Jasper hissed through his teeth. For some reason that pleased me. 'In any case, this new evidence from St Clements

Park doesn't support the theory that she was abducted while at work. No-one saw her after lunch on the day she disappeared. Perhaps that was deliberate on the part of the kidnapper to mislead us. Everything I've found indicates Lydia DuChamp was taken violently from that park.'

I sighed. 'Except you don't want us to go to the park, do you? You want us to go and talk to the boogeyman. He might not have had anything to do with her actual disappearance but he might have been the reason why she was there in the first place. If he wasn't, then we know to look harder for who might have arranged to meet her there.'

Jasper smiled. 'You're really are smarter than you've been given credit for. If your boogeyman spends as much time as he seems to in that park, he might have seen Lydia getting kidnapped.'

'Hmm. Given his proclivities, he wouldn't want to report what he saw either to the police.' It did make some sense. A brief thrill ran through me. Maybe we were onto something.

Jasper sensed my excitement. 'Ready to play detective, Saffron?' His fingers twitched in my direction.

I grinned at him. 'Suit me up.'

The Devil's Advocate was no ordinary faery. Whereas I could rarely perform a glamour upon myself, even with the magical boost I was granted when I was on duty, he managed to conjure one up for the pair of us with ease. It wouldn't fool another faery – no glamour could manage that. It would, however, be more than anything to serve our purposes in getting past the local human police so we could talk to the boogeyman.

'I don't know his real name,' I cautioned. 'But he'll definitely have been taken to the Goddard Street station. It's the main police station for this area and it has a large number of cells where people are held.'

Jasper crooked up an eyebrow. 'Dare I ask why you know so much about local incarceration tactics?'

'I know a lot about national incarceration tactics,' I told him. 'I was a dope faery, remember? I could tell you about most of the different police headquarters up and down the country.' I paused, my thoughts darkening. 'We work all across the United Kingdom. All faeries do. It can't be a coincidence that Lydia went missing right on our own doorstep.'

'No,' he agreed grimly. 'It can't. Whoever is behind all this snatched her from under our noses for the same reason that they sent us her ear. They're taunting us.' His lip curled. 'Showing off.'

'Well,' I said, 'let's hope that makes them more likely to trip up and make a mistake.'

We exchanged glances then, in focused silence, headed for Goddard Street, marching abreast and causing various passersby to scoot out of our way. Under other circumstances, I'd probably have enjoyed myself. It wasn't every day you got to pound the pavements with the Devil's Advocate by your side. I checked my surroundings, part of me hoping that I was being followed so that the spy faeries could take note of my new companion and be suitably admiring. Alas, however, the coast seemed clear. I was no longer officially at work and therefore no longer at supposed risk. Then I told myself that five faery godmothers were either dead or in dire peril and the last thing I should be worried about was how I looked to others. I grimaced and pushed those sorts of self-involved thoughts away. There were far more important matters in hand.

The station on Goddard Street was a large, rambling sort of place. From the outside it appeared almost pokey but once you entered it was a labyrinthine maze of corridors and rooms. To reach that inner sanctum, however, you first had to get past the front desk. With Jasper's glamour in place, I didn't think it would be a problem.

'Good evening,' I said to the uniformed officer scribbling at something on a clipboard from behind the glass at the front desk. 'I'm Detective Inspector Sawyer and this is my colleague PC Advocate. We are to speak to a gentleman who was arrested earlier today at St Clements Park.'

'Name?'

'I don't know his name,' I answered honestly. 'We've not been given that information. It's possible, however, that he may have knowledge of another case we are investigating. It's imperative we speak to him as quickly as possible.'

The police officer, whose blonde hair had been gelled to within an inch of its life, looked from me to Jasper and back again. 'You got ID?'

'Of course.' I pulled out my wallet and showed him my gym membership card. He peered at it for a long moment before nodding. 'Let me check the records.' He turned away and began to tap at a nearby computer.

I nudged Jasper. 'Look at that,' I marveled. 'Your glamour held up.'

'Of course it held up,' he muttered. 'Tell me. Why do you get to be the DI while I'm the lowly PC?'

I smirked.

'Vincent Hamilton,' the police officer said. 'He's in the holding cells before his court appearance tomorrow morning. I'll buzz you through.'

'Thank you.'

'No problem.'

I dipped my head at him and waited for the door to be opened. Then Jasper and I strolled through. It was as easy as that.

The cells, which were in the eastern wing of the building, smelled strongly of cheap bleach. A second officer unlocked Hamilton's cell door and gestured in towards him.

'Hamilton! You're up. This way.'

There was a muffled grunt then the boogeyman himself shuffled out, an expression of bored disgust on his face. Then he caught sight of me waiting at the end of the corridor and his mouth twisted into something far uglier. 'You!' he spat. 'I knew this was down to you all along. What are you? Some kind of undercover pig chick?'

I raised my voice. 'Let's save it for the interview room, Mr Hamilton.'

He rolled his eyes. 'Bitch.'

Yeah, yeah. If he thought I was a bitch, he should come and meet more faery godmothers. I reckoned I was remarkably sweet by comparison.

He grumbled all the way behind us and then grumbled some more when he was deposited in a chair in the drab interview room. Jasper and I took our seats opposite him.

'I want a lawyer. I ain't saying nuthin till I've seen my lawyer.'

'He's on his way, Mr Hamilton.'

He glared at me. 'My lawyer's a woman.'

I cursed inwardly. It was galling when even I made sexist assumptions. 'I'm glad to hear you're an equal opportunities drug dealer.'

Hamilton's nostrils flared. 'Yeah. I got female lawyers. Female customers. Female pigs.' He leaned forward. 'I also help out the odd female faery.'

Beside me, Jasper stiffened. I didn't miss a beat. 'You're a helpful sort, Vincent. So why don't you help us out again now?'

'Why the fuck would I wanna do that?'

'You help us, we help you,' Jasper said.

Vincent Hamilton jerked his chin sharply upwards. 'You'll get me out of here?'

'We can't promise that. But we can perhaps mitigate your current circumstances.'

He narrowed his eyes in suspicion. 'How?'

I smiled. 'I'll forget that you tried to sell me some of your ... wares. You can argue they were for personal use only rather than possession with intent to supply.' Considering how much his pockets had been bulging, I very much doubted that sort of argument would wash with anyone. Mr Hamilton was going away for a very long time. He didn't need to know that though.

'I had too much on me,' he sneered. 'I'm going down no matter what. Unless you do for me.'

Fuck a puck. I'd under-estimated his knowledge of the system. I flicked a side glance at Jasper. 'Will he remember this?' I asked. 'Or will your magic cover us?'

'He wouldn't have remembered a thing,' Jasper said tightly. 'Except for the fact that you already told him directly that you're a faery yourself. You neglected to mention that part. I thought you'd just discussed the idea with him. That was a dick move, Saffron. You knew you weren't covered by memory magic at the time. What you've done is incredibly dangerous and foolhardy. You have no idea what the consequences might be.'

'He didn't believe what I told him,' I protested, feeling my cheeks grow irritatingly warm. 'Anyway, it was the fastest way to find out if he had anything to do with the abductions. I didn't think I'd ever see him again.' I gestured helplessly. 'What does it matter?'

'His subconscious believes it. It will interfere with the memory magic. The CCTV is automatically covered by my magic because I'm here on official Devil's Advocate business. The police officers' memories are covered by me for the same reason.' He pointed at Vincent. 'But because you already told him you're a faery, you've blown any chance that he'll forget about this. You've also blown any chance we had to manipulate this situation to our favour.'

Oh. My shoulders sagged slightly. 'I didn't know that was a thing.' It had never come up before. Let's face it, I'd never introduced myself as a faery to a human before unless I was working. Why would I? It simply wasn't the done thing. Any human I told would have thought I was looney.

Vincent was staring at both of us as if we were crazy. 'What the fuck are you two on about?'

'If I'd known about this beforehand,' Jasper muttered under his breath, 'you'd have stayed outside.' He shook his head, unable to believe how stupid I'd been, and raised his voice. 'My colleague here is a faery godmother. She will grant you a wish in return for your cooperation in answering a few questions with full and honest detail.'

Vincent laughed derisively and folded his arms. 'Yeah, yeah. I didn't believe her the first time around. Why would I believe you?'

'Because you want to,' Jasper said simply.

Vincent's mouth curved into a mocking smile. 'Sure. Well, then I wish to be released without charge. Do that and I'll answer any questions you've got.'

I glared at Jasper. 'I'm not granting him any wishes. Certainly not that one. I'm not even on the job right now. The magic probably won't work.'

'It'll work. You've got your wand, don't you? And unless you have a better plan as to how to get him to talk, this is how it's got to happen.' His expression hardened. He was very pissed off with me. 'The lives of several faery godmothers are on the line.'

'Fuck a puck.' I rolled my eyes. 'Fine,' I said to Vincent. I took out my wand and gave it a quick swish. 'Your wish is granted.

But if you ever tell anyone about this, it will immediately be rescinded.'

'Re-what?'

'The wish will stop working and you'll be taken back into custody.' I frowned at him. 'And if you commit any more crimes you'll also end up here. Got that?'

'Sure.' He laughed. 'I got it.' He waved an arm around. 'I'm still here though, ain't I? Some faery godmother you are.'

There was a knock at the door and it opened. 'Sorry, Detective,' said one of the police officers. 'We don't have enough to hold Mr Hamilton any longer. He's being released as of this minute.'

Vincent's mouth dropped open. 'I don't believe it.'

'It's your lucky day,' the officer said, with another apologetic look at me. 'Come on. We'll sort out your paperwork and you can crawl back under whichever rock you came from.'

Vincent smiled so broadly, I thought his face was going to crack. 'Awesome.'

I sighed. 'Great. Just great.'

CHAPTER EIGHTEEN

'Look,' I said to Jasper as we waited outside for Vincent Hamilton to exit the police station, 'that memory business was an honest mistake to make.'

He pressed his lips together. 'Mmm.'

'I didn't know it was a thing! It's not like I usually go around introducing myself as a faery whenever I chat to humans.'

'It's the most basic rule of first impressions. You can't overwrite them. We might be magic, Saffron, but we're not God.'

'I didn't know.'

He sent me a dark look. 'You should have.'

Yeah. Probably. I wrinkled my nose and sighed. 'We could have found another way to get Hamilton to tell us what we need instead of granting his wish.'

'Not quickly. Five lives are hanging in the balance. Assuming they're actually still alive.'

I cursed. He really didn't need to remind me of that. 'What a fuck up.'

Jasper ran an irritated hand through his hair. 'Worse things have happened. We can't change it now so let's forget about it and hope that Mr Hamilton doesn't capitalize on his new knowledge in ways that will cause us more problems down the line.'

I dreaded to think. I wrapped my arms round myself. It didn't look like my first week in my dream job was improving in any way, shape or form.

The front door of the police station opened and Vincent Hamilton appeared. He cupped his hands together, lighting a cigarette, then swaggered down the steps with his trenchcoat flapping behind him.

'Thanks, faeries,' he said, raising a hand towards us and then pushing past us.

Jasper shot an arm out and hauled him back. 'We had a deal, human. Quid pro quo. You have a few questions to answer.'

Hamilton shrugged amiably. 'Maybe tomorrow. I lost a lot of time being locked away in there. I've got things to do and places to be.'

I narrowed my eyes at him. I couldn't help noticing that time wasn't the only thing he'd lost. His thick accent also appeared to have vanished and his grammar was considerably improved. I supposed all of us were now able to drop our facades. We all knew the truth.

'Fat chance, buster. We got you out of there and we can put you right back. Either answer of questions or go down.' I shrugged. 'It's your choice.'

Hamilton huffed loudly to emphasise that all this was a terrible inconvenience to him. 'Fine,' he eventually said. He gestured towards us. 'Ask away.'

Jasper stepped towards him. He was at least a foot taller than the drug dealer and managed to cast an impressively threatening presence. 'We will know,' he said, 'if you lie.'

'And if you do,' I added, 'it won't go well for you.'

Hamilton held up his hands, palms stretched outwards. 'I won't lie.' He offered us a toothy grin. 'I'm a good boy.'

I rolled my eyes. As if.

Jasper reached into his inside pocket and drew out a photo of Lydia. From the background, it looked like it was also her office ID although her picture was considerably more aesthetically pleasing than mine was. 'Have you ever seen this woman?'

Hamilton barely glanced at it. 'No.'

'Look again,' Jasper growled.

He muttered something and took the photo, his dirty fingers with the nails bitten down to the quick oddly incongruous against the fixed, smiling glamour of Lydia. Then he sighed and passed it back. 'I don't know her name. I didn't speak to her.'

My entire body tensed. Jasper's expression grew more watchful. Maybe all this would be worth it after all.

'I saw her in St Clements Park three days running,' Hamilton said. 'She looked like she was waiting for someone. She hung around for a few hours or so on each day before leaving. She didn't speak to anyone but she seemed watchful.' He shrugged. 'She was pretty. I enjoyed watching her too. She didn't ever approach me though. It wasn't me she was interested in.'

'What days were these?'

Hamilton raised his eyes up as he tried to think. 'Not last week but the week before. Wednesday, Thursday and Friday. I remember that Friday was the last day because on that day I almost got knocked out by some prick who was trying to muscle in on my turf. He thought that he could set up shop here. Here! I've been selling on this spot for two years! Ratty bastard thought he could steal my space and...'

'Let's stay focused on this woman, shall we?' I said. 'Her name is Lydia,' I told him, hoping that making her appear more like a real person would encourage Hamilton to open up further. The Friday he'd mentioned was the same day Lydia had vanished. The grimy drug dealer might have been the very last person to see her.

'Is she a faery too?' he asked.

'Who she is doesn't matter,' Jasper said. 'What happened to her does. What time was it that you saw her? What time of day was she in the park?'

Hamilton waved his bare wrists towards Jasper. 'I don't know. Half past a bloody freckle. I don't wear a watch, do I?'

From what I could tell, Jasper was barely keeping a hold on his temper. 'A rough estimate will do. Morning? Evening?'

'Early evening, I suppose.'

So not dark yet then. I frowned. Given the blood that Jasper had discovered, there had clearly been a struggle of some sort. That was bold. As dodgy as this park was, there were still enough passersby that someone would have noticed. Some Good Samaritan would have intervened.

Jasper took out some more photos. 'What about these people?' he asked. 'Have you seen any of them?'

Hamilton rifled through the pictures of the other missing faeries. 'Yeah. I might have.'

Tension clawed at me. 'Where?' I demanded. 'In the park too?'

Hamilton was starting to pout. 'Just how many questions are you going to ask?'

'As many as we need,' Jasper told him, with such a dangerous undertone that the drug dealer stopped whining and yielded to the inevitable.

'Yes,' he said. 'In the fucking park. And, no. I didn't see what happened to them.' He pulled out one of the photos and held it up. 'This one spoke to me. He asked if I was Bernard.'

'That's Boris, right?' I murmured to Jasper.

He nodded. 'What did you say to him, Vincent?'

'The truth. I don't know anyone called Bernard. I'd have pulled a fast one on him but I thought it might be some Grindr date thing so I said I didn't know him.' He leered at me. 'I like women. Not men. Don't go getting any ideas though, darling. I don't go for women with hair like yours. Yours is a bit messy.'

I stared at him. 'While you are a dapper gentleman who's the very epitome of a sleek, manicured style.'

'Yeah.' He grinned with a slight hint of self-mockery. Apparently good ol' Vincent was still playing something of a role.

'When exactly did you see these others?'

He splayed out his arms in a massive shrug. 'I don't know. It was a while back. I didn't see them together. They were always alone. They were always waiting for someone. They'd be there for three days on the trot then I wouldn't see them again.'

'Who else have you seen loitering around the park, Vincent?' Jasper's voice was softer now. More coaxing. We were getting somewhere. We had a name if nothing else. Bernard. I savoured it in my mouth. Watch out, Bernard. We were coming for you.

'I'm not telling you about my customers. I don't grass on them and they don't grass on me. I don't care who you are or what you've done for me.'

I didn't think it was Vincent Hamilton's customers we were after. 'Not them,' I said. 'Tell us about the others.'

He scratched his groin absently.

'The ratty bastard for one. The one I told you about already. Middle aged woman who works at the accountancy firm across the street. She comes and sits here most evenings. There's also some old biddy who walks a Yorkshire terrier. She's been coming here for years. It's why there's no decent plants left in this place. Her dog pisses over them all. Kills them stone dead.'

'Yeah, yeah. Anyone else?'

'A few teenagers. I'd try and sell them some stuff. A starter pack, if you like. I don't do kids though.'

I nodded. 'Because you're a man of principles.'

'That I am.' He put his hands in his pockets. 'That I am.'

'The ratty bastard. What does he look like?'

'White guy. Bald like me. Big ears.' He jerked his chin at Jasper. 'About the same height as you. He's better looking than you though.'

Jasper didn't smile. I did.

'Are we done here?' Hamilton asked. 'Can I go?'

Jasper took hold of the lapels of Hamilton's trenchcoat. 'Sure,' he said. 'If you want to go, you can go. Just a little warning first though, Vincent.'

'A teeny tiny one,' I said.

'Don't go telling all your friends about us,' Jasper told him. 'If you do, the wish will stop working. You'll be picked up by the police again and no amount of wishing will put you back on the streets.'

'And,' I said, 'no more drug dealing. Find yourself a proper job. One that's legal and above board. If I see you in this park again, I might wave my wand once more and you'll end up in a cell.'

'Finally,' Jasper said, 'You've never heard of faeries. You don't believe in faery godmothers. If I hear otherwise, then,' he tightened his grip, 'what do you think will happen, Vincent?'

'I'll be arrested again,' Hamilton answered sourly. 'I've got it.' He looked at us both. 'For what it's worth, I *don't* believe in faeries.'

'Good,' I said. 'Now scat.'

Jasper released his hold. Hamilton smoothed down his trenchcoat and smiled congenially at both of us. Then he began to cross the street. About half way over he glanced over his shoulder. When he realised we weren't following him, he started to sprint, his legs moving faster than they probably ever had before. Within moments, Vincent Hamilton had disappeared.

Jasper looked at me. 'We don't make a bad team.'

'It was a shaky start,' I agreed, 'but we got there. Do you think he'll keep his mouth shut?'

'Actually,' he said, 'I do. Not because he's afraid of the consequences if he blabs but because he's recognizes we've got power. Power that he might want to make use of again.'

I snorted. 'Blackmail, you mean? His continued cooperation for more wishes granted. That won't work.'

'No.' Jasper's mouth crooked up. 'It won't stop him trying though. Don't worry about it. I'll keep an eye on him. Besides, he did give us a lot to work with.'

'Mmm. There are still plenty of unanswered questions though.'

He glanced at me. 'Why don't we grab a drink somewhere and talk it all through?'

'A drink?' I asked. 'Like a real drink? An alcoholic drink? The high and mighty Devil's Advocate resorts to alcohol? I didn't think a man like you would have any such vices.'

Jasper's eyes darkened to a smoky green. 'You'd be surprised, Saffron. I'm no saint.'

I smiled. 'I'm pleased to hear it.'

I TOOK him to the Stagger Inn. It was a popular faery hang out, not to mention my local, so it would have been rude not to. When I walked in with Jasper right behind me, however, Harry's eyes just about popped out on stalks. Perhaps coming here had been a mistake.

'We can go somewhere else,' I said to Jasper under my

breath, as every single other faery in the dark pub turned towards him and stared.

'Why?' he asked. 'Here seems as good as anywhere.' He lifted up his chin and met every single stare with a hard-eyed gaze of his own. Everyone, apart from Harry, turned hastily away. 'What would you like?'

'Pint of Demon's Ale, please,' I said.

'Coming right up.'

I left Jasper to talk to the barman and get out drinks while I wandered over and joined Harry in the corner. I hadn't even sat myself down when he leaned over and, in a stunned whisper, said, 'Saffron! What the fuck is going on?'

I smiled primly. 'The Devil's Advocate and I are working together.'

'What?' His whisper rose to a near shriek. 'What do you mean you're working together?'

'We're going to solve the kidnappings and save the day.' I grinned. I was enjoying this.

'Solve the...' Harry shook his head. 'I thought the Devil's Advocate was one of the bastards who was setting you up as bait?'

'Actually,' I began.

Jasper appeared, placing two pints down on the table in front of us. 'Hi,' he said.

'This is Harry,' I told him. 'Harry, this is Ja...'

'The Devil's Advocate,' Jasper interrupted, holding out his hand. Harry took it and both men shook. 'Nice to meet you.'

'Likewise,' Harry muttered. He shot me another look and then took a sip of his drink. We all pretended not to notice the brief tremble in his hands as he raised his glass. Honestly, Jasper wasn't that scary.

'Harry,' I said overly loudly, 'did you know that if you introduce yourself as a faery when you first meet a human, and then later on you have to deal with them during the course of your job, memory magic doesn't work?'

Harry blinked at me. 'Er, no.'

I smiled, satisfied. 'See?' I said to Jasper.

'Although,' Harry added, 'I'm a rainbow faery. I don't deal with humans so it would never actually come up in my line of work.'

Jasper raised an eyebrow in my direction. I coughed. 'I think I've made my point regardless,' I said.

We all took another sip of our drinks, the awkward silence stretching out. Well, this wasn't weird at all.

Eventually, Harry put his drink down and straightened his shoulders. 'So,' he said, apparently now having had enough Dutch courage to address Jasper directly, 'is Saffron's life still in danger then?'

Jasper looked mildly astonished. 'I'm not sure it was ever in any real danger.' He glanced at me and I shrugged.

'I've told Harry everything that's been going on,' I said. 'We don't have any secrets.'

'Apart from,' Harry said, 'the fact that I enjoy a little sadomasochism at weekends.' He paused, his slight grin causing his eyes to dance. 'Oops. Did I say that aloud?'

I rolled my eyes. 'Don't mind him.'

Jasper frowned. 'You know I'll have to put that in my report.'

Harry instantly looked alarmed. Then he seemed to realise that Jasper was pulling his leg and relaxed once more. 'Fill me in then,' he commanded. 'What's been going on?'

I quickly outlined the last day or two. Harry nodded, listening carefully without interrupting. This was one of the many reasons why I liked him. He knew when to keep quiet and pay attention. It was a surprisingly rare skill.

'I've never heard of anyone called Bernard,' he said, once I'd finished.

Jasper took another drink. 'There's Bernard Wallace, a tooth faery who comes from Wales. He's about sixty, however, and as thin as a rake. Even Saffron here would manage to best him in a fight.'

'Oi!' I punched him lightly in the arm. Harry looked horrified but I reckoned that Jasper was secretly delighted. He didn't smite me on the spot anyway so I'd count that as delighted.

'There's also Bernard Moss,' he continued. 'But he's fifteen years old and more concerned with girls than with anything else. Including studying for his luck faery exams.'

'He probably doesn't need to study,' I mused. 'Considering he's about to become a luck faery.'

Jasper gave me a look. 'Everyone needs to study. Luck magic only extends to humans.'

'I was making a joke,' I told him.

He snorted. 'Not a very funny one.'

I'd give him that. 'So what's our next move then?'

'I'll check out both Bernards just in case. I think it's highly unlikely that either one of them is our man but it's worth being sure even though our kidnapper must be using an alias.' He tapped his long fingers on the table top. 'What we really need to work out is how each victim was lured to St Clements Park in the first place. If we knew that then we'd be some way closer to finding out who's behind all this. And rescuing those godmothers before anything worse happens to them.'

Harry glanced at us both. 'I've been thinking about that.'

'Go on.'

He fidgeted. 'When did the first disappearance happen?'

'Three months ago,' Jasper answered, without missing a beat.

'And all in that time, there's been no communication from

the kidnapper? No ransom notes? No letters? The ear that arrived this week has been the only thing?'

He nodded. 'Yes.'

'So why now?' Harry asked. 'Why send a body part now after all this time?'

'It's obviously some kind of message,' I said. 'Maybe a ransom note is about to follow.'

Harry scratched his head. 'How many kidnappers do you know who wait three months, looking after their abductees for all that time, without getting in touch?'

'I don't know any kidnappers, Harry.'

'You know what I mean.'

Jasper's expression was grim. 'Lydia was the last one taken. It could be that the others are already dead and he's changed tactics with her because killing is no longer enough.'

We all thought about that for a second. Up until now, I'd allowed myself to believe that the others were still alive, as Lydia had been at least up until the point her ear was sliced off. Jasper was right, however. It was perfectly plausible that the other faery godmothers were dead. It was even logical.

I drew back my shoulders. 'Whether they are still breathing or not, Harry makes a very good point. It doesn't make sense for the kidnapper to get in touch now. Unless...' my voice trailed off. I bit my lip.

'Unless,' Jasper finished for me, 'he's sending us a message because he's escalating matters.'

'It doesn't bode well,' Harry said.

No. It really didn't. I sighed heavily. 'I'll go back to the park tomorrow,' I said. 'We know that Lydia hung around for three days running before she was taken. Maybe I need to loiter there for longer before I'm approached.'

'You mean,' Jasper said, 'put yourself out there as bait. I thought that was the very thing which enraged you.'

'I'm choosing to do it this time,' I said. 'That's entirely different from being forced unknowingly into the same position.'

He inclined his head in brief acknowledgment. Harry looked highly entertained.

'I'll ask around the office too,' I declared, keen to change the subject. 'Maybe one of the missing godmothers mentioned something to someone else that can give us a clue as to why they went to St Clements Park in the first place.'

'Good plan,' Jasper agreed. I didn't argue. It wasn't a good plan but it was the best we had for now. 'Now that we know godmothers aren't being attacked when they're out on jobs, I'll get the Director to release you from your other clients. We should put our full attention towards this investigation.'

I started. 'You want us to work together full time?'

He turned his green eyes to mine. 'It makes sense.' His tone dropped a notch. 'Until you got yourself involved, we've been spinning around in circles. Now we're actually getting somewhere.'

Most of that was purely by coincidence. I decided not bother pointing that out, however. 'The thing is,' I began.

'What?'

I raised my shoulders awkwardly. 'I don't want to abandon my faery godmother duties entirely. I still want to be a faery godmother.'

Harry smiled. 'The best damn faery godmother in the world.'

'Amen.' I smiled back. 'If I abandon that work and we solve the case then it's entirely possible that I'll then be turfed out on my ear for not doing my real job properly.'

Jasper's expression darkened. 'That wouldn't happen. I wouldn't let it.'

Where there was a will, there was a way. I knew how most

of my colleagues felt about me. Not to mention the way the overly nice way Director spoke to me which suggested she actually despised me underneath her smiling mask. Adeline's snarky attitude towards me was far more trustworthy than the Director's. It was honest. 'All the same,' I said, 'I think I can do both. It's still possible that someone from within the office is involved. If I alter what I'm doing too obviously then it might alert them to the fact that we're getting closer. Not to mention that I've still got Lydia's old client, Luke, to worry about.'

'Then,' Jasper said, 'continue working with him alone. You'll have a hand in your godmother work should anyone question it but you'll have more time to focus on the investigation.'

I could cope with that. 'You'll clear it with the Director?'

'I will.'

Harry beamed at me. 'Look at you, Saffron! From dope faery to faery godmother to bona fide faery investigator with the Devil's Advocate in her back pocket.'

Jasper's brow furrowed. I raised my glass. 'Mad skills, Harry. Mad skills.'

CHAPTER NINETEEN

I arrived at the office ridiculously early the next morning. I was buzzing with anticipation at my plans for the day. By five o'clock, I told myself, I'd have rescued all the missing faery godmothers – all of whom would still be alive and well, minus one sole ear – and I'd be feted as the most wonderful faery the world had ever seen. I allowed myself a moment of picturing the other godmothers raising me up onto their shoulders and parading me around the office, while loudly singing 'For She's A Jolly Good Faery'. A girl could dream. Then I walked into the office lobby and realised that, despite my early start, Mrs Jardine was still here before me and I didn't feel quite so buoyant.

'Good morning, Saffron,' she said primly as I walked up to the desk.

'Good morning, Mrs Jardine,' I answered. I crossed my fingers, part of me hoping that she would now afford me the same latitude which Alicia enjoyed and ask me to call her Miranda. Alas, no such nicety was forthcoming. 'How are you this fine morning?'

She sniffed. 'I'm alright, I suppose.' She pursed her lips. 'How are you?'

'Good.'

She glanced behind me as if expecting to see someone behind me. 'And the Devil's Advocate? How is he?'

I repressed a grin. 'I have no idea. I didn't spend the night with him, if that's what you're wondering.'

She stared at me. 'I wasn't wondering that at all. I couldn't give a single fig for your sex life. What I do care about, however, is this office. Is he likely to be joining us today?'

I looked down. Despite her professional demeanour, her fingers were so tightly curled around her fountain pen that her knuckles were white with the tension. 'I don't think so,' I said softly. I debated whether to tell her that I was no longer being used as unwitting bait and was now entirely ... witting, if that was a word. It seemed wise to keep the plan to myself for now, however. After all, we still didn't know everything that was going on or who was involved.

I pressed my thumb down onto the sign in sheet before heading up to the office. When I stepped out of the lift, which had managed to make its way all the way up without any sort of incident or mishap whatsoever, I realised that Mrs Jardine wasn't the only one who'd come in early. At least half of the office was already here. I gaped. The official start time was 9am. It wasn't even seven yet and the place was already remarkably full. Perhaps I'd not given the other faery godmothers enough credit for how hard they all worked.

Pleased that I'd at least remembered to bring my own mug in this morning, I headed first to the little kitchen to make myself a coffee. I'd barely managed to flick the kettle on when Rupert appeared, leaning against the doorway with his hair falling across his forehead and at least one curl hanging over his eyes so that he was looking at me with some sort of faked squint which I supposed was meant to come across as both artless and sexy.

'Hello Rupert,' I said. I pointed at his hair. 'Isn't that annoying? I know the name of a good barber if you need one.'

He blinked at me and pushed the curl back. 'Thank you but no,' he muttered. He watched as I busied myself with measuring out a teaspoon of coffee into my mug. He obviously wanted to say something but was waiting for me to ask him what it was first. He'd be waiting for a while.

'How are things going?' he said eventually. 'It's still only your first week but I hope you're settling in.'

'I'm getting there,' I answered cheerfully. 'It's hard with everything that's been going on but I feel like I'm starting to get a handle on everything.'

'I'm really pleased to hear that, Saffron.' He reached out and put a hand on my arm, squeezing gently. Then his head tilted and he gazed at the thin material of my shirt. 'Is that a tattoo?'

'Yes.' I pulled up my sleeve to show him, hoping that the horror of the image would imply enough of my supposed bad taste that he'd leave me in peace.

'A dog! It's so cute,' he cooed. 'It suits you. Does it hurt?'

Damn it. 'A bit,' I said. I covered up again. 'And it's a cat. Not a dog.'

He smirked. 'I love a bit of pussy myself.'

I counted to ten in my head.

'If there's anything I can do to help, do let me know,' Rupert continued, blithely unaware of my growing irritation. 'Maybe we can go out for lunch together. The canteen is good but there's a lovely little café around the corner. We could go out just the two of us and get to know each other better.'

I hastily poured out some hot water from the urn into my mug and smiled at him. 'That's *so* kind of you, Rupert. I'm going to be busy all day today though.'

'You have to eat. I'm sure you can find some time.'

I pondered this. 'Yes,' I said. 'I'm sure I could. You know what though?'

He half smiled at me. 'What?'

I shrugged. 'I don't want to.' I grabbed my mug and walked off. I didn't want to be rude to the guy but I would be if that was what it took to shake him off.

I was pleased to see that Delilah wasn't at her desk. At least she started work at a normal time unlike all these other faeries. I plonked down my mug and started up my computer to check Luke's file and update it with the information I had on him so far. I'd try some more research and see if I could uncover any useful information before I visited him again. If I could sort him out this morning then I'd be free to concentrate on the missing godmother investigation for the rest of the day. Before the screen had flickered into action, however, there were raised voices behind me.

'I've had it enough of it! Can't you keep quiet?'

'I'm humming, Sarah. It's only humming. I'm allowed to hum.'

'You're doing it deliberately to annoy me. I know you are.'

'The fact of my humming has nothing to do with you.'

I glanced round and spotted two faery godmothers squaring off against each other. Honestly, it looked to me as if they were about to descend into fisticuffs at any moment. I gulped down my coffee and grabbed my bag. It would be safer to get out of the office as quickly as possible.

THE METAFORA ROOM transported me directly outside Luke's flat, a small student type affair that he shared with five others. Unfortunately, while I might be up and about and raring to go,

I'd temporarily forgotten that he was still a university student. He'd be fast asleep for the next few hours at least. It was the way students rolled. I gazed at the closed door for a moment. Just because he was sleeping didn't mean I couldn't still be working on his case.

I tried the door but, sensibly, it was locked. Flicking my fingers towards it, I used a swirl of faery magic to jiggle the mechanism. A moment later I was in, carefully closing the door behind me so as not to wake up any of the flat's occupants.

The flat seemed surprisingly well kept. I knew from Luke's file that the parents of one of his flatmates owned it and rented rooms out to the others at reasonable rates. Perhaps that was the reason why it was so neat and tidy. I peered at the handwritten rota which had been pinned up onto a wall in the kitchen. The chores had been divided up equally between all of them. I tapped thoughtfully at Wednesdays. It was Luke's job to take the rubbish out on that day. It should have been done yesterday. I strolled over to the bin and flipped the lid open. It was brimming full with squashed packages and empty takeaway cartons. Hmm. Luke's flatmates might be conscientious when it came to housekeeping but it appeared that Luke himself was slipping.

I nosed around the rest of the flat, opening cupboards here and there and rifling through various bits of paper which had been left lying around. As pleasing as it might have been that these students looked after their home, temporary though it may be, it didn't make it easy for me to find any clues as to what Luke really wanted. I gave up on what I was doing and headed for his bedroom instead. I opened the door and peeked in. There was a strong smell of feet and, troublingly, the same stale alcohol reek which I'd noted in the study carrel the first time I'd met him. Luke himself was curled up in a foetal like position, his thumb in his mouth. I considered waking him up but from what I'd seen of him yesterday and the gaunt look to his face which was visible even through his repose, I decided to leave him be. I could wait for an hour or two at least to see if he would wake up.

Ambling back to the living room, I sat myself down on a comfy chair. There was no doubt in my mind that Luke's wish would have something to do with his demands at the tattoo shop. He was tracking something – or rather someone – down. The question was who. His file hadn't indicated anything helpful when I'd looked through it.

I crossed my legs as I tried to sift through the information in my mind. Just then, however, the living room door opened and a young woman wearing a fluffy purple dressing gown appeared. I stiffened but she merely offered a vague sleepy smile in my direction and curled up in the chair opposite.

'Hey,' she said.

I licked my lips. 'Hey.' I was taken aback by her lack of reaction at a stranger in her flat. She might not remember this encounter given that I was officially on the clock but I'd have expected more wariness from her.

'I'm Lucy,' she said. 'I take it you're one of Luke's friends.' There was a faint emphasis on her last word. Ah. Now I understood.

'Yeah,' I said. 'I woke up before him so I thought I'd come through here and wait.' That was sort of true.

She tutted to herself and threw me a look filled with little but sympathy. 'He does this a lot, you know,' she said gently. 'He has a lot of ... friends.'

I searched for a way to keep her talking. 'He and I have a connection,' I said finally. 'But I'm under no illusions. I'm here to help him.'

'I don't know that anyone can help him at the moment. You're welcome to wait until he wakes up though.' She sighed and reached for the remote control, turning on the television and effectively barricading any further attempts at conversation.

I watched her for a moment as she flicked though various channels and programmes, before settling on some sort of horrific chat show which seemed to involve a lot of yelling and cushion throwing and very little else. Then I arced my wrist and cut the power. The television flicked off and Lucy cursed. She got up and began fiddling with the plug. I let her try for a moment or two and then tried again.

'Luke told me about his search,' I said, testing the water.

She paused briefly in her attempts to re-start the television and glanced round at me. 'He did? He won't say very much about it to any of us.'

'He's getting close.'

Lucy's mouth tightened. 'I'm not sure that's necessarily a good thing.'

'Why not?'

She tugged at her ponytail. 'Sometimes you have to be careful what you wish for.'

And then some. I nodded wisely. 'True.' I ploughed on. 'But I don't think Luke's wish is all that unreasonable.'

She frowned. 'He hasn't seen his real dad since he was five years old. I don't think any parent who walks out on their child at that age is someone who deserves attention. Even if Luke finds him, I think he'll end up regretting it. His stepdad has been more of a father to a him than his real dad ever was.'

Bingo. I resisted springing up to my feet and doing a little jig at finally discovering what Luke wanted. The file I had on Luke suggested that both his parents were still at home – but if Luke's mum had re-married and they'd all taken on his step-dad's name then everything made sense. All Luke wanted was to find his real father. And with one snap of my fingers I could achieve that for him.

'It's been lovely meeting you, Lucy,' I said. 'I think I'll head home and get a shower. I'll catch up with Luke later.' I flicked my fingers and the television sprang into life, forestalling her from questioning my sudden decision to leave.

'Huh.' She frowned at the screen. 'That's weird.'

I slipped out of the door. She'd already have forgotten who I was. I grinned to myself. Now all I had to do was to find out whether Luke's father was someone worth knowing and I'd have achieved success. In this at least.

CHAPTER TWENTY

Armed with my new information on Luke, I was able to narrow down my research once I was back at my computer. Fortunately, the bickering from earlier had come to a halt and the office itself was reasonably quiet. It made it easier to focus on my search and, when I finally found the information that confirmed Luke had been adopted by his stepfather when he was seven, I leaned back in my chair and breathed out. If I'd had more time to research him in the first place, I could have discovered this on my own. I'd felt pressure from Adeline to perform, however, and I'd rushed things. Next time, I resolved, I would do far better.

'You're still wearing those shoes,' Billy said, appearing silently behind me and causing me to jump half out of my skin.

I glanced down at my feet. Oh yes. Shiny, patent leather. 'You can't seriously have a problem with these,' I said. 'Where in the rule book does it say I can't wear patent leather?'

'Section four, sub section f, line 23,' he answered without missing a beat.

'You're not lying, are you?' I asked. 'You actually have that memorized.'

'What can I say?' he shrugged. 'I have a lot of time on my hands.'

'So what's the issue with patent leather?'

He grinned. 'Who the hell knows? It was probably some Director in years gone past who had a weird aversion to it. Honestly, most of the rules in there are completely nuts.' He arched an eyebrow towards me. 'Haven't you read through them all yet? I know that HR gave you a copy.'

'I haven't had time.'

He bent down towards me. 'That's the beauty of it,' he said. 'No-one ever has time. Frankly, I could make any old shit up and people would believe it's a rule. Not that I need to,' he added. 'There's so much daft crap in there that I doubt even my imagination could match the reality.'

'Well,' I murmured, 'it's good that we have you on hand to keep us all on the straight and narrow then.'

He chuckled. 'Indeed.' Then his expression sobered up. 'How are things with you really, Saffron? You're spending a lot of time with the Devil's Advocate. If he's bothering you, I'm sure I could find a rule that would help your situation.'

'Actually, he's alright.' At Billy's disbelieving look, I laughed. 'Honest. In fact, it's far better spending time with him than staying here. I get that everyone is on edge because of the kidnappings but you could cut the atmosphere in this office with a knife.'

Billy's mouth downturned further. 'It's been like that here for a long time. The kidnappings are the icing on the proverbial cake.'

I chewed on my lip. 'Those godmothers who went missing – Lydia, Boris, Alistair, Edwina and Jane?'

'What about them?'

I picked up a pen and began twirling it in my fingers. 'Were they feeling the pressure too?'

He sighed. 'And then some. Jane burst into tears on the morning she vanished when she spilt a cup of tea all over keyboard and got bawled out by Adeline. I caught Alistair actually sleeping here so that he didn't have to worry about the time he lost commuting. They were all under a great deal of stress.' He waved a hand around and I noted several heads quickly duck behind their cubicles to avoid Billy's notice. 'Everyone's under a great deal of stress.'

I squinted at him. 'Don't you think your stickler for the rules attitude adds to that stress?'

'Actually,' he said, 'for a while it was quite the opposite. I was the perfect stress release. Most offices need a scapegoat. You know, someone to despise and vent about. Sometimes complaining about others can be a useful pressure valve. Grumbling about a shared enemy can bring a place together. Of course, that shared enemy used to be me. Now it's you.'

I grimaced. 'Gee. Thanks.'

He shrugged. 'Think of yourself as providing a valuable service to others. If their unhappiness is focused on you then they're not thinking about how utterly shite everything else about their job is.'

The pen in my fingers snapped in half. I cursed and threw it onto the desk. One half of it rolled off and landed onto the floor with a soft plop. 'This is supposed to be the best job a faery can have.'

'I know,' he said sadly. 'It sucks, doesn't it?' He patted me on the shoulder. 'If there's anything I can do to help you, let me know.'

I nodded and watched him wander off. Then I bent over to pick up the fallen half of the pen. It was just out of reach. I scowled and stretched my hand out further, finally managing to scoop it up. I tossed it in the wastepaper basket and started to straighten up. As I did, however, something caught my eye. No wonder the chair I'd purloined was a bit wonky. There was something stuck in one of the wheels.

Frowning, I hunkered down further and used the tips of my fingers to try and yank it out. I tugged at it but, when that didn't work, I grabbed a pair of scissors instead and poked at the thing. With enough frantic jabbing, I managed to free it. I picked it up and held it up to the light. It was little twist of brown paper. My stomach tightened. I opened it up to see if there was anything written on it, or if there was anything clinging to the paper itself. It was clean. I could still hear my blood roaring in my ears, however. Unfortunately, that sound was quickly replaced by the panicked murmur of my colleagues around me.

I hastily pulled myself up to my feet. Both the Director and Adeline were striding out of their respective offices. Their faces were pale and grim. I looked round the rest of the room. Figgy was clutching Rupert's arm. Angela, and the other HR faeries, were staring out from the doorway that separated them from the rest of us. Even Alicia looked worried, one bejeweled hand wrapped around her own throat. What did they all know that I didn't?

I spotted Delilah over by the kitchenette and quickly walked over to join her. She looked as unsettled as everyone else. 'What's going on?' I asked.

'Miranda called up from downstairs,' she whispered. 'There's another delivery.'

The blood drained from my face. 'You mean...'

Delilah nodded. 'I think so.'

Just then the lift dinged and the doors slid open. The mutterings immediately silenced and a grim hush descended across the office as we all waited to see what happened next.

Mrs Jardine was there, holding a package in her outstretched hands as if it were some kind of bomb. An unhappy looking delivery faery was standing next to her. He might have been wearing the same sort of Spandex as the last guy but he was considerably older.

'All I did was pick it up,' he said. 'You can't pin this on me.'

Nobody paid him any attention. Everyone was wholly focused on the package. It looked to be almost the same as the one which had transported Lydia's ear although it was slightly thinner and longer.

The Director, who for the first time looked genuinely upset, reached out and took the box. She turned to take it to her office. I realised she wasn't going to open it here. She was prepared to leave the rest of us in the dark, wondering just what gruesomeness the package contained. For a few moments everyone watched her go. Then I felt my feet propelling me forwards.

'No.' My voice rang out, bouncing around the room and rather louder than I'd intended.

The Director stopped moving, her head snapping in my direction.

I'd started so I'd finish. 'If that's what we think it is,' I said, my voice trembling ever so slightly, 'then we have the right to see it too. This affects all of us.'

Adeline stiffened. 'You've been here for three days, Saffron. This hardly affects you.'

I raised up my chin. The last thing I'd ever intended to be was a trouble-maker. They had to see that hiding away whatever grim delivery had been made would only make matters worse for everyone though. The trouble that hours of morbid speculation would create would be far worse than the truth. 'It feels like it's been a lot longer than three days,' I said. 'And it *does* affect me. You made sure of that.' I gave both Adeline and the Director heavy, pointed looks designed to tell them that I knew exactly what my role here was supposed to be.

Adeline looked guilty. The Director actually looked annoyed.

'We all work here,' I reiterated. 'We all should see what's in that box.'

'That's not for you to decide,' the Director said. Her brows were drawn together and she was paler than before. I understood the anxious stress she was under. She wasn't the only one feeling that way though.

When another voice spoke up to support me, I almost fell backwards in shock. 'She is right,' Alicia said. She glanced across the office at me and, while her gaze was not warm, I recognised a flicker of kindred spirit in her eyes. 'You can't keep us in the dark over this.'

'You almost had a breakdown the last time,' Adeline muttered.

'Only from the shock,' Alicia returned. 'Whatever is in that box could belong to one of our friends. We should see what it is.'

Delilah moved up towards me and reached out, grasping my hand in hers and squeezing it so tightly she almost cut off all the circulation to my fingers. 'I don't need to see what it's in that box,' she whispered to me. She was unable to drag her eyes away from it. 'But I want to know what it is.'

'You don't have to look,' I said, trying to reassure her.

'What if it's a heart?' she shuddered. 'A heart would fit inside that box.' Her hand squeezed mine even more and I let out a pained gasp. 'What if it's two hearts? What if it's five hearts?'

'Delilah,' I said in a strained voice, 'please let go of my hand.'

She didn't seem to hear me.

'How many of you feel like Alicia and ...' the Director turned to me, 'Saffron?'

Slowly, bit by bit, hands went up all over the room. Thankfully, Delilah let go of me and also put her hand up. The Director pursed her lips and I thought I detected a flicker of sadness on her face. 'Very well,' she said. She shifted the package to one hand and used her other to open it up. She stared at the contents. Several of us shuffled towards her to get a quick look. I hoped I wasn't going to regret this. I craned my neck, catching a glimpse of the bloody contents before dropping back.

'What is it?' Delilah asked. 'What's in the box?' She had her hand over her eyes but she was peeking out from under her fingers.

'It's not a heart,' I said. 'And it's good news.'

Delilah's hand dropped. 'Really?' she asked hopefully. 'It's not body parts?'

I grimaced. 'It is body parts. But unless the kidnapper has been keeping five faery corpses in a freezer then I think he's telling us that his captives are all still alive. He's sent us fingers. There are ten little fingers in the box.'

'Little...' Her hand moved to cover her mouth while she gasped.

'Pinkies,' I said grimly. 'Ten pinkies.'

In the far corner of the room, someone began to retch noisily. The Director shot me a look as to ask if I was happy now. I swallowed.

'Get this to the Devil's Advocate,' she said aloud. She closed the box and passed it back to the delivery faery, who tried to shrink away from the task but faltered under the weight of her gaze. 'Saffron Sawyer,' she called. 'My office. Now.'

Fuck a puck. Somehow I didn't think I was about to get a commendation for speaking up. I squared my shoulders. It was okay though; I was in the right and she'd be able to see that. She was an intelligent faery. I nodded to myself. I could do this.

'Don't bother sitting down,' the Director said, taking her own chair behind her massive mahogany desk. 'This won't take long.'

I drew in a breath and moved to the centre of the room to face her properly. I didn't drop my head though. I wasn't cowed. I didn't think I'd done anything wrong. I'd take my lumps and then I'd get myself back out there.

'The Devil's Advocate has been in touch,' she said to me. 'He has informed me that his investigations have uncovered the fact that the missing godmothers were not abducted while working for this office. Their kidnappings occurred outwith their jobs.'

My mouth felt inexplicably dry. 'Yes.'

She sniffed. 'Clearly you are now aware of the real reason why you were employed. It was not because we thought your skills as a dope faery would enhance our office. It was because we thought you might help us uncover the kidnapper and draw him out.'

'I was bait,' I said flatly. 'You put my life in danger and didn't tell me.'

She drummed her fingers irritably on her desk. 'Your life was never in danger. You had a team of faeries following you at all times. I would never allow any of my faeries to be put in danger.'

I pointed towards the door. The box might have left with the delivery faery but its existence still sat ominously between us, making the atmosphere in the room even heavier. 'I rather think you have had evidence of that which is entirely to the contrary.'

Her expression hardened. 'Do not get clever with me.' She glared. 'You might have believed that getting close to the Devil's

Advocate and spending time with him would insulate you. I can assure you that this is still my office no matter what he or you may think.'

'I don't think that...' I began.

'On reflection,' she interrupted, 'this is not the right place for you. We no longer require the ruse of your presence and it's obvious that you are not fitting in. It is time for you to return to your previous employment. It's far more suitable for you.'

Oh no. 'That's not true,' I protested. 'I'm making inroads here. I've started to get along with some of my colleagues. I've made headway with my clients.'

The Director raised a single manicured eyebrow. 'Adeline informed me that you granted your first client a wish.' She paused for dramatic effect. 'You gave him a cup of coffee.'

'That was a mistake! I'm correcting it! I've found out that he's looking for his father who abandoned him when ...'

'Ms Sawyer,' the Director said, 'nobody cares. And as for your colleagues, you manipulated Rupert into taking you into the Adventus room, did you not?'

'I ... er ...' I shuffled my feet.

'Didn't you do that?'

'I did,' I said, 'but I had very good reasons for it.'

'It was not your place to go there,' she said coldly. 'Access is restricted to the Adventus room for good reason.'

'But,' I said, still seemingly unable to prevent myself from digging a massive hole from which there would be no escape, 'shouldn't we all spend more time in there? If we can learn from previous wishes and from the deeds of faery godmothers in time gone past, then won't we become better ourselves?'

'The Adventus room is not for the likes of you!'

Jeez. 'Fine,' I muttered. 'It won't happen again.'

She didn't blink. 'I know. Now, give me your wand and your ID and clear out your things.'

'I think I'm onto something with the kidnapper,' I said quickly. 'I found something in my chair and ...'

'Your wand and your identification.' She held out her palm.

My head was beginning to throb, a pulsating pain from behind my eyes. No tears threatened, however. I was too stunned for anything like that. 'I'm sorry I spoke up out there,' I said. 'I wasn't trying to cause trouble. I made a mistake. It's just that everyone is stressed and there's nothing like the fear of the unknown to make people feel even worse. I knew what was in that box would be gruesome but you have to see that our imaginations were capable of conjuring up far worse than what was really in there.'

The Director's expression didn't change. Her hand remained outstretched. I stared at it. I hadn't messed up that badly. Had I? Moving stiffly, I walked up to her desk, drawing out my wand and unhooking my lanyard from around my neck. I dropped both into her hand.

'Thank you,' the Director said. 'I wish you the best of luck in your future endeavours.' She dropped her head and began to read the papers which were in front of her.

For a moment I remained where I was, staring at her as she pretended to do some work. I couldn't stay forever though. Eventually I turned on my heel and left.

Adeline was waiting outside the Director's office. She took one look at my face and her expression dropped. 'I'll escort you to your desk,' she said. 'You can collect your things before leaving.'

I looked at her. 'You know this isn't fair, right?'

'We're all under a lot of pressure,' she said stiffly. 'The Director is no exception.'

'That's not my fault.'

Her response was quiet. 'I know.'

I half snorted. 'That might be the kindest thing you've said to me.' I brushed her off. 'I can collect my things on my own,' I said. 'I don't need a damn escort.'

The office itself was as quiet now as it had been when the box had arrived. Every single pair of eyes watched my walk of shame. I held my head up high all the way to my desk. Delilah stared at me as I reached for my bag and began to scoop up the few things that were personal to me.

'Have you actually been sacked?' she breathed.

'It would appear that way.' I stuffed my mug into the top of my bag and tried to zip it up. The zip jammed and I cursed, trying to unsnag it. Eventually I gave up and left it as it was.

Angela appeared from HR, unable to conceal her glee. 'I'll have all the relevant paperwork sent to your home,' she said. 'We don't want you hanging around here for longer than is necessary.'

'Heavens forbid,' I muttered. I pushed past her, shouldering my bag and heading directly for the lift. Billy was already there. 'Here to wave me off?' I asked.

He frowned at me, clearly unhappy. Welcome to the club. 'I wasn't expecting that to happen,' he said. 'The Director isn't usually so petty. She's under a lot of ...'

'Pressure,' I said for him. 'I keep hearing so much about that. It's beginning to sound a lot like a poor excuse.' The bitterness in my tone landed between us like acid.

'I'll try and speak to her on your behalf,' he said. 'There are rules about this sort of thing.'

'I was on probation,' I told him. 'Anything goes.' I forced a smile that wouldn't have fooled a blind person. 'Don't worry about me. I'll be fine.' I turned and looked round at the office, my gaze meeting that of Alicia's. Her mouth tightened momentarily then she gave a shrug to indicate that she didn't care. I raised my voice. 'It's the people who are staying here who have to worry.'

Billy winced. 'Saffron...'

'Nice knowing you,' I told him. The lift opened and I stepped in. He said something else but I didn't quite catch it. The doors closed and, finally, I was on my own. When I reached the ground floor, I was expecting Mrs Jardine to be there to add further useless homilies. It appeared, however, that she'd made herself scarce. I shrugged to myself and pretended I didn't care about any of this. I didn't want to be a stupid faery godmother anyway.

CHAPTER
TWENTY-ONE

I'd barely gone fifty metres from the office when my phone began to ring. I ignored it. I didn't want to talk to anyone right now. I stomped along the pavement, glaring at anyone who dared to veer even slightly into my path. I'd been fired for virtually no reason whatsoever. Those damn faery godmothers had set me up to fail from the outset. The Director hadn't turfed me out because of what had happened with the box. I hadn't been good enough to be one of them. I wasn't from the right sort of faery family. I didn't have the right sort of name. Then my anger gave way to doubt. Maybe I wasn't as skilled as I'd thought I was. Maybe I'd been kidding myself all along that I could ever make a go of this.

I thought about calling my mother so I could pour out my woes to her. Yes, I was an adult. Yes, I still wanted my mum. She was away for the day with her friends though. I didn't want to interrupt her fun with my tears. Harry would be working, his head filled with ways to improve his lot in the rainbow faery world. I couldn't bother him with this either. I was, to all intents and purposes, on my own. I supposed I should check in with Jasper. Except I couldn't face him. The thought of trudging home to sit alone on my sofa didn't appeal very much either.

'You are good enough,' I whispered to myself, startling a woman who walked past me and who quickly steered herself away from me. I paid her no attention. 'You did the very best that you could.' Luke Wells' face flashed into my mind. I was the second faery godmother he'd supposedly had. And the second one who'd failed him. He hadn't presented himself as a nice guy but if he'd had his wish granted then perhaps he'd have been able to sort himself out and get onto the straight and narrow. That would probably never happen now.

I walked along for a few more steps. Then I stopped. The last person any of this was fair on was Luke. The least I could do was to help him out. Without my wand, I might no longer have the full bounty of magic invested in me as a faery godmother at my fingertips. I wasn't entirely useless though. I gritted my teeth. Screw the Director. I'd been given a job to do and I was going to do it. It would be my last hurrah as the world's shortest lived faery godmother. Luke Wells would get the wish he wanted. It would help me to sleep at night if nothing else.

Spinning round, I changed direction. Without the Metafora room, I couldn't transport myself in an instant to Oxford. There was still public transport, however. Trains ran regularly enough and the station wasn't far away. I set my chin. I also pulled out my phone. The missed call had been from Jasper. I glared at his name as if all this were his fault. I still didn't want to talk to him. I sighed. Unfortunately not all of this was about me. I pressed the button to return the call. I had to tell him my suspicions about the kidnappings. Five pinky-less faery godmothers couldn't be blamed for my current woes.

The call went straight to voicemail. I reminded myself that he was now occupied with ten little fingers and another traumatised delivery faery. I calculated travel times in my head, along with how long it might take me to sort out Luke, and left Jasper a message, telling him to meet me in St Clements Park later in the evening. I didn't mention my firing. If I didn't say it out loud then I could pretend for a little longer that it happened. Almost.

It was almost two o'clock in the afternoon by the time I arrived in Oxford. I'd spent most of the train journey in a state of furious anticipation, my mind churning over what had happened. I had the distinct feeling that if I'd not spoken up about the second gruesome delivery, I'd still have ended up in this very same place. I questioned myself over and over about what I could have done differently to achieve a more optimum outcome. Unfortunately, the answer I kept arriving at was nothing. My fate had been sealed before I'd even stepped through those faery godmother doors a mere four days before. I kept telling myself that I should be grateful I was still free and still in possession of all my fingers. It wasn't much of a comfort but it worked for a while.

Rather than seek out Luke, who I was certain would be actually out of bed by this hour, regardless of his university timetable, I strode out of the train station and made a beeline for the tattoo parlour. He'd been certain they had the information he'd needed so that was where I'd return also. This time, I told myself, I definitely wasn't going to get another tattoo. One dodgy cat emblazoned on my arm for the rest of my life was bad enough.

If anything, the tattoo parlour looked grimier and more desperate than it had on my first visit. I didn't waste any time in loitering around outside it. I pushed open the door with dramatic purpose and strode in.

The tattoo artist who had created the supposed art which I now displayed on my skin was already in the front room, fiddling with some of the photos as if their arrangement would make the tattoos they advertised appear more desirable. When he caught sight of my face, he didn't smile or greet me in any way which might suggest some form of decent customer service. In fact, I could swear the sound that emitted from his throat was actually some sort of growl. He was more bear than human then. It accounted for his clumsy fingers, I supposed.

'Want a tattoo?' he asked.

Somewhat belatedly, I realised that he wouldn't have any memory of my previous visit because I'd officially been on the job at the time. Thanks a bunch, memory magic. It didn't work when I needed it to and when I needed it not to work, it did. That about summed up my life right about now.

I rolled up my sleeve and showed him my misshapen cat. He squinted at it, obviously recognising his own work. His gaze snapped to my face then back at the cat and I could see him struggling to remember. He frowned and scratched his head. Then he shrugged. The tattoo was obviously fresh and still healing. Perhaps he'd decided he had been drunk at the time and that was why he couldn't remember. It would certainly account for the state of the tattoo, I supposed.

'No refunds,' he said. 'If you're not happy with your art then it's tough shit for you.'

Hmmm. From the manner of his speech and his words, I could only presume that his customers often returned unhappy. I tilted my head and smiled, although my own mood meant that I was physically unable to take off the unpleasant edge which I knew was visible in my eyes. 'Actually,' I said, 'I'm here to get a matching tattoo for my other arm.'

The artist stared at me, his nose wrinkling in disbelief. 'Really?'

'No. Not really. In fact,' I said, getting up closer to him, 'I strongly suggest you seek out a new career. I'm not convinced that being a tattoo artist is your destiny.'

He snarled at me, his muscles bunching up. I could see, however, that there was the faintest glimmer of hurt in his face. Vague guilt spluttered through me and I felt a sudden odd kinship with him. I was a useless faery godmother and he was a useless tattoo artist. We had more in common than I could have realised.

'I'm sorry,' I said. 'I can't tell you that I love my new tattoo because I don't. It's not a good tattoo. But you already know that yourself. It's not my place to tread on your dreams, mate. Maybe you just need more practice. Ask your boss for more support and training and who knows what might happen.'

My words had the opposite effect to what I'd intended. He growled again and puffed out his chest. 'You're still not getting a refund.'

I held up my hands. 'I don't want a refund. I want information.'

His eyes narrowed suspiciously. 'What?'

'When I was here before, there was another guy here. Young-ish. He was trying to trace your records relating to an old tattoo. He was speaking to your ...' I took a stab in the dark based on what I'd earlier surmised, 'brother about it.'

'And?'

I smiled again, more genuinely this time. 'I'd like to see those records.' I paused. 'Please.'

He looked me up and down. For a brief moment, I thought he was going to manhandle me back out of the door. For some reason, however, he decided otherwise. 'Wait here.' He turned round and walked through to the back.

I breathed out. Maybe I'd get what I wanted without using any magic whatsoever. That would indeed be a bonus.

I didn't have to wait long. Less than a minute after he'd disappeared, the tattoo artist returned, this time with the second burly man in tow. 'What's so special about these records?' he demanded, without so much as a hello. It must be a family trait to launch directly into conversation without any of the niceties that other people spent their time on.

'You don't need to know that,' I responded calmly. 'And I won't take up much of your time. I only want to see who had that tattoo done.'

'I wouldn't give that kid that information. I'm not going to give you it either. Piss off out of here.'

On comparison, the brother who'd done my tattoo was by far the more congenial of the two. 'There's no need to be obstructive,' I said. 'It's an old tattoo, right? What does it really matter?'

'You the police?'

'No.'

He raised his massive shoulders. 'Then you don't get to see the records. We don't go back that far anyway. I don't know who had that tattoo done.' He pointed behind me. 'Now piss off. I won't say it again.'

I hissed through my teeth in irritation. He was lying. I was certain of it. Once Luke Wells had visited, this man would have looked through his records and found what Luke was after. He knew exactly what I was talking about. I'd lay money on it. I quickly debated my options. I could continue trying to wheedle my way into getting what I needed or I could take a short cut. Alright. Perhaps I did need some of that magic after all.

I raised my hands and drew on my own personal magic. While both brothers glared at me, I snapped my fingers. They froze. An instant later, I gasped and bent double. Bloody hell. No wonder faeries didn't tend to use much magic when they weren't working and no wonder our wands were so vital to proceedings. My head swam and the burst of energy it had taken me to bespell the pair of them left my whole body trembling. I tried to catch my breath, grimacing all the while. Then I slowly stood up straight again and examined the hapless duo.

Now that I had time to examine the pair of them together, it was obvious that they were closely related. It wasn't just their similar features. They held themselves in the same way, each one dropping their left shoulder enough to be noticeable. Both of them had almost comical expressions on their face, mouths half open and nostrils flaring. I poked the nearest one. He didn't move. I knew I didn't have long before the magic wore off though. Tick tock, Saffron.

On legs that still felt like jelly, I wobbled through the inner door and towards the back. I ignored the two tattoo cubicles, especially the one where I'd been given the daft cat tattoo, and instead walked towards the third door, which I presumed led to some sort of office.

I wasn't disappointed. Although it was even darker and shabbier than the rest of the tattoo parlour, I'd definitely found the tattoo jackpot. Filing cabinets lined the walls, several of them with their drawers half open thanks to the many overflowing files which had been jammed in. There was single desk sitting against the wall, although it had two chairs beside it. Clearly, both brothers shared it. I sat down on the nearest chair and spared a thought for what Adeline would think about the mess. She'd complained about the boxes and files on my desk. That had been nothing compared to this, however. Every inch of the surface was covered.

I shuffled around some papers, uncovering a small silver photo frame which had been hidden by a brown envelope. I picked it up and peered at it. Younger versions of both boys grinned out at me. In between them was another man, whose face also looked similar. Dad, no doubt. I examined the sign above all of three of their heads. It was this same tattoo parlour. So it was a family business. Their father had run the shop and they'd taken it on after him. That probably explained a lot.

I lifted up various other envelopes. A lot of them displayed scarlet words and capitalized fonts. The tattoo brothers were in trouble. No wonder they didn't give refunds. I wasn't entirely surprised. I couldn't imagine anyone rushing to this place to get their skin branded. I did, however, feel some sympathy for their situation.

Shaking myself, I focused on the reason why I was here. I was still banking on the fact that one of them would have already looked out the records that Luke had been searching for. Without any clue as to when the tattoo in question might have completed, or the name of the person who had it done, the last thing I wanted to have to do was to start flicking through the overflowing filing cabinets. I cursed to myself and hastily scoured the other bits of paper, praying there was something here that wasn't a final demand.

I was about to give up hope when I came across a single sheet of A4 with an old Polaroid photo clipped to the front of it. The photo was faded and its edges were curling up. There was no doubt that it was what I was looking for, however. It displayed an elaborate tattoo of an insignia. The same insignia which Luke Wells had been doodling in his study carrel.

Buoyed by my success, I scanned the details. The recipient of the tattoo was Mark Countman. It had been inked by A.G. in May 2005. Presumably, A.G. was the tattoo brothers' father. The tattoo itself was far too neat and well designed to have been created by either of the boys themselves. I squinted at the faded words. There was an old address there. Bantam Road. I checked my phone. It was only a few streets away from here. Mark Countman had to be Luke's dad. It was who he was searching for.

I committed the address to memory. Maybe I'd get lucky and he'd still be living in the place. Or someone in the area would remember him. Either way, I smiled to myself in grim delight. Take that, faery godmothers. I could still get the job done without the power of the office behind me.

I got up to my feet, leaving the little room behind as I'd found it. Out in the front, the brothers were still frozen in the same position. I took a deep breath and snapped my fingers once more. Almost immediately they shifted, changing from unmoving statues to living, breathing humans who were fully aware of their surroundings. And of me. I felt another wave of nausea assail me. Fuck a puck, that magic was hard-going.

'Go on. I'm not saying it again,' the second brother said. 'Get the fuck out of here.'

I refrained from pointing out that he had indeed said it again and started to shuffle towards the door. 'Fine, fine. I'm going.' I felt both their eyes on my back. I put my hand on the door knob and then looked round. 'Actually,' I said, 'before I go, there's just one other thing.' I hesitated. Without my wand, this would be nigh on impossible. It would definitely make me sick as a dog. I reckoned it might be worth it though. 'You both took this shop on after your father died, didn't you? He was a great tattoo artist.'

I noted the brief identical spasm of pain on both their faces. 'Yeah. So what?'

I reached down inside myself and raised my hands one final time, twirling my fingers in the air, one hand for the brother on the right and one for the brother on the left. 'Now,' I said, 'you're as good as he was. Your skills match his.' My vision was blurring but I managed a small smile. 'It's up to you what you do with that.' Then I turned again and lurched out of the door, seconds before I started throwing up.

CHAPTER TWENTY-TWO

I wasn't sure what happened to ex-faery godmothers who granted wishes off the books. I'd never heard of anyone performing such a feat. I had certainly learned why that was the case. I doubted very few had ever tried it before. I might have felt dizzy earlier, after causing time to halt for both brothers. Now, however, I had the definite feeling that I was dying. My head pounded and my vision was no longer just blurry. It had narrowed to tiny pinpricks of light. I stumbled away from my pile of vomit, staggering along the street and rounding the corner. I barely made it before my knees gave way and I felt, rather than saw, the pavement rushing up towards me. It was very cold and very hard. I closed my eyes, moaning slightly. Then I felt a pair of hands at my waist and someone hauling me back upright.

My eyelids fluttered. 'Wha – at?'

'For fuck's sake, Saffron,' Jasper snapped. 'What the hell have you done?'

I blinked and tried to focus. 'Wha ... ooo.... ere?' I frowned. That didn't make any sense. 'Wha are oo doing ere?' Damn it.

'I might ask you the same question. Have you been

performing magic?' he demanded roughly. 'Did you grant a bloody wish without your wand?'

I tried to answer but my stomach heaved and I began to retch once more. I felt Jasper's hands reach for my head, gently pulling my hair out of the way. I was dimly aware of my own bile splattering the pavement. He lifted me up to face him and placed his hand against my forehead, muttering something under his breath. My body jerked as a buzz of warmth spread across my skin. A moment later, my equilibrium started to return. Slightly.

Jasper's face swam into view. His expression was dark and angry. 'It appears,' he said icily, 'that breaking rules is something you regularly do.'

I pulled away from him, regretting the sudden motion, and smoothed back my hair. I still felt shaky but I was definitely better than before. 'It was worth it,' I said weakly. 'Besides, what's the worst that can happen? I've already been fired.'

Jasper cursed. 'So I heard. That wasn't supposed to happen.'

'Tell me about it,' I muttered.

'I only gave the Director the most basic information about what we'd uncovered. I thought if I held some details back, she'd avoid doing anything rash, including where you were concerned. Clearly, I was wrong. The woman seems to think she is above reproach.' He continued to glower. 'Not that it's any excuse what you just did. What are you even doing here?'

'My job.'

'The job you've been fired from?'

I shrugged. 'There's no other.'

'I can sort that out for you and get the Director to take you back,' he bit out. 'I told you before that I wouldn't let you lose your position and I meant it. I can't help you if you're going to run around performing off the books wishes though.'

I straightened my posture. 'I do not want or need your help,' I told him.

He gazed at me with exasperation. 'A moment ago, you couldn't stand up without my help.'

'Everyone's a critic.' I met his eyes. 'I mean it. I can handle this on my own. I don't know why you've come here anyway. I told you that I'd meet you later.'

His expression darkened further. 'I wanted to make sure you were alright. It's as well that I did.'

'I am fine.'

'You won't be if you do any more godmother magic.'

'Then,' I said, rather huffily, 'I won't do any more magic.'

He folded his arms. 'Good. I'll get you to Colchester. You can tell me about this new information that you've found about the kidnappings. I presume that your moonlighting means that you are still happy to work with me on the investigation?'

'Of course I am. I'm not going back yet though.'

Jasper stared at me. 'Why on earth not?'

'Because,' I answered calmly, 'I've not finished here yet.'

He took a step towards me, his heady cinnamon scent swirling round me. Goodness. I must still be feeling light-headed.

'I told you. No more magic. Your body can't take it without the protections afforded to you by your job.'

'I don't need to use magic for what I've got to do.' I hoped.

'What do you have to do? Is this related to the disappearances?'

I shook my head. 'No.' I raised my chin. 'This is about professional pride. I started something so I will fucking finish it. I won't leave my client in the lurch. I'm not forgetting about the kidnappings. But I'm not forgetting about my client either. He desperately wants to find his long lost father. That's his wish and I will grant it for him.'

Several beats passed. A tiny muscle throbbed in Jasper's cheek. 'I can get behind that,' he said finally. 'Will it take long?'

'Honestly?' I said. 'I have no idea.'

He sighed. 'Then we'd better get a move on.'

I looked at him. 'We?'

He rolled his eyes. 'Clearly, you need a lot of help.'

Actually, I didn't. But it would nice to have him around. I smiled slightly and pointed down the street. 'Down there.'

He gestured to me. 'Lead the way.' Then he added, 'I really hope I won't regret this.'

'You don't have to come.'

'I know,' he said.

I licked my lips. 'Thank you, Jasper.'

There was a pause. 'You're welcome, Saffron.'

DESPITE JASPER'S TIMELY INTERVENTION, I still didn't feel quite right. The last thing I wanted was for him to know that I was still woozy, however. He might have kept his castigation to a minimum so far but I knew I didn't need to give him cause to berate me further. He was still the Devil's Advocate after all, even if our interests currently merged and we were working well together. I concentrated on putting one foot after the other and maintaining a straight line. I reckoned I just about pulled it off. In any case, Jasper didn't produce any further comments on my state of health or my foolishness in attempting to grant a wish while faery godmother non grata.

Fortunately, it didn't take long to reach the address which Mark Countman had given the tattoo parlour all those years ago. I walked up the few stone steps to the front door, leaving Jasper to wait behind me on the pavement. There was no doorbell so I rapped loudly on the wood with my knuckles. Then I tightly crossed my fingers. It was almost too much to hope for that Luke's dad still lived here. There was always a slim chance though.

When the door opened and the wizened face of an older gentleman appeared, my heart sank. He was too old to be Luke's dad and there wasn't the slightest resemblance to my client. I kept my expression friendly, however, and ignored the continuing churn in my stomach. I did not feel sick. I did not feel sick. I did not feel sick.

'Hi,' I said.

'Hello?' The man blinked at me. 'Can I help you? I'm not interested in buying anything and I already donate to charity. And if you're a Jehovah's Witness...'

'I'm not,' I said hastily. 'I'm actually looking for someone. A former occupant of this address.'

'I've lived here for eighteen years.' He held himself away from me as if he were still unsure about my intentions. 'So I don't know who you could be looking for.'

'Mark Countman,' I told him. 'I'm looking for a man called Mark Countman. He's probably in his forties or thereabouts. It's really important that I find him.'

'What do you want with Mark? He's not in trouble again is he?'

Hope flared in my chest. 'No,' I said quickly. 'No trouble. He's an old friend of the family and I'm trying to locate him.' I put on my best 'harmless young woman' expression. That might have worked if Jasper wasn't looming behind me.

'If you give me your details,' the old man said, 'I'll pass them along to Mark and then he can choose whether to get in touch with you or not himself.'

Fuck a puck. That wouldn't work for me, even if it was the most eminently sensible thing for the man to do.

'Time is of the essence here,' I told him. 'It's to do with Mr Countman's son. If you could just...'

He glared at me. 'I already told you what I'll do. If you get off my doorstep then I'll do it a hell of a lot quicker.'

I wasn't going to change his mind. Frankly, if I pushed any further I might not get anywhere at all. Ever. I gritted my teeth in irritation and then reeled off my phone number. The old man made a note of it and then all but shut the door in my face. Well, that sucked. All I could do now was hope that he kept his promise and did contact Mark.

I turned round. Jasper was watching me, his hands in pockets and a slight smile on his face. He should smile more often. It made him look far less intimidating. 'Humans are a lot more suspicious of strangers than they used to be,' he said. 'I'm sure our jobs would have been far easier a few hundred years ago.'

I met his eyes. 'I appreciate what you're trying to do,' I said, 'but I don't need you to make me feel better. I'm perfectly fine.' I raised my eyebrows meaningfully. 'I'm not defeated yet either.'

'I wouldn't dare to suggest you were.' He took his hands out of his pockets and straightened his broad shoulders. 'Let's head back to Colchester and...'

I shook my head, interrupting him. 'No. Give me another hour first.'

'Hour? To do what exactly?'

Good point. 'Ninety minutes then.' I jogged down the steps and tugged at his arm. He glanced down at my hand with a curious expression on his face but he didn't pull away. 'Nothing is going to happen with Bernard, our evil kidnapper, for a few hours yet anyway.' I tugged again. 'Come on.'

This time, he allowed himself to be moved. Part of me wished I was still being followed. I'd have loved for other faeries to witness me leading the Devil's Advocate around the streets of Oxford. I pulled him across the street and then ducked down behind a car which was parked not too far from the old man's house. Jasper remained standing.

'Saffron,' he said, 'what are you doing?'

'Hiding, of course. Ninja faery style.' I swished my arms through the air in a simulacrum of a karate chop. 'I need you to do the same.'

This time he didn't follow my lead. 'I am not a ninja faery. And I am certainly not hiding behind a car like this one.' His mouth tightened.

'Ohhhh,' I said, with a knowing, sarcastic air. 'You only like to hide behind sparkly clean sports cars as befits your status?'

He muttered something under his breath before rolling his eyes. 'I don't like to hide behind anything. Generally because I don't need to.'

I stood up again, frustration getting the better of me. 'Look. I didn't ask you to join me although I'm happy that you're here. But this is my operation and I need you to fall into line. It's not for long. It's only for an hour and a half then we'll go back to Colchester, save some faeries and everything will be right with the world once more. Just do what I say.'

'Saffron,' he murmured. 'You do remember that I'm the Devil's Advocate?'

'So?'

He tutted and raised his hands. 'I don't need to hide behind cars. And when you're with me, neither do you.'

I frowned, opening my mouth to continue arguing while he twirled his fingers in the air. Then I glanced down at myself and realised what he'd done. Oh. 'You've made us invisible.'

'Just so.' His voice was the very epitome of smug satisfaction. I looked back but could no longer see either him or what was no doubt his matching expression. That was probably as well. 'Can you sense it? Can you still see me?'

I shook my head. 'Not a thing.'

'Ah.' I thought I detected a trace of disappointment. 'Some faeries can.'

'Not this one.'

'I can't either,' he admitted. 'But it's important for me to remember that no magic is foolproof.'

I began to nod before remembering that he couldn't see me so it was a pointless gesture. Then another realisation hit me. 'Wait,' I said slowly. 'You didn't use a wand. You didn't use one for the glamour last time either.'

'I'm the Devil's Advocate.'

I sighed. 'You know you can keep saying that over and over again but it still doesn't make it any more of an explanation.'

'Well,' his disembodied voice said somewhere over my head, 'I could stand here and tell you more about it or we could follow your old man and hope he will lead us to your client's dad.'

I whipped round. He was right. The old man had already exited his house and was fumbling with a key as he locked up. My fists clenched in sudden anticipation. He really was going to tell Mark Countman about our visit as he'd promised.

Without saying another word to Jasper, I took off. The old man might be moving with a slow, shuffling gait but I wasn't taking any chances. I wanted to be absolutely sure that I didn't lose him. For all I knew he was about to start sprinting down the narrow street and out of sight. Then, however, he halted at the very next house down. I came to a skidding halt in the middle of the road, almost toppling over in the process and planting my face onto the tarmac, just as the old man pressed the doorbell.

When the door opened, my breath caught. The face that looked out was the exact same as Luke's, only about twenty years older. He lived right next door. Maybe he always had and the details at the tattoo parlour had been written down wrong. Either way, I'd found the man I'd been looking for. I rocked back on my heels and breathed out. Bingo.

With less haste this time, and remaining on the balls of my feet so that the sounds of my own footsteps didn't alert Mark Countman or his elderly neighbour to anything out of the ordinary, I drew closer to try and hear what they were saying. I didn't get very far when Mark beckoned the older man inside. I threw myself forward, sneaking in behind them in the split second before he closed the door behind them. Damn, but this invisibility shit was handy.

'It was a young woman,' the old man quavered. 'With crazy brown hair that didn't look like it had been brushed in the last year.' I scrunched up my face in his direction that was a bit uncalled for, wasn't it?

'There was a man with her,' he continued. 'Dangerous looking sort. Not the type you'd want to meet in a dark alley. He was more interested in the woman than in anything else though. He was staring at her arse with the sort of expression that suggested he could barely hold himself back from lunging forward and grabbing it.'

I blinked. He should put on his glasses before he answered any knocks at his door.

Mark Countman scratched his head. 'She said it was to do with my son?'

'Yes. She was mightily desperate to talk to you.' He handed over a crumpled piece of paper. 'Here's her number if you want to call it. It's up to you.' The old neighbour shrugged. 'I've got to get home. I'm in the middle of my favourite programme.'

I smiled to myself. Antiques Roadshow. Betcha.

'The Dark Demon is about to take down the Guardian and I don't want to miss the fight. Last time he ripped out a hunk of his hair and broke his nose. There was blood everywhere.'

Okay then.

The old man smiled. 'I'll see myself out.'

Mark Countman mumbled a farewell. He was still staring down at the piece of paper. Fuck a puck. If he called me right now, then things could get incredibly awkward. He wasn't reaching for his phone, however. He wasn't doing very much at all.

After a few moments of frozen inactivity, he stumbled through to his living room and then sat heavily down on a chair, still gazing at my scribbled number. I followed him in and stood staring at him, my arms folded. Did he even care that his son was desperately searching for him? He seemed like he did but if he was that bothered then why hadn't he contacted Luke himself? I didn't think that I was mistaking the expression of guilt on his face. I peered more closely. That wasn't just guilt, I decided. That was also fear.

Mark Countman rubbed his hand across his forehead and sighed, making a sound that was so heavy it filled the tiny room. Then he reached down the side of the chair and pulled up a small wooden chest. It was plain and unvarnished but, from the way that he held it, it was also as heavy as the sigh he'd emitted. He flipped it open and stared inside at the contents for a moment. I bit my lip and stepped forward, trying to peek in myself. Before I could, however, he dropped the scrap of paper inside and snapped the lid shut again. He returned the chest to its original position and leaned back in his chair, taking a remote control from the side and flicking on the television.

My mouth dropped open. What the hell was he doing? This wasn't the time for television, no matter what the Dark Demon was up to. Pick up your fucking phone, I wanted to scream. It was no use, however. Whatever moment had just been had passed entirely. I ground my teeth in bitter frustration. Then I quietly let myself out of the house.

CHAPTER 23

Unable to see Jasper out on the street, as a result of his own invisibility magic that still affected us both, I was forced to shout to try and locate him. 'Jasper!' I yelled. 'Where are you?'

A tabby cat sitting on top of a red brick wall next to Mark Countman's house freaked out completely, its fur standing on end as it tried to locate the source of the noise. I ignored it and opened my mouth to shout again.

'I'm right here,' Jasper murmured quietly in my ear.

I jumped. 'Can you remove the magic?'

The cat began to growl, as my skin prickled and Jasper came into view. I looked down. My body was still there. I still had hands and feet and a slightly protruding belly. I breathed out. The cat was less impressed, however, and drew back on its haunches, preparing to pounce. Jasper turned his head and looked at it. A moment later, the cat backed down and began to groom itself. Huh.

'What happened?' he asked, looking at me.

I took out my phone and waved its still darkened screen in his direction. 'Nothing happened. He's got my phone number. He knows it's to do with the son he's not seen in almost two decades. And he's not called. He's thrown the number into a box and forgotten all about it.' I could barely keep the frustration out of my voice.

Jasper's expression didn't alter. 'What did you think would happen? That he'd call you up immediately and explain how he suffered from a traumatic car accident followed by amnesia and that's why he's not seen his son? That he's been searching for him for years and now his life is complete because he can speak to him again?'

Well, okay, I knew that was unlikely. I gestured helplessly towards him. 'I expected more.'

Jasper continued to study me. 'You were a dope faery. You must be used to being disappointed by clients.'

I grimaced. 'That man's not my client. Besides, I'm not a dope faery any longer. I'm a faery godmother.'

'And only the pious and worthy deserve to come to your attention?' he asked softly.

'No.' I cursed. 'Yes.' I screwed up my face. 'I don't know. Maybe.'

'They're all human, Saffron. They all make mistakes and screw up.'

My shoulders dropped. 'Faeries aren't any different.'

'No,' he agreed. 'We're not.' He waited for a beat. 'What now? Will you tell your client where his father is?'

I sighed. 'I don't know. It's what he wants. It's what he thinks he wants anyway. But does he really need to know that his father still doesn't care about him? I could be consigning him to a worse hell than he's already in.' I looked at him. 'What do you think?'

'You're his faery godmother, not me,' Jasper said. 'It's up to you to decide.'

Yeah, I supposed it was. 'Thank you,' I said quietly.

He quirked up an eyebrow. 'For what?'

I shrugged. 'For not giving me an easy way out or telling me what to do.'

'That's not my job.' He continued to watch me closely.

Growing uncomfortable with the intensity of his green-eyed stare, I shook myself and stepped away. 'Come on,' I said finally. 'Let's head back to Colchester and St Clements Park. I think I have a good idea about how those godmothers have been lured out there. If I'm right, it'll make our plan to use me as bait more likely to succeed.'

His gaze darkened. 'I'm no longer sure that's such a good idea.'

I smiled slightly. 'Actually, when you hear what I've discovered, you'll change your mind. I might even have the inside track.' I hoped so anyway; it would certainly make a damned change.

With Jasper's Devil's Advocate powers in play, there was no need to hang around waiting for crowded trains. Being whisked to the park in the blink of an eye made me realise how much I both missed and relied upon faery magic. It made the pain of losing my job and all the power that went with it that much harder to deal with. I tried not to think about it. Or Luke. Or the five godmothers who may or may not still be alive. I could only deal with one problem at a time.

'I found something,' I told Jasper, as we walked through the now almost empty park. 'Back at the office.'

I could sense his sudden tension. 'Go on.'

I reached into my pocket and pulled out the twist of brown paper which had been caught in the wheels of my office chair. 'Here,' I said grimly.

Jasper took it from me, his fingers brushing against mine as he did so. I felt a brief electric shock as our skin and connected and hastily drew back. He didn't seem to notice. 'I don't get it,' he said. He frowned at the paper, holding it up and examining it. 'What is it?'

'You've never audited the dope faeries' office, have you?' I twisted my mouth. 'Sometimes our clients get their drugs in plastic baggies. Sometimes they get them in little twists just like this one.'

Jasper's brow furrowed further. 'You mean...?'

I nodded. 'All I kept hearing in the godmothers' office was how much pressure everyone was under. There's the targets to be met, the threat of special measures, the reputation to uphold,' I snuck him a side glance, 'not to mention the upcoming audit.'

'Go on.'

I swallowed. I was certain I was right but I still felt like I was trading on dangerous ground here. 'I saw it for my own eyes. The atmosphere in there isn't what you'd call friendly. You even commented on it yourself the first time we met.'

His expression was growing darker. 'Indeed.'

'Humans make mistakes and screw up,' I reminded him gently. 'And so do faeries. Especially when they have long hours and lots of pressures at work. One way that they could improve their situation, or at least think they could improve it, is by taking some sort of substance that could buoy them up. Increase efficiency, decrease the need for sleep, make them feel happier.' I shrugged. 'Whatever. If I wanted to lure a faery godmother out so I could kidnap them, I'd get them away from their office with the promise of something that would make them feel better. Illegal drugs would make sure they told no-one where they were going which is where the misdirection about being abducted on the job would come about. We already know Lydia sneaked out and hung around the park for three days. We also know from Vincent Hamilton that some other drug dealer was muscling in on his turf at the same time.'

'Bernard,' Jasper bit out.

I nodded. 'Bernard.' I fiddled with my cuffs. 'It's not a pretty explanation but it does fit.'

Jasper ran a hand through his hair and looked away. 'Yes,' he admitted. 'It does indeed fit.'

'So,' I said, pretending as I were making light of the situation, 'I really am the perfect fit. Drug dealing is a world that I understand. If we stick to the same plan where I set myself up as bait then we can catch the bastard who's behind the abductions.'

'Assuming,' he said, 'that Bernard the bastard doesn't already know you've been fired.'

'It's only been a few hours since I was given the shove,' I said. 'I reckon I can still get away with it.'

Jasper bunched his hands into fists. 'Or I can get you reinstated and ...'

'No.' On that point, I was adamant. 'If you intervene, it'll make me miserable, make the other godmothers miserable and solve no actual problems. I have to deal with the issue of my job all on my own.' Even if it meant I never got another chance at being a faery godmother. Frankly, at the moment, that might not be a bad thing.

'Fine.' His mouth flattened. 'You have to be careful though. The last thing I need is for you to be abducted.'

I held up my hands up and wiggled my fingers. 'I like all my digits where they already are, thank you very much. Besides, that's why you're here.' I smiled. 'It helps that I've already been loitering around here. If anyone's been watching then they'll think that I'm like the others and looking for a quick hit of something to perk me up.'

'If anyone's been watching,' he pointed out, 'they'll have seen me with you as well.'

'That first time we both ended up here by default. I wasn't following you and you weren't following me.' I smiled confidently. 'I reckon I can explain it away if need be. I doubt anyone is watching this place twenty-four seven, however. The abductions will all happen around the end of the working day when the park is almost empty.'

'Like now.'

I bobbed my head. 'Like now.' I gave him a little nudge. 'But we can't have you scaring off our target. There's a little café across the road. You get a good view of the park from in there so you can come running if need be. It's better not to use your invisibility magic. We still don't know what kind of faery we're dealing with here and they might still sense your presence even if I can't. If they're watching now, we want them to see you walking off anyway. I don't think we should call in anyone else either. We don't want to scare Bernard off.'

Jasper folded his arms across his chest. 'I'm not leaving you here on your own.'

'You'll only be across the road. Besides, I've got some moves. If Bernard shows up then I can do something to delay him till you get back.'

'I don't think that's a great plan.'

'It's the best one we've got,' I asserted. 'It'll be fine.'

He glowered. 'It had better be.'

I pointed towards the café. 'Go on. They're open until eight and they do a great cheese sandwich. I'll wait on the bench and keep my fingers crossed this works.'

'And that you don't die in the process.'

'Something,' I said with a straight face, 'I always aim for.'

Jasper clenched his jaw and then reached for my hands, squeezing them tightly in his own. 'Bernard could be watching us now,' he said. 'He could be wondering why we're together in this park. Why we're alone. We'd better give him a reason just in case. Then I'll leave and double back for the café. It's better to be safe than sorry.'

'If you think that's a good idea,' I said with a shrug, 'then sure. But why would we be alone in this park together?'

He leaned towards me. Oh. Okay. That was as good a reason as any, I supposed. I shivered.

Jasper dropped my hands, his arms going round my back. He pulled me in more closely so that my body was pressed against his.

'You really do smell very nice,' I told him.

'Good.' He smiled at me then his mouth descended on mine, gently at first, then more insistent. I pushed myself up onto my tiptoes, my knees going strangely weak at the same time. Then my hands were in his hair and I was groaning, pulling him towards me even more closely. Part of me had been expecting him to taste dark and spicy, like a fiery chilli sauce. Instead, however, along with the faint tang of mint, he tasted more like deep, dark chocolate. I wanted more. I could feel his hands at my waist, then his teeth nipping at my bottom lip. Fuck a puck. Forget those abducted faery godmothers. This was all I actually wanted. Then I winced and gently pulled away.

Jasper's chest was rising and falling faster than normal. He wasn't the only one who felt like that. His fingers reached for his mouth, brushing against his lips. He shook himself and dropped his hand. 'Hopefully that worked,' he murmured.

I met his eyes. 'It certainly worked for me.' I shivered again and looked away. 'It'll be a real coup for Bernard if the thinks he can abduct the Devil's Advocate's latest squeeze.' I avoided looking at him directly again. 'You should go.'

'Yes.' He reached one last time, his hand briefly taking mine. 'Don't get kidnapped,' he said.

I nodded. A moment later he turned and walked away.

I watched him go. Say what you like about the man, I mused, he could definitely kiss. And he still walked like the he owned the world. He was the Devil's Advocate though. He virtually did. I sighed. I could still taste him in my mouth. I supposed at least the kiss would give me something to think about if this did all go pear-shaped. I licked my lips and strolled towards the nearest bench, sitting myself down and avoiding the splatter of bird poo at the far end. Come on then, Bernard. Let's be having you.

CHAPTER 24

An hour later, I'd decided that this was the most stupid plan anyone could ever have come up with. I was freezing cold and the damp from the wooden bench was seeping through my trousers. The windows of the café were all steamed up so it was doubtful Jasper would be able to see anything from there no matter how hard he was looking. I wrinkled my nose. There wasn't anything interesting to look at. A family had trundled through about twenty minutes earlier but since then, the park had been empty other than me. At this point I'd even welcome good ol' Vincent Hamilton back into the fray. At least it would give me something to do.

I was on the verge of giving up completely when I spotted a figure edging hesitantly towards the main park gates from the other side of the road. Whoever it was, they were coming from the direction of the faery godmother offices. I squinted. This had better be Bernard, I decided. I'd much rather get all this shit out of the way now than have to come back again and try tomorrow evening as well. Then the figure drew closer and my breath caught. No. Way.

For a brief flailing moment, my mind went entirely blank. I

didn't know what to do. My entire body was tense, as if it couldn't decide whether to run and hide or stand and fight. One thing was certain; the plan to throw myself out as bait was no longer going to work. Not now. So much for the mysterious Bernard.

I managed to spring into action in the nick of time, throwing myself towards the single tree in the entire park to use as a shield. At least it was growing a bit darker now. It was barely dusk but anything was better than full sunshine. With luck, she wouldn't glance over and I'd be able to stay concealed. Not that it appeared luck was on my side.

I crouched down, attempting to make my body as small as possible so that there was less chance the Director would spot me. I didn't take my eyes off of her though, tracking her every movement as she walked slowly through the park. Had she already seen me? Had I already screwed all this up? I knew she was a good actress from the way she'd treated me in the office – pretending to be sugar sweetly nice while waiting for the right excuse to throw me out on the streets where I'd come from. I was still finding it hard to believe that she was one responsible for the kidnappings. I supposed in a way it made a sort of sickly nefarious sense, however. It would draw attention away from the other faery godmother failings of her office. It would garner her sympathy in droves. Or maybe she was just an evil bitch who took joy in the misery of others.

She didn't once glance in my direction. Her posture was stiff but I didn't get the sensation that she knew she was being watched. I breathed out as she sat down on the very same bench that I'd vacated. She kept her eyes trained dead ahead, not glancing around her like I had done. Then another thought struck me. What if I'd gotten all this wrong? What if the Director wasn't here as Bernard but had instead been lured out as another potential victim? Fuck a puck. Jasper had told me himself he'd withheld details of our investigation from her. No doubt the location of this park as the abduction point was one of those details. I glanced over at the café but I couldn't see it from this angle. I sent out a plea for silent help in Jasper's direction. Unfortunately it appeared that none was immediately forthcoming.

I got up to my feet, my legs stiff. I'd have to approach the Director myself. If she were abducted then all hell really would break loose. And if she was here as the abductor instead of the victim, well, then, even more hell would free itself. Either way I was in a disastrous maelstrom of potentially catastrophic consequences. I couldn't hide behind a tree and do nothing though. It wasn't in my nature.

I dusted down my clothes and ran my hands through my hair. There was no reason to look disheveled and unkempt, I decided. She was still the faery godmother Director. It was just as well that I took that time to sort out my appearance, however. The delay was long enough for a white van to pull up outside the park's entrance. Four figures jumped out and began striding towards the Director. The lead one was male. White. Bald. Big ears but good looking. I squeaked. It was Vincent Hamilton's ratty bastard. It had to be. The Director really was a victim then. This was Bernard and he was here for her.

I glanced back at the café. There was still no sign of Jasper. The Director was already on her feet and moving towards Bernard. I couldn't waste any more time. I had to help her.

'Hey!' My voice was high pitched and panicked, more of a screech than a shout. The Director heard it and frowned, turning in my direction. Unfortunately Bernard heard it too. His head snapped towards mine, eyes narrowing. Then he started to raise his hands.

'Run!' I yelled to the Director. Except she did no such thing. She froze, suddenly unsure of what to do. I had no time to do anything myself other than pitch dramatically to the left, avoiding whatever Bernard was trying to throw at me. There was a sizzle somewhere beyond my left ear. I hissed and looked round, registering the smouldering patch of weeds where I'd been standing moments earlier. I shook my head in dismay. What the hell had that been?

The other three ran at the Director. She finally seemed to realise the gravity of the situation and began to move, racing to join me, her face a white mask of fear and determination. She was too late, however. She was still at least thirty metres from me when the fastest of the bastards lunged for her, bringing her body slamming down to the ground in a vicious rugby tackle. The Director spun, her hands scrabbling in her pockets for her wand. I sprang up to my feet and began sprinting forward once more, zigzagging to avoid any more magical incineration bolts. The wanker who had a hold of the Director hauled her up to her feet, one hand encircling tightly round her wrist and forcing her to drop her wand with a sharp cry of pain. The other hand held a gleaming, curved dagger to her throat. He allowed the blade to slice into her skin, beads of blood forming across her pale neck. I skidded to a halt, my heart hammering against my chest.

'Come any closer,' Bernard called out, in a chillingly calm voice, 'and we'll slit her throat and be done with this.'

I swallowed. My mouth felt painfully dry and my hands were shaky. I stared from Bernard to the bastard holding the Director to the other two women who were staring at me with a mixture of morbid glee and undisguised hatred. They weren't faeries. I didn't need to get up close and personal with them to be able to tell that. But they weren't human either. They had an indefinable, ethereal quality about them. I couldn't pinpoint it exactly. But it was definitely there. What the fuck was going on here? And where was Jasper?

'You don't have to do this.' My words came out more as a

croaked whisper than an assured command. 'You can let her go and we'll forget all about this.'

Bernard threw his head back and laughed. 'But we don't want to forget about all this. That's entirely the point.'

I looked at the Director's face. She was still pale but she somehow seemed less frightened now. Her expression was calmer. She gazed at me. 'It's alright, Saffron. Just stay back.'

Bernard raised a single, dark eyebrow. 'Saffron?'

'She's the new one,' one of the women muttered. 'The transfer.'

He looked amused. 'Ah, yes. Such a shame. It's not even been a week as a faery godmother and it's already ended in disaster.' He grinned. 'That should put off any other faeries from rushing to join the godmother ranks.'

'Can we kill her?' the woman asked, clearly hopeful that I was about to meet my maker.

Bernard tapped his mouth thoughtfully. 'Hmm. I've not made up my mind. Her presence is rather ... unexpected.'

There had to be a way out of this. I just wasn't seeing it yet. The best thing I could do would be to keep the bastard busy. Any extra seconds I could scrape up might give Jasper enough time to put his own plan into action. Because surely he had a plan. He was the Devil's Advocate after all. We might not have been expecting this many adversaries, or the Director herself, but we could still adapt. Couldn't we?

'Why are you doing this?' I asked, my voice stronger this time. It was a daft question. He was doing it because he was a psychotic bastard. If I could get him talking, however, I could perhaps delay matters enough for Jasper to join us and use his powers to save the day.

Bernard grinned. 'That's the million pound question, sweetheart.'

'You've kidnapped five godmothers,' I said. 'And you've not asked for any ransom.'

He pointed at the Director. 'Six godmothers,' he said. 'Don't forget about your boss.'

He hadn't taken her just yet. I nodded my head, however, pretending to concede the point. 'Six then. Why?'

Bernard strolled nonchalantly over to his goon, taking hold of the Director's right hand. He began to stroke it. Even from here I could see her shudder. 'Don't you know who I am?'

'No,' I said. 'I don't.'

He looked at me. 'You're telling the truth,' he said softly. 'You don't know.' He flicked his eyes at the Director. '*You* must know who I am.'

She didn't say anything. All she did was press her mouth into a stubborn line and resolutely refuse to meet his gaze. Bernard's expression didn't change. He simply pulled her hand up to his mouth then, without taking his eyes off of mine, he bit down hard on her pinky.

The Director screamed. She yanked her hand back, blood everywhere. Bernard chewed thoughtfully more a moment and then spat out the tiny digit. It bounced off the ground, coming to lie between us, the bastard's teeth marks visible across its length. I fought against my own rising nausea. Was this really happening?

'Who am I?' Bernard asked her, his barely accented voice so soft it was almost a caress. A caress of pure evil.

For a moment, she didn't respond. He shrugged to himself and reached over to take hold of her other hand. The Director licked her lips. 'You're a troll,' she whispered.

Bernard beamed from ear to ear. 'You do know!' He released his grip on her unharmed hand and began to clap. 'I knew you were old enough to know of our kind.' He gestured towards his grim companions. 'We're all trolls.'

I stared at him. I thought all the trolls were dead. That they'd all been killed in a single freak accidents decades ago. How on earth could they possibly exist now?

He laughed at the look on my face. 'You see what we're fighting against here, folks?' he said. 'This one didn't think we were real. That's how low we have fallen.' His eyes gleamed. 'It won't be long before every faery in the land knows of our kind and knows that we still survive despite their best efforts to the contrary. We are the stuff of faery godmother nightmares.' He bared his teeth. 'We won't kill her. It's time to let them all know. Our anonymity has served its purpose in creating an appropriate climate of fear. Now it's time to draw back the curtain. With the Director of the esteemed faery godmothers in our grasp, the terror our very names can unleash will do enough to strike fear into every faery heart. The reign of faery is almost over. The reign of troll is about to begin. It won't be long before there isn't a single faery left on this planet who will dare to be a godmother or to grant any wishes. Your entire organisation is on its last legs. Thanks to us.'

The man was mad. Utterly, stark raving crazy. I gaped, shuffling over to the left ever so slightly as I did so. Not far from the Director's severed finger lay her dropped wand. If I could grab it then there might still be a chance. There was no doubt in my mind that it was a powerful instrument. In my hands it could become the lethal weapon we needed.

'You will spread the word,' Bernard told me. 'Make sure everyone knows what has happened here. Make sure every faery godmother knows what's coming for them. It won't merely be a few disappearances they have to worry about now.'

'I still don't understand,' I said, finally getting the toe of my shoe to touch the edge of the Director's wand. 'Why do you have it in for faery godmothers?'

He snarled. 'You all think you're heroes. You don't understand that you're the villains. You always have been.'

I moved my feet, dragging the wand a few inches towards me. 'You're right. I don't understand.'

Bernard's mouth down-turned. 'No, I don't suppose you do. You will though.' He said this last part ominously. I had no idea what he was referring to. 'For now, you might not have the knowledge but you have the resources. The magic. The manpower. You faeries think you're in control of this world.' He spat on the ground, some of the Director's blood still in his saliva. 'Not for much longer. Humans have revered you and despised us for too long. We will change all that.'

The Director's gaze momentarily flicked downwards and her head moved imperceptibly. I didn't waste any further time. I lunged down, grabbing her wand up in one swift movement before thrusting it out towards the group of trolls. I didn't have a conscious thought about what I was doing. I just wanted to get the Director free and attack the bastards who were attacking us. There was a loud roar and, pounding the ground from directly behind me, the large green monster who'd terrified Duncan and my dope faery trainees appeared. It thundered towards Bernard and the other trolls, rage reverberating through its body.

'Get the Director into the van!' Bernard shouted.

I jerked forward, trying to reach for the Director and pull her back out of harm's way. My fingers brushed against her arm before she was abruptly dragged away towards the still waiting vehicle.

'Jasper!' I shrieked. 'Jasper!' Where the fuck was he?

I ran towards the trio of trolls, desperate to protect the Director in any way that I could while the green monster roared at Bernard. It raised one massive, quivering thigh then kicked him smack bang in the chest. He went flying backwards. As he fell, however, he flung his arms upwards. My monster choked, coming to an abrupt halt with its massive hair paws reaching for its chest. I didn't look back to see what happened. I just continued to pelt for the other trolls. Then something hit me from the side, slamming into my skull. I toppled to the ground, agony tearing through me. I blinked, managing to see the Director as she was bundled into the back of the van. Then I screeched in pain as a hand grabbed a hank of my hair and lifted up my head for me. It felt like my scalp was being ripped out.

'Neat trick,' Bernard said, his face looming over mine. A trickle of blood ran from the corner of his mouth and a large bruise was already forming down one side of his face. It wasn't enough to stop him, however, and I couldn't tell what had happened to my own monstrous conjuration. 'I wouldn't have expected a faery godmother to be capable of such a clever feat. It doesn't matter though.' He shrugged. 'I still win.' He leaned in even more closely. 'Interesting that you were calling for the Devil's Advocate. He won't help you now any more than your Director will.' He bared his teeth in a smile and dropped me. Then he aimed a sharp kick towards my stomach and more pain screamed through me. I curled up into a foetal position in a weak bid to protect myself. Bernard just laughed. 'Don't forget to tell all your little faery friends that the trolls are coming.' He aimed another kick at my side, as if for good measure. 'Toodle pip, sweetheart.'

CHAPTER 25

I didn't know how long I stayed there on that cold, hard ground. There was little coherent thought in my head. In truth, I couldn't think beyond the agonizing pain that had all but shattered my body. I drifted in and out of consciousness several times, my breath ragged as I wheezed through several broken ribs.

'For fuck's sake. What's happened to you?' A familiar face swam towards mine.

I blinked and tried to focus. 'Wha – at?'

'Should get yourself a pair of wings, faery. Then you can fly to casualty and get yourself fixed up.'

'Vincent?' I croaked.

'Who else? Hang on. I'll call an ambulance.'

I clutched at his leg. 'No. No, ambulance.'

'You're in a bad way. Unless you want to bleed out right here, you need to get to hospital.'

'No,' I repeated. 'Help me up.'

He hesitated. Then his hands reached under my armpits and he pulled me up to a sitting position. 'That's what happens when you go interfering on other people's business,' he told me. 'I could have seen it coming a mile off.'

'Yeah, yeah.' I raised my head and looked over at the café where Jasper had supposedly gone to wait. 'Help me across the road. I need to see inside that coffee shop.'

'I don't recommend it. Their food is shite and their coffee is worse.'

'Please,' I whispered.

He sighed as if all this was a great burden to him. He should walk in my shoes. 'Alright then.' He raised me up to my feet. 'Can you even walk?'

I nodded. 'Yes.' I took a step and my knees gave way. Fuck a puck. Maybe not then. My gaze snagged on something lying on the ground. The Director's wand. I must have dropped it when I'd been struck in the head. Bernard screwed up massively by leaving it with me. Then it occurred to me that it might have been deliberate. He wanted me alive so that I would spread the word about him. After all, he was already long gone now. I couldn't do anything to stop him. I had no idea where he'd gone either, and no way of tracking him.

I pointed at the wand. 'Can you get that for me?'

Vincent pursed his lips. He did as I asked though, bending down and retrieving the wand. 'This is how you do that magic shit, right?' he asked. He waved the wand around in the air. 'Nothing's happening.' He sounded disappointed.

'You're not a faery,' I said, barely managing to get the words out. 'Give it to me.'

'You're not going to turn me into a frog, are you? I'm trying to help you. And I've not sold any drugs since I spoke to you.' He said as if I should be proud of his accomplishment. He'd only been released yesterday.

'Just give me the fucking wand.'

Vincent huffed. He did, however, place it into my

outstretched hand. I heaved in a pained breath and squeezed my eyes shut. Then I waved the wand around me. This had better bloody work.

The pain eased almost instantly, my bones re-knitting back together again. I'd be sore for a long time yet and no manner of wand waving would resolve the ugly bruises which I knew had already formed all down my body. I'd be able to walk now though. And think. That was something.

'Thank you,' I gasped.

Vincent peered at me. 'You've got some colour in your cheeks. You still don't look great though. I can still call that ambulance.'

'No.' I heaved myself upwards once again. 'The café. Now.'

'Honestly,' he said, as I began to stagger out of the park and towards the orange glow of the coffee shop, 'this place is not worth it. You don't need food poisoning to deal with on top of everything else.'

He meant well. I couldn't prevent myself from turning towards him and snarling, however. He stepped back and held up his palms. 'Fuck you then.' He turned on his heel and began to walk away.

I scowled. Damn it. 'Vincent,' I called. 'Please don't go. I'm sorry. I'm just still hurting. Something very bad has happened and I'm worried. Can you help me out? Stay with me for a while longer?' I couldn't face being on my own on these streets, even if the alternative was a grubby drug dealer with loose morals.

He crossed his arms and pouted. Actually pouted.

'Please?'

'What do I get in return?'

Damn it. This wasn't worth it. 'Never mind. I'll manage on my own.' I turned away and continued shuffling to the café.

Vincent swore again and caught up to me. 'Fine,' he said.

'I'll stay with you. Just remember that I helped you out though. Okay?'

'Okay.' I was more relieved that he was staying than I'd have thought possible. I swallowed. 'Thank you.'

'That's more like it.' He took my arm and helped me over.

Vincent pushed open the café door and looked inside. Then he drew back. 'This is more of a bad idea than I thought it was. The place has been trashed.'

My heart sank to the bottom of my boots. 'I have to see.' I sidled past him and walked in, barely managing to stop myself from crying out when I saw the devastation inside.

The few tables and chairs were overturned and there were shards of glass all over the floor. One of the plaster walls had several holes which appeared to have been punched through it and the fridge which contained cans and bottles of drinks was lying face down. Vincent knelt down, dipping his finger in a pool of liquid.

'It's blood,' he said unnecessarily.

'Yeah.' I heaved a sigh and blinked back tears. 'I figured.' I scanned the room. Jasper had put up a hell of a fight but whatever had happened here had happened quickly. Those trolls were stronger than I'd thought if they could best the Devil's Advocate. Maybe they'd followed him in here and attacked him before he even knew what was going on. Then I thought about the man who'd served me when I'd come in for lunch before. I briefly closed my eyes. The trolls didn't have to follow him. One of them had already been waiting in here. The entire café was probably a set up to keep an eye on the park. No wonder the food was so bad. They didn't want customers. They only wanted an excuse to be here.

'How long has this place been open?' I glanced at Vincent.

'Couple of months, maybe more.' He frowned. 'Why?'

I passed a hand over my forehead. 'It doesn't matter.' Not

now. I grimaced. Despite the magic I'd performed on myself, I still had a horrific headache. I looked round the café once again. I couldn't deal with all this on my own. I'd have to get some more help from somewhere.

Vincent bent down and picked something up. He held it up towards the light. 'Check this out,' he said. 'It's some sort of dart.' He reached out to touch the tip of it.

I hissed at him. 'Don't touch that!'

He instantly dropped it. 'Why not?'

Because it seemed almost inconceivable that Jasper could have been taken - but that dart explained it. If he had his back turned to the slimy bastard who'd worked here and he'd been shot with some sort of poisonous projectile, then he could have fallen unconscious – or worse – before he could have defended himself properly. I glanced round the devastation once more. He'd still given it his best shot though.

'Just don't,' I said.

Vincent shrugged, using his hand to push back a limp hank of hair which was falling into his eyes. I stared at him. Fuck a puck. Why hadn't I paid attention to that before? I was a prize idiot.

'I need to get to my office,' I said faintly.

Vincent blinked at me. 'You want to go to work? Now?'

'There are people there who can help with ... this.' I waved a hand around.

'Whatever this is,' he muttered. 'Is it far? This office of yours?'

I shook my head. 'Only a few streets away. Can you help me?' It was hard to believe I still needed his help but the last thing I wanted was to collapse in the middle of the street before I could raise the alarm.

'Then let's go. I don't want to be anywhere near here when the coppers arrive. They'll think I did this.' He scratched his head. 'Unless I pin the blame on you.' He offered me a tiny grin.

I tried to smile in return but I didn't do a very good job of it. Vincent seemed to realise how much I was struggling and put an arm round my shoulder. 'Come on then. You've got this, Alicia.'

I sniffed. 'Saffron.'

'You told me your name was Alicia.'

'I lied. It's Saffron.'

I was waiting for some snippy remark in return. He only dipped his head though in acknowledgment. 'You've got this, Saffron.'

I swallowed. I really didn't. But I would – if only because failure was not an option.

I wasn't sure if anyone would be left in the office but I was banking on the faery godmothers' propensity to work late. Mrs Jardine was still at the front desk and I suspected there were plenty more people upstairs. I hoped so anyway. I was going to need them. She didn't look particularly pleased to see me lurch in with Vincent by my side. Unfortunately, I didn't think anything I said would improve her mood.

'You can't come in here, Saffron!' She rose to her feet. 'Not now and certainly not after hours. If the Director hears about it, there will be hell to pay.'

Vincent paid her words no attention. He whistled loudly and gazed round at all the shiny marble. 'I've walked down this street a thousand times,' he said, 'and I've never noticed this building before.' He goggled about himself. 'It smells so good. And it's so ... clean.'

Under any other circumstances, Mrs Jardine's horror would have been comical. 'You brought a *human* here?'

'Is she another one of your faery types?' Vincent asked me. 'She's kinda hot.'

Mrs Jardine looked even more shocked. 'You told him what we are?' She threw her hands up in dismay. 'You're not protected by the memory magic any more! Saffron, I know you must be upset at being fired but this kind of behaviour will have serious consequences.'

Vincent looked at me. 'You've been fired?' He gave me a nod of approval. 'Kudos.'

I rolled my eyes. I wasn't quite sure how getting sacked earned me any brownie points whatsoever. 'Thank you so much for your help in getting me here, Vincent. I'm not sure I would have made it without you.'

A flicker of hope lit his eyes. 'Does this mean I get another wish?'

'It means next time I see you, I might buy you a coffee.'

He grunted. 'I'd rather have a pint.'

'I can manage that. Now,' I added, aware of Mrs Jardine's pursed lips and bristling disapproval, 'you have to remember not to...'

'Tell anyone about any of this. Yeah, yeah. No-one would believe me anyway.' He looked over at Mrs Jardine then blew her a kiss. 'Hope to see you again, doll-face.' He jabbed me. 'Don't get yourself killed, faery.' He spun round, his trenchcoat flapping round his ankles. Then he exited.

'Saffron,' Mrs Jardine was still shaking her head. 'What have you done?'

'That human is the last of our worries,' I told her. 'I need to speak to every faery who's still left in this office. It's urgent.'

Her frown deepened. 'You know that's not going to happen.

And before you suggest it, I can't even ask the Director if it's okay. She's already left for the night.'

'I know,' I said grimly. 'But unless we do something now, she won't be coming back.'

'What on earth ...?' She took another look at my face and sank down in her chair. 'Oh no.'

'Oh yes.' I set my jaw. 'Get everyone down here.'

It didn't take long. When Mrs Jardine wanted something done, it happened quickly. She made the wise decision not to inform the other faeries as to why she was requesting their presence in the lobby. When the small group of around ten faeries exited the lift and caught sight of me, their expressions pretty much said it all.

Before they could start throwing their magical toys out of the pram, I hastily spoke up. 'The Director has been abducted by the same wankers who took the others. There's not just one kidnapper. There are several of them.' My mouth flattened. 'I think they've got the Devil's Advocate as well.'

For one long moment, everyone stared at me. Then there was an explosion of noise.

'What the fuck?'

'No way. That wouldn't happen!'

'What the hell are we going to do now?'

I held up my palms in a bid to silence them. Unbelievably, it worked. Even Alicia stopped talking.

'I saw it all happen,' I said. 'I tried to stop it but I was attacked in the process.' I reached into my pocket and took out the Director's wand. There was another collective gasp of horror. 'She was lured out there and then she was taken. Thrown into a van and driven off. The tosser in charge wanted me to tell everyone what he's done. He's on a mission to spread terror amongst every faery in the country.' I waited for a beat. 'His name is Bernard and he said he was a troll.'

Almost every single face looked confused. The only two faeries who didn't were Mrs Jardine and Billy.

Rupert ran a hand through his hair and stepped forward. 'Saffron,' he drawled, 'as much as I want to believe all this, trolls don't exist.' He gave me a kindly look that swept in my entire body. He still seemed to think that he might be in with a shot to get into my knickers, despite my new unemployed status and supposed tall tales.

I looked at Mrs Jardine, raising my eyebrows. 'Care to add anything to that?' I inquired.

'I thought they were all dead,' she said quietly. 'I was working here at the time and we were told they were all dead in the same way that you were told that at school.' Every single eye turned towards her. Mrs Jardine wrung her hands. 'There were never very many of them. They tended to keep to themselves and stay out of our way. Most lived in caves and tunnels. They didn't like humans and didn't appreciate that we essentially work to improve humans' lives. They didn't bother us though.'

'But?' I prodded.

She sighed. 'But about forty years ago, there was a terrible accident. A landslide in the hills in Wales. The trolls had all been gathered there for some sort of meeting to elect a new leader. That's what I heard anyway. They were all caught in the landslide.' Her voice dropped. 'They all died.'

'We know all this,' Delilah said. 'It was covered in school.'

Indeed. Clearly they didn't all die though. I opened my mouth to ask her more when Billy broke in. 'That's not the full story.'

Mrs Jardine looked away.

'The full story,' Billy continued, 'is that the landslide occurred because of a wish that went wrong. A wish that the faery godmothers granted. The reason that you've never heard of it before now is because it was covered up to avoid any taint attaching itself to this office.'

I shook my head in disgust. Unbelievable. 'This,' I said, 'is why it's vital for history to be full, transparent and available to all. Otherwise no-one learns from their mistakes and sooner or later your past deeds come back to bite you on the arse.'

'It wasn't a deliberate cover-up,' Mrs Jardine said. 'Not exactly. It just wasn't spoken of again. The truth is that the trolls died in an accident. The fact that it was an inadvertent result of a wish gone wrong doesn't change that fact. Most faeries barely knew that the trolls existed in the first place. The faery godmothers who knew what had occurred were simply too embarrassed and horrified by what had happened to dwell on it. There was nothing sinister behind the omission. Not intentionally, anyway.'

'Those surviving trolls might beg to disagree,' I muttered. It seemed to me that faery godmothers spent a great deal of time hiding the truth from both themselves and others. I shivered. I felt light-headed and ill and it wasn't simply because of the unpleasant revelations. 'I need a chair.' I wavered over to the uncomfortable seats I'd been forced to wait in less than a week ago and slumped down. 'Regardless of their underlying motives, these trolls want us terrified. Bernard and his buddies want to destroy us, root and stem. They want revenge for what we did to their kind.'

'What do we do? What *can* we do?' Figgy's voice was rising along with her panic. 'What the fuck can we do?'

'We find the trolls' hideout,' I said quietly. 'With as much haste as possible. I know who we can ask. I just need a bit of help to get there before I pass out again.' I raised my head and gazed blearily at them all. 'I need all your help.'

Alicia strode out in front of the group. 'The Director needs us!' she bellowed. 'We have to help her. We will help her. We are faery godmothers! We are faery godmothers!'

Everyone else joined in, the chorus of voices growing. 'We are faery godmothers!'

My eyes met Billy's. Given the revelations we'd heard, I wasn't convinced that anyone should be proud to be a faery godmother. However, if Alicia's rallying cry meant that we could work together to save the Director, the other faeries, and Jasper, then I guessed it would be worth it.

CHAPTER 26

One small group went with Rupert to the Adventus room to scour the archives for any historical mention of trolls which might help us. One small group went with Mrs Jardine to investigate both St Clements Park and the café for any clues I might have missed. The rest of us went to see Duncan. It would be an education for Alicia, Delilah and even Billy, if nothing else.

'Are you feeling any better?' Billy asked me in a low voice, when we pulled up to Duncan's building.

'I don't feel like I'm about to faint any more so I suppose so,' I said. I tried to smile cheerfully at him but we both knew I didn't really mean it.

'I don't understand,' Alicia said, with a disgusted expression on her face, 'why are we coming to see a drug addict again?'

'Because,' I answered calmly, 'I think he might know where we can find the trolls.'

'Even if he does know anything, won't he be too off his face to tell us anything?'

I shrugged. 'He tends to stick to shrooms and avoid harder substances.'

'He takes drugs,' Alicia sneered.

I opened my mouth to tell her that the Director herself was probably lured out to her own abduction on the promise of some drugs. Then I thought better of it. 'Duncan is an intelligent guy.' I laughed humourlessly. 'Frankly, if I was as smart as him, I'd have spoken to him again before now and we might have avoided all of this.'

Alicia snorted. 'Well,' she said, '*frankly*, we all wish that you were smarter.'

'If only I spent more time thinking about hair, then maybe I would be.'

She glared at me and tossed her head, apparently thinking I was making some sort of dig at her shiny golden locks. 'What on earth does that mean?'

I sighed. 'Never mind.' I rang Duncan's buzzer. Come on, I prayed. Please be in. Last time I'd spoken to him I'd not officially been working so there would be no memory magic to block his mind. He would remember me from that encounter. It was something I was counting on.

'Who is it?' his voice asked, trembling through the speaker.

'It's Saffron. Your mate. I thought I'd pop by with a few friends.'

There was a pause. 'Those mushrooms you brought last time were shite.'

I winced. 'Sorry.'

'I don't want to talk to you again.'

'Wait,' I said, 'Duncan, I just ...' I cursed. The lack of static noise told me that he'd already clicked off.

'What now?' Delilah asked.

I tightened my jaw with resolute determination. I had to speak to Duncan. There was no other choice. 'Wait here,' I said.

'What will you do?'

I drew back my shoulders in preparation. 'I've still got the

Director's wand.' I smiled grimly. 'I will cast some faery godmother magic.'

Billy reached into the bag on his shoulder and pulled out a wad of bright pink fabric. 'You might need this then.'

I shook out the cloak and placed it round my shoulders. 'Fabulous. Thank you.' I glanced at the three of them. 'Keep an eye out down here for any passersby.' Then I waved the wand and began to rise up through the air, the cloak billowing out behind me. Hey, I was a faery; I had to fly at some point.

Duncan's dirty window was only just ajar. It certainly wasn't a wide enough gap that I could fit through. Rather than attempt to open it further from this side, I leaned over and tapped it with my wand. A moment later, Duncan peered out. When he saw me, he fell backwards. 'Wh .. what?'

'Let me in, Duncan.' I smiled at him, noting his dilated pupils. He might not have appreciated the mushrooms I'd given him but he'd gotten something more potent from somewhere. That was good. It meant this would go easier. 'It's Saffron. Remember?'

Duncan began to violently shake his head from left to right. 'I'm not letting you in. You might be evil.'

Yeah, Duncan was indeed intelligent. 'I'm really not. But we can chat while I'm out here if you prefer.' I supposed it would waste less time, even if it was a considerable effort to keep myself afloat like this, despite the handy help the Director's wand granted me.

'I came to see you before,' I said, 'about the boogeyman.'

'Yeah?' he edged over on all fours to the window and peered down, as if expecting to see a ladder propping me up.

'I made a mistake. I thought the boogeyman you were talking about was a guy called Vincent. But I was wrong. Vincent has shoulder length grey hair. When I spoke to you before and I mentioned the boogeyman's hair, you threw me out. That's because your boogeyman is bald, isn't he? And his name isn't Vincent. It's Bernard.'

Duncan swallowed, his Adam's apple bobbing up and down. He seemed reluctant to answer but something about the bizarreness of this situation must have persuaded him otherwise because he finally nodded. 'Yeah,' he said, sitting up on his knees. 'Bernard the boogeyman.'

I breathed out. I'd been on the right lines all along. If I'd had more faith in my own long shot from the start then I might have found Bernard days ago. I shook myself. I couldn't focus on what had already happened and what I'd already missed. I had to worry about what would happen next.

'You told me to avoid St Clements Park in order to avoid him,' I said urgently.

'He's there a lot,' Duncan muttered. 'Don't go there. It's a bad place.'

I wondered if Duncan had witnessed Bernard and his team abducting any of the other faery godmothers from the park. I decided that I didn't need to know. It wouldn't help. 'When he's not at St Clements Park, Duncan, where is he?'

'I can't tell you.' He shook his head with vehement denial. 'It's too dangerous.'

'Duncan,' I pressed, 'Bernard has kidnapped some friends of mine.' Jasper's dark features flashed into my mind and I felt a sudden pulse of pain ripple through me. 'I think he'll hurt them. I have to find him and find them before it's too late.'

Duncan looked upset. 'I don't want anyone to get hurt.'

'Then tell me where I can find Bernard. Where does he live? Where else does he hang out?'

Duncan blinked. He wasn't going to tell me. I could see his continued denial written all over his drawn, haggard face. I clenched my fists. 'I'm floating like this, Duncan, because I'm a faery godmother.' I licked my lips. If Jasper could hear me now, he'd throw another fit. I wished he would. 'I'm a faery godmother,' I repeated. 'Tell me where Bernard is and I will grant you a wish. Any wish.' Another off the books wish wasn't a great idea but I had to give him something. This was getting desperate.

'You'll give me a wish?' he asked doubtfully.

'Anything,' I said. 'Just say the word and I'll give you whatever you want.'

'I don't want anything.'

'There must be something.'

He seemed puzzled. 'I've got a roof over my head and food to eat. I've got friends and family. I have fun tripping on some shrooms from time to time which takes the edge off the problems I've got. Why would I want anything else? Things could be a hell of a lot worse. I'm lucky.'

There was a lesson in there for all of us. 'I can give you what your heart desires.'

A tiny smile lit his mouth. 'My heart is happy.' He looked at me. 'Actually, there is one thing.'

That was more like it. 'Go on.'

A calculating light came into his eyes. 'Your cloak.'

I blinked. 'Huh?'

'Give me your cloak. I like the colour. Give me it and I'll tell you where the boogeyman is.'

'That's what you want?' I asked stupidly.

From behind the window, Duncan folded his arms. 'That's what I want.'

I all but ripped it off my body. 'Here.' I shoved it through the small gap. 'Take it. It's yours.'

He grabbed it, before holding it up and stroking the material with his fingers. 'It's so soft.' He wrapped it round his shoulders and grinned. 'I love it.'

I watched him for a moment. 'I wish I knew more people like you, Duncan,' I said softly.

'You ought to get out more,' he advised.

'Saffron!' Billy hissed from below. 'Some people are coming! You have to get down from there.'

'Please, Duncan,' I said quickly. 'Where can I find Bernard? I have to find him.'

He glanced up, his eyes meeting mine. 'Bridge To Nowhere,' he said. 'Nightclub on Fore Street. He owns the place.'

I felt renewed surge of adrenaline race through my veins. 'Thank you,' I whispered.

Duncan just smiled.

It was too early for Bridge To Nowhere to be open, even though night was fast approaching. The four of us stood across the street, staring at the darkened façade. The other faery godmothers were on their way. It wouldn't be long now.

'Maybe we should wait,' Delilah whispered. 'Come up with a proper plan first.'

'Don't be such a coward,' Alicia snapped. 'That's our Director they've got in there. Not to mention the Devil's Advocate and the others. We storm the place and rip the guts from those trolls.' Her jaw tightened. 'There's no other choice.'

Damn. Alicia was braver than I'd realised. Especially considering I could see her hands shaking from here.

'We need to have something in mind. What is the actual plan for now, Saffron?' Billy asked. 'What do we do?'

I looked round the expectant faces. They seemed to think I had some sort of actual battle blueprint in mind. Perhaps they believed that I was used to storming the citadels of my enemies. I swallowed. If I could act confident and knowledgeable in the office then I could do it here. Without some sort of self-belief, then we were all already doomed to fail.

Clearing my throat, I raised my chin. 'We have no idea of the trolls' numbers. We have no idea of what's inside that place or even if our colleagues are still alive. We don't know for sure if they *are* here at all.' I saw everyone's faces fall further. Way to boost morale, Saffron. 'So,' I said hastily, 'we need to be clever. And careful. We don't want to get spotted by anyone. Our goal is to be sneaky and to avoid detection. We can't hope to beat the trolls in a fight without knowing more about them. We're going to find our people and get out of here without spilling any blood.' Or losing any body parts.

'Okay. Yes.' Delilah nodded. 'That makes sense.' She hesitated. 'So do we go through the front door?'

I shook my head. 'Definitely not. There must be a back entrance. We're not stupid enough to waltz in through the front door. Let's head round the back and find another way in.'

Five minutes later we were at the front again. There was no handy staff door round the rear of the club. There were a few windows but they were blackened out and sealed shut and didn't seem like any sort of appealing entrance point.

'So,' I said cheerfully, 'the front door it is then.'

Alicia, Billy and Delilah stared at me. I shrugged. It was either that or go home and we all knew that wasn't an option.

'Maybe we should wait for everyone else,' Delilah hedged again.

'We'll only be more likely to be detected. You three are welcome to stay out here and wait for the cavalry if you want, however.'

'No.' Billy was adamant. 'I'm coming in with you.'

Alicia tossed her head. 'I'm not letting you bag all the heroic glory. Let's do this.' She smoothed her still shaking hands down her sides.

Delilah sighed. 'It'll be good to see what's really going on in there first hand.' She was clearly trying to convince herself.

'Last one in the door is a rotten faery,' I whispered. 'Come on.'

We jogged across the road and up to the door. I led the way, like the ninja warrior I was pretending to be. Naturally, the heavy door itself was locked. Surprisingly, it was Billy who stepped forward. 'I've got this,' he said. When I shot him a look, he just shrugged. 'The amount of times you godmothers lose your keys has made me adept at lockpicking, whether doors are magically sealed or not.'

I inclined my head in brief admiration and moved to the side. Billy lifted one finger. He didn't have a wand. In his line of work as general office dogsbody, I supposed he didn't need one. In any case, it didn't matter. Although beads of sweat broke out on his forehead as he strained to break the door seal while remaining quiet, it was mere seconds before it sprang open. We each exchanged grim glances and then entered.

Delilah carefully closed the door behind us, wedging it ajar a fraction with a ten pound note she extracted from her pocket and folded up just enough to prevent the lock from returning to its original position. To anyone looking in from the outside, it would appear as if the door were still firmly closed. I nodded approvingly and her cheeks glowed in the shadowy gloom. Maybe I was better at this management crap than I'd realised.

'Let's go left,' I said decisively. I was on a roll now.

'Don't be ridiculous,' Alicia snapped. 'The toilets are to the left. If our people are here, they will be that way.' She pointed to the right and the interior door marked Staff Only. Ah. Yes, that did make more sense.

I gestured to her to go ahead and take the lead. She shook her head. Alicia was no fool. There was only faery around here who was stupid enough to take the lead as potential cannon fodder and I guessed that was me. With my heart in my mouth, I sucked in a breath. Then I tiptoed through the door.

If I'd been expecting blood dripping from the walls and various body parts pinned to the noticeboard, I was sadly mistaken. The staff quarters we found ourselves in were no different to any others around the world. Curling healthy and safety posters which no-one ever read were tacked up to the right and the beige paint gave the long corridor in front of us a depressing air. If anyone ever wondered what hell was like, I knew deep down that it would definitely involve beige.

I strode ahead, glancing in the different rooms leading off from the main corridor itself. There was a reasonably large staffroom with some chairs, dirty cups and old magazines. There were also several little offices apparently used by the nightclub's own management team. There was no glowing neon sign marked dungeon, however.

We investigated every nook and cranny, moving silently and swiftly through the darkness but still coming up short. I hissed through my teeth. Perhaps I'd been right the first time and there was indeed a secret entrance leading from the restrooms. Then, however, Billy trod on something and there was a dull thud. Something about that had sounded off.

Beckoning to the others and indicating to Billy to step aside, I carefully lifted up the threadbare carpet. A trapdoor. This had to be it. Without wasting any more time, in case I lost my bottle entirely, I crouched down and flipped it open. A ladder led straight down. If I'd thought the nightclub had been dark and gloomy before, it was nothing compared to the yawning chasm which lay in front of us now.

'We need light,' Delilah whispered. She took hold of her wand and flicked it through the air. All at once, there was a bright white flash.

'Not like that!' I whispered urgently, shielding my eyes.

'Sorry,' she muttered, waving her wand once more and reducing the brilliant shine to a much softer glow. I bit my lip. I hoped no-one outside had seen that spasm of light. It was just as well the windows were darkened after all.

Checking below me and registering nothing, I began to lower myself down the ladder's rungs, one foot after the other. I descended a good twenty feet before I found solid ground again. Instead of roughly hewn stone walls and a damp, mouldy atmosphere, I was gazing round a large opulent room, with soft red carpet, elaborate antique paintings and gilt edging. It was about as far removed from the bare staff rooms over our heads as it was possible to get. This was definitely the trolls' lair. I prayed that it was also definitely where Jasper and the others were being held.

I beckoned to the others to join me. One by one, they lowered themselves down the ladder, gaping when they hit the floor and saw what I did.

'Nice,' Alicia whistled. She pointed at one of the paintings. 'I swear that's by Van Gogh.' She walked over and began to prise it off the wall.

'Leave it!'

She turned round and gave me an irritated look. 'They're trolls. They can't possibly appreciate this level of art.'

'Alicia...'

She rolled her eyes. 'Fine.'

There was only one door in the entire room, a paneled mahogany affair that looked incredibly solid. I edged over and opened it slightly, peering out. Another corridor stretched out. It all but mirrored the staff one above our heads. The interior decorator for this section of the building had again done a far better job down here though.

Shuffling out, and staying as quiet as I possibly could, I strained my ears for any sound of any sort. It was just as well no expense had been spared. The rich, luxuriant carpet helped mask my own footsteps. I sneaked along. I didn't know what I was looking for but I reckoned I'd know it when I found it. At every closed door, I paused and listened. The only sound which rebounded was the hum of silence.

'There are too many doors,' Billy said behind me in a low voice. 'This place is a maze.'

I opened mouth to answer him when I saw Alicia's eyes flare in sudden alarm. She gestured frantically. A moment later, I heard something too. From the other end of the corridor, someone was coming.

We didn't waste any time. Delilah flung open the nearest door and threw herself in. The rest of us followed, squashing ourselves into a tiny space filled with brooms and mopes and overflowing hanging shelves. I grabbed the door and closed it but the size of the cupboard and the size of our bodies meant that it no longer shut properly. I was forced to keep hold of the handle to avoid the door from springing back open and giving us away. Alicia was standing on my feet and my head appeared to be rammed into Delilah's armpit. I could already feel the panic of claustrophobia setting in. Two sets of footsteps could be faintly heard plodding towards us.

'We're going to have to kill them. I don't care what Bernard and the others say about the plan. We can't continue holding them all here.'

'If we kill them, then we're bad as those fucking faery godmothers themselves.'

'It'd be easier if they were dead.'

'I won't argue with that.'

Both the voices and the footsteps melted away. I breathed out. They were still alive. They were all still alive. Jasper's face flashed into my mind and my stomach lurched, although whether through fear or relief, I couldn't have said.

'I. Can't. Breathe.' Delilah's words were muffled.

Alicia sniffed. 'This is closer than I ever wanted to get to any of you.'

Ditto. I released my hold on the door handle. Then I pointed down the corridor in the direction the trolls had come from them. 'They're down there,' I said quietly. 'They have to be.' I clenched my teeth. 'Let's go save our friends.'

CHAPTER 27

The last door at the end of the hallway was unmarked. I couldn't fail to notice the scratches in the woodwork frame, however. Almost like someone had dug their nails in to prevent themselves from being thrown inside. With a painfully dry mouth, I turned the handle, steeling myself from whatever horrors might lie inside.

There were six mattresses. Each one was occupied by a body. Even with the aid of Delilah's light magic, I couldn't see any facial features.

'What now?' a female voice muttered from the closest mattress. 'Haven't you already bothered us enough today?'

'Lydia?' Alicia called. 'Is that you?'

It seemed as if everyone in the room, captives and rescuers all, held their breath. Then a tiny voice spoke back. 'Alicia?'

Thank fuck. All the tension in my body was released in a whoosh. We'd found them. We'd done it. Now all we had to do was get them out. All of the figures turned and sat up, chains jangling. They were each manacled to the wall. That was okay. I had the Director's wand with me after all.

'Jasper?' I asked, my heart in my mouth.

'Who's Jasper?'

Fuck a puck. He wasn't here then. Bernard and the others must be holding Jasper and the Director somewhere else. I curled my hands into fists, feeling the bite of my fingernails as they cut into the fleshy part of my hand. Then I released them. First things first.

'We're here to get you all out,' I said. 'Just hang on. We've got you.' I motioned to Billy, Delilah and Alicia. They all nodded and immediately began to work on releasing each faery godmother's restraints.

'Who are you?' An older male faery blinked at me, confusion in his face. I recognised him immediately as Boris.

'Saffron,' I told him. 'I'm a new faery godmother.'

There was a faint snort from Alicia's corner. Now that we'd actually found who we'd been looking for, her natural personality was beginning to reassert itself. 'Actually, she's not. She's already been fired. She was a faery godmother for about five minutes. Now she's not.'

'But,' Billy interrupted, 'she is the reason why we're here rescuing you all now.'

'Tell me, Billy. How many rules have we broken by letting ourselves get kidnapped like this?' Lydia asked.

He let out a brief laugh. 'I'll write up all my reports later,' he said. 'For now let's concentrate on getting you all the hell out of here.'

'How many trolls are there?' I asked, fumbling with the last chains on the faery next to me.

'We've counted at least a dozen,' he answered. 'But different ones come and go.'

I flicked my wand one last time and the manacles finally sprang free. He groaned in relief and began to rub his wrists. 'And the Director?' I asked urgently. 'Or the Devil's Advocate? Have you seen them too?'

He stared at me through the gloom. His face was pale and drawn and there were two painful looking stumps on his hands where his little fingers had once been. Other than that, however, he seemed alright. At least physically anyway.

'They've been captured too?' he whispered, patently horrified at the thought.

'Where might they have been taken? We have to find them as quickly as possible and get out of here before any of the trolls notice what's going on.'

'The nightclub floor.' He jerked his head upwards. 'We were all brought there to start off with. And when they took...' he swallowed and held up his hands, 'and when they took our fingers they did it up there too.' His face twisted. 'They like to put the music on loud. I'm not sure if it's to drown out our screams or because it makes it all more enjoyable for them. They hate us. They want us to hurt.' He shook his head. 'I don't know why. I didn't even know trolls still existed until they grabbed me in the park.'

This wasn't the time for half-baked explanations. I only had a few of the facts anyway. It was pointless – and too time-consuming – to speculate.

I turned to Billy. 'The three of you have to get these guys out of here. Get them as far away as possible.'

He nodded. 'What will you do?'

'The Director and the Devil's Advocate are probably upstairs. I'm going to get them.'

'On your own?'

'Get these godmothers out of here, Billy. That's what's important right now. They've been here for long enough. Once you've gotten them away, you can always come back for the rest of us.'

He gazed at me for a moment. Then he bit out a nod. 'Come on, people,' he said. 'Let's skedaddle.'

I helped the godmother beside me up to his feet. 'You're Boris, right?'

'Yes.' He smiled at me. 'It's nice to meet you. It's a shame it's under these sort of circumstances.'

I smiled back. 'Tell me about it.' Although actually this was a warmer welcome than the one I'd had in the actual office. I smiled again. 'Come on. Let's get you out of here.' I edged over to the door and peered out. The corridor remained thankfully empty. 'There are a few trolls wandering around. We'll have to be quick and careful.'

'Have you heard,' Delilah murmured to Lydia, 'that Caroline from Accounting is doing the dirty with...'

'Delilah!' I snapped.

She blinked at me. 'What? I'm trying to keep everyone's mind off the fact that we're still in mortal danger.'

'A nice thought.' I rolled my eyes. 'But stick to the escape. You can gossip later.'

Alicia took the front this time, leading everyone in single file down the corridor and to the ladder. Just before she began to ascend it, she glanced back, her eyes meeting mine. Then she nodded once and turned away. One by one, each faery godmother disappeared upwards. I tightly crossed my fingers. All they had to do was make it out of the building without being detected. Freedom was only a few breaths away.

By the time I hauled myself up to the staff corridor, Billy, who was taking up the rear, was already slipping out of the door. I caught up, watching as they all sidled out of the main entrance and into the cool night air. Five captives gone. Only two more to go. I cracked my knuckles before drawing out the Director's wand once again and holding it in front of me like the weapon it had the potential to be. I was ready. Or at least as ready as I'd ever be.

I tiptoed through the main hallway, past the empty cloakroom and desk. Two saloon style doors covered in silver glitter lay just up ahead. There was no scream covering music thumping out, which I presumed could only be a good thing. I pressed forward before peered over the doors.

The public part of nightclub was smaller than I'd expected. A bar had been built along one side, its back mirror lit up and displaying all manner of gins and vodkas and whiskies. There was an emergency exit to the other side and a smattering of tables and built in benches. Some sort of mezzanine floor hung over half of the space, where I presumed the VIP area and the DJ's booth were located. Other than the two slumped over figures in the middle of the dance floor, whose appeared to still be breathing, I couldn't detect anyone else in the vicinity. I knew that there were still at least two trolls in the building, however. But I didn't know where they'd gone. It was a gamble whether to run towards the Director and Jasper and free them, or to be more cautious. The longer I waited, I decided, the more peril I was putting us all in. There was no point in wasting any more time.

I pushed open the doors and ran forward, kneeling down first by Jasper. His nose had been broken and there was a considerable amount of bruising all over his face. His right arm was lying at an awkward angle. As far as I could tell, however, he still retained all of his body parts. Be thankful for small mercies.

'Jasper,' I whispered.

He groaned.

'Jasper, I need you to wake up. I can't carry you out of here on my own.' I poked him. 'Come on, buddy.'

His eyelids fluttered open, dull green irises filled with pain fixing onto me. His pupils flared and his body jerked. 'Saffron?'

'The one and only.' I grabbed his uninjured arm and tried to pull him up. 'Let's go.'

'When I kissed you before,' he croaked, 'in the park. It wasn't because I thought anyone was watching. It was because I wanted to kiss you. I just wanted you to know that.'

'I already knew that, you daft bugger. This is real life, not a romance novel.' More's the pity. I glared at him. 'Stop with the dying declaration. I'm getting you out of here.'

'No.' He shook his head. 'Her first.'

'I'll get the Director right after you.'

'She's lost a lot of blood. And,' he added weakly, 'she's the one they really want to hurt. Get her out of here.'

'But...'

'I'm the Devil's Advocate. You have to do what I say.'

I glared at him. 'I really don't.'

'Please.'

I sighed. Arguing wouldn't help matters. 'I'll only be a minute.' I scooted round. The Director was barely conscious. I felt for her pulse. Jasper was right. It was weak and thready. She needed urgent medical help. I could use her own wand to repair some of the superficial damage but I couldn't do very much about blood loss. 'I want you to remember,' I whispered in her ear, 'that I'm saving you right now. Me. Saffron Sawyer.'

She moaned. I pointed the tip of the wand at her, allowing a gentle surge of magic to leap forth and encircle her. That would have to do for now. I bent over and scooped her up in a fireman's lift, staggering up to my feet. Ex-employee of the year. That was me.

I began moving back towards the saloon doors, albeit considerably more slowly now. I didn't get very far. The sound of footsteps and voices drifted over. I threw myself and the Director towards the nearest cushioned benches. A moment later, Bernard, flanked by two other trolls, strode through the door.

'I'm baaack!' he called out. 'Did you miss me? I do hope so.

We'll get started now. In fact…' he faltered. 'Why is there only one faery in the middle of my dance floor?' he whipped round, immediately catching sight of me. To be fair, it wasn't much of a hiding place. His eyes narrowed. 'You again.'

I left the Director where she was and pulled myself up to my feet. I made a show of dusting myself off and then gave him a disarming smile. 'Me. Hello again. I was feeling a little left out that you didn't want me so I thought I'd come and join the party anyway.'

Bernard's head snapped to the side. 'Check on the other godmothers.'

'They were all there half an hour ago.'

'Check them!' he roared. 'Now!'

The troll to his right scuttled off.

'Call the others,' he commanded the other one. This time, his minion didn't wait. He sprang to order, sprinting out of the room. Uh oh.

'I know what you're thinking, little faery,' Bernard said, taking a step towards me. 'But you can't beat us. You can't beat *me*. I'll crush you into the ground before you can lift that wand even an inch.'

I raised my head and met his eyes. 'You don't really think I'm here on my own, do you?' I managed to inject a note of amusement into my voice. 'Every faery godmother in the country is converging on this building. We're a team. We support each other and work together. We aren't faery godmothers so we can be average. The only real competition we have is when we look into the mirror and see ourselves.' I tutted. 'If you're not willing to learn any of that, Bernard, then no-one can help you.'

He stared at me. 'What the fuck are you on about?'

'There's no I in team.'

'No,' he agreed, 'but there is in dimwit.'

'You have to look through the rain to see the rainbow.'

Bernard put his hands on his hips. 'Alright, that's quite enough of that.' He glared at me. 'You're stalling.'

Oh yes. Yes, I was. I changed tack. Motivational phrases would probably only add to his fury. They certainly never helped me in the slightest. 'Why didn't you kill any of them?' I asked. 'You could have. But you didn't. Why not?'

He smiled unpleasantly at me. 'You noticed that, then. I haven't killed anyone up until now because I'm not a faery godmother. I don't decimate other races just because I feel like it.'

'I don't think...'

'Shut up!' he roared. 'I've not killed anyone up till now. I'm about to change my mind though.'

The saloon doors burst open and the other troll reappeared, panting. 'They've gone,' he said. 'They've all gone.'

'So be it.' Bernard advanced towards me. 'You've left me with no choice. Whoever you really are.'

'Saffron,' I said. 'My name is Saffron.' I began to dip into a curtsey. At the same time I raised my hand which was still clutching the Director's wand. Unfortunately, however, I wasn't fast enough. A stream of magic jetted out from Bernard's hands, smacking into my side and sending me flying through the air. My spine hit the far wall and I crashed down to the floor. Bernard stalked over to me and knelt down. 'You know what the best thing about being a troll is?' he inquired. He raised his hand once more. 'We don't need wands to perform powerful spells.' He slammed more magic into my body and I doubled over, seizing up with agonizing pain. Then he began to circle round me.

'Boss,' the other troll said nervously. 'I'm not sure this is a good idea. You know we're not supposed to hurt any of them that badly. We're only supposed to terrorise them into submission.'

'Oh,' Bernard snarled, 'I'll terrorise them. Have no fear on that score.' Then he muttered to himself, 'I always knew it would come to this. You godmothers won't understand anything until we do start killing you. You think you're so superior because you grant wishes for humans. You should realise that makes you little more than slaves. Well,' he bared his teeth, 'soon you'll all be slaves for us trolls instead.'

From outside there were several loud shouts. The others had returned, and hopefully with the rest of the faery godmothers in tow. Bernard turned his head, momentarily distracted. I took full advantage, using every last vestige of energy left in me to throw myself at him. I lifted my hands, aiming my thumbs at his eyeballs. His hands reached up, his fingers encircling round my wrists and squeezing. I yelped.

'They're here,' the other troll said, his eyes darting fearfully from side to side. 'The other faery godmothers are here.'

'Then you know what has to happen.'

'Boss...'

Bernard gripped my wrists even tighter. I could feel my own bones being crushed. I tried to wriggle free but he was too strong. From behind me I could see Jasper trying and failing to raise himself up. The Director hadn't moved from the bench.

'I want you to know,' Bernard sneered in my face. 'That you brought this upon yourself.' He released his grip on me. 'But don't worry. Your sacrifice won't be for nothing. Our policy is indeed to cause terror amongst the godmothers without killing. I will continue with that policy, at least as far as the outside world is concerned. Now we'll all die here.' He grinned. 'But you'll be blamed. This will only serve as a catalyst to bring the other surviving trolls round to our way of thinking. We either destroy the faery godmothers by subverting them to our will or we all die. For good this time.' He lifted his head and raised his hands into the air. At first I didn't think anything was happening. Then he pointed at the giant glittering disco ball perched above our heads. 'Devil's Advocate!' he called. 'What did I tell you was packed into that innocuous looking little sphere?'

I looked at Jasper. His eyes flicked to mine. 'Explosives,' he whispered.

Bernard smiled. 'Indeed.' He seemed to be salivating over the prospect. 'None of us are walking out of here now. But we will be martyrs for our cause.' Then he flicked his wrists one last time.

I screamed. I ran at Jasper, grabbing him by the scruff of his neck and hauling him backwards. Neither Bernard nor the other troll tried to stop me. Billy burst back in. I didn't waste any time. 'Get the Director out of here now!'

He spotted her immediately and hauled her upwards. We were all just reaching the saloon doors when there was a loud whomp. It felt like all the air had been sucked out of the room. A split second there was heat, deadly skin blistering heat. All four of us were thrown forwards. I felt rather than saw hands reaching out and pulling us towards the nightclub's doors. There was a strange ringing in my ears. I stumbled out into the night as Bridge To Nowhere went up in flames. I gasped for breath, desperately looking round me. The Director was there. So was Jasper. And Billy. We'd all made it out. We were all still alive.

'We've won!' Delilah's face appeared hovering in front of me then she pulled me into a hug which did nothing for my pain wracked body. 'We've won! We beat the troll bastard!'

My tongue darted out in a pathetic bid to moisten my cracked my lips. 'No,' I whispered. 'I don't think we've won at all.'

CHAPTER 28

The Director gazed at me from behind her desk. Her hand, with its missing finger, was tightly bandaged but other than that and a new haircut as a result of her singed hair, she appeared unscathed from her ordeal. She was a tough cookie.

'You came through for us, Saffron,' she said. 'For that I have to thank you. If it weren't for you, things would have been a lot worse.'

I inclined my head and bit back the temptation to mutter that it had been nothing. I *did* come through for them and I *did* deserve thanks. This wasn't the time for false modesty. I wouldn't allow my deeds to be brushed under the carpet.

'You're welcome. I am glad that no-one on our side died.'

'Mmm.' A tiny frown marred her smooth forehead. I knew what she was thinking. The fact that not one faery had died was a big deal. Especially given what happened with Bernard. How ever many trolls actually remained, his showy martyrdom would only spur them on against us. Plus, it would allow them the opportunity to pretend to themselves that they were still on morally higher ground and that they weren't killers – unlike us. They'd gloss over the actual kidnappings and minor dismemberment issues and use the events at Bridge To Nowhere to solidify their intent to subjugate and destroy the faery godmothers once and for all. The battle had been won, but the war was only just beginning. I had the uneasy feeling that I wasn't willing to voice that the trolls were going to prove to be far more intelligent than we were.

Beside me, Adeline coughed. 'Perhaps, Director,' she said awkwardly, 'this is an opportunity to re-consider Saffron's position here.'

I glanced at the office manager with some surprise. Obviously, I'd been hoping for this outcome. I just hadn't expected it to come from Adeline.

'The audit is still going ahead. The Devil's Advocate likes her,' she continued. 'That could be helpful for all of us.'

The Director herself didn't blink. Her lack of discomfort at the suggestion that I return to my original position had me holding my breath. Come on, I prayed. Give me my job back. This place was a horror and my colleagues were nuts. It had potential though. And, despite everything, I could still see myself sitting in the Director's own chair. One day. I could make the faery godmothers live up to their much exaggerated reputation. I had it in me. I knew I did. Assuming the trolls didn't destroy us first, of course.

'Leave us, Adeline.'

She started. 'But ...'

The Director's gaze narrowed. Adeline all but sprinted from the room. Honestly, Bernard had been made of stronger stuff than I'd given him credit for. If one look from the Director was enough to make Adeline turn tail then daring to abduct her was an action that only a steel hearted person could accomplish.

Once the door had closed behind her, the Director turned to me. 'You understand why you were initially recruited.'

It wasn't a question, but I nodded all the same.

'You also understand that things are not ... easy within this office.'

I nodded again.

'Despite all that has occurred, I still expect the very best from my faery godmothers. I remain unconvinced that you are capable of delivering that.'

Unbelievable. What more did I have to do?

'Still,' she murmured, 'regardless of the mistakes you have made, you do know how to keep your mouth shut. You could have told everyone why I had ventured out to the park in the first place.' She eyed me as if testing to see if I even knew the answer at all.

'You wanted drugs,' I said. 'You needed to take the edge off whatever it is you're feeling. Or to escape.' I kept a straight face. 'Or to just get buzzed.'

The Director winced. 'I went to St Clements Park as part of the investigation into the disappearances,' she said carefully.

Uh huh. 'Yes.' I wasn't completely daft. Not always anyway. 'You were very ... brave.'

She picked up a pen. 'You will be reinstated. I suppose we owe you that much.'

I couldn't prevent the giant grin from spreading across my face. She might think she was buying my silence about her attempted venture into the world of trippy drugs. I didn't actually care. Revealing her secret wouldn't be anyone best's interests, regardless of what happened to me. I wanted this job though and if this sort of prevarication was what it took then so be it.

'You will remain on your initial probation,' she added. 'Don't think that this means you can do whatever you want and get away with it.'

'Of course not.' I lifted up my chin. 'As long as I am treated fairly and given the same opportunities as everyone else then I have no complaints.'

'Indeed.' She sniffed.

'What about the trolls?' I asked. 'What's happening with them?'

'We are searching for them. We will find them. They will not put us in that position again.'

They'd stayed hidden for nigh forty years. I reckoned they had the upper hand when it came to magical hide and seek. There was no point saying that aloud, however. The Director knew it as well as I did.

'You don't have to worry about the trolls,' she continued. 'They will be dealt with sooner or later. You should worry about your own position here and concentrate on being the best faery godmother that you can be.'

I inclined my head. 'I will.' There was no doubt in my mind.

She pursed her lips. 'Well, with that in mind, there are a few matters to iron out. You say you want to be treated fairly. Even with the fawning eye of the Devil's Advocate upon you, that is important.'

Fawning eye? That wasn't how I'd ever thought of Jasper's feelings towards me. I doubted he'd think much of that phrasing either.

'Yes,' I said aloud. 'Equality is vital for the future of this office.' In more ways than one.

'Good.' She pressed the buzzer on her desk. The door opened and Billy appeared.

'Ms Sawyer,' he said formally to me. 'We welcome you back into the office. Just a few things to be aware of.' He avoided meeting my eyes. 'Your wages are to be docked at the end of this month...'

My mouth dropped open. 'Why?'

'There's the matter of a missing pink cloak.' He consulted

the clipboard in front of him. 'I believe you gave it away to a human. A Duncan Smith?'

I shook my head in faint disbelief.

'You deny giving the cloak to him?'

'No.'

Billy shrugged. 'Well, then.' He looked at his notes once again. 'Then there's damage incurred to a magical wand belonging to the Director herself.'

'What damage?'

'Some scrapes. A crack along one side.'

Fuck a puck. 'Fine,' I muttered. 'Is that it?'

'You are also to attend six human sensitivity training sessions. You revealed our existence to the afore-mentioned Duncan Smith and another human named Vincent Hamilton. That is completely unacceptable and entirely against the rules. Any further fall out from these actions will be on your head.'

I folded my arms. I had the distinct sensation that if I stood here and argued about any of this, it wouldn't go well for me. 'Alright.'

Billy passed the clipboard to me. 'Sign here.'

I sighed. I did as he asked, however. When I gave it back to him, his hand briefly met mine and squeezed.

The Director opened a drawer and took out my ID and my wand. 'Here you go, Saffron. Congratulations.'

I was no longer feeling quite so delighted. I took both items anyway. 'Thank you.'

The Director looked at me. 'Well? What are you waiting for? There are wishes waiting to be granted.'

Despite her cool manner, a brief thrill ran through me. She was right. I was still going to be the best damn faery godmother this world had ever seen. I reckoned I was already halfway to proving it.

'Yes, ma'am.'

CHAPTER 28

I took a deep breath and knocked sharply on Luke Wells' front door. His flat mates had already left the building – I'd made sure of that. It would just be me and my client alone together. I prayed that this would go well.

He opened the door and blinked blearily out. 'Yeah?'

'Hi Luke.'

His body stiffened in suspicion. I wondered whether his subconscious was pushing away the memory magic and telling him that I was some sort of madwoman and the best thing he could do right now was to slam the door in my face. 'Who are you?'

'You don't remember me.' I managed a sigh. 'I don't suppose that's surprising. You were so little the last time I saw you.'

My comment only served to make him even more distrustful. 'Eh?'

'I'm Saffron,' I told him. 'You used to call me Aunty Saff.' I smiled hopefully to disguise the lie. 'Does that ring a bell?'

'No.' He folded his arms and I sensed he was on the verge of giving me another brutal brush-off.

'I'm a friend of your father's,' I quickly said.

Luke's demeanour changed within a flash. 'You know my dad?' His expression was no longer that of a stand-offish, grumpy student. Instead he actually looked more like an eager puppy dog. I could feel myself softening towards him. 'My real dad?'

If biology was what it took in Luke's mind to be real. I was rather of the opinion that his stepdad was the real parent. I wasn't here to judge, however. That wasn't in my job description. 'Yes. Mark Countman.'

Luke sucked in a breath, his hand shooting out to grip the door frame as if to steady himself. Later, he'd wonder how on earth I'd found him. Now he only had one question burning through his skull. 'Do you know where he is?' he demanded. 'Do you know where I can find him?'

'I do.' I gave him a half smile. 'In fact, I can take you to him right now if you like. He's less than twenty minutes away from here.'

Under any other circumstances, Luke would have assumed I was trying to scam him and refused to come with me. He certainly possessed a suspicious enough nature to suspect only bad things of others. His desperation to find his father supplanted everything else, however. I'd said the magic words and, as a result, he'd all but sprinted out with me to the taxi I'd booked earlier and which was already waiting for us. It wasn't long before I was stepping back out onto Mark Countman's street. I could tell from Luke's expression that he recognised the area from his investigations at the tattoo parlour. Now he truly did believe that I was taking him to his dad. In fact, his entire body was quivering with anticipation.

'Which house?' he demanded. 'What number is it?'

'Let's hold off for just one second, Luke.' I put a soothing hand on his arm. 'Before we knock on his door, I want you to be prepared. He doesn't know we're coming. He might not react ... well.'

Luke opened his mouth to argue with me then seemed to think better of it. He was silent for a moment before looking at me. 'You know,' he said slowly, 'I think I do remember you, Aunt Saffy. You used to bring me bacon rolls, right? And coffee.'

I supposed it was fortunate that Luke didn't have much experience with little kids. There wasn't much wisdom in giving toddlers caffeine. 'Er, yes. That was me.'

'You looked after me,' he murmured. 'You're still doing it. You're like my faery godmother.'

I coughed. 'That's right.' I raised my eyebrows at him meaningfully. 'It's your side I'm on in all this. You can still walk away. You have a dad at home who loves you more than anything. This one has been absent for almost your entire life.'

Luke's shoulders sagged slightly. 'I know. I should hate him. He abandoned us. He abandoned *me*.' His chin was trembling. 'But if it wasn't for him, I wouldn't exist. I'm not always a nice person. Sometimes I'm fucking horrible. I wonder if that's because I've got so much of him in me. I'm not here to play happily families, Aunt Saffy. I'm here to find out what he's really like and what really happened all those years ago. I'd like to get to know him.' His head dropped. 'Even if he's still the same bastard he always was.'

Blood ties ran thick. I nodded. At least I could be assured that Luke was aware his biological father wasn't a hero. He could still get hurt badly here but he wasn't a babe in the woods either. Either way, meeting his dad was his wish. His real wish. 'He's at number twenty-three.'

Luke was already halfway across the road before I'd finished my sentence. So much for taking things slowly and thoughtfully then. I followed him, watching as he raised his fist to Mark Countman's door. He wavered in mid-air, hesitating for a few seconds. Then he set his chin and knocked loudly.

It seemed to take an age. Eventually, however, the door opened and Luke's father appeared. 'Good morning,' he said. 'Can I help ...' His voice stopped abruptly and he stared at Luke, his face turning white as a sheet.

'Hi Dad.' Luke didn't smile. 'Can I come in?'

Panic flared in Mark's eyes. I knew he wanted to refuse. He was seconds away from letting his worse instincts get the better of him. I did the only thing that made any sense. I stepped up, pushing past Luke and offering Mark a brilliant smile and before striding into his house without waiting to be invited. Mark was so surprised at my actions that he didn't stop me.

'I'll make some tea, shall I?' I bustled into the kitchen, immediately filling the kettle from the tap, listening to the awkward silence as both Mark and Luke also shuffled in after me and headed for the little living room.

'You shouldn't have come here, Luke.'

Fuck a puck.

'Why not? I'm your only son. Don't you want to get to know me?' Luke's voice was rising. 'Or do you have other kids I don't know about? Do I have any little brothers and sisters?'

'You're the only one.' Mark sighed. 'How's your mother? And Jonathan?'

'Mum's fine, not that you'd care.' I winced. Now that he had his foot in the door, Luke's fear of being rejected again was coming to the fore and presenting as antagonism. That wasn't going to help. 'And Jonathan's great,' he continued. 'He's been a wonderful father to me all these years.'

Mark's answer was quiet. 'I knew he would be. I knew you'd always be alright.'

Luke growled. 'You couldn't have known that.'

A growing silence filled the air. I peeked round the corner. They were like a pair of nervy street cats, staring at each other and unsure if they should walk away or start scratching each other's eyes out. They were so similar it was uncanny. From what I could tell, they were both terrified.

'I don't know why you've come here, son. I don't have any money. I'm not your dad either. Not really.'

'I don't want your fucking money. And I know you're not my dad. It takes more than a lucky shag to become a real father.'

'So what do you want?'

Luke drew in a ragged breath. 'Did you care?' he asked. 'Did you ever care about me at all?'

Mark looked away. 'No,' he said. 'I never wanted you. I never cared.'

He was a terrible liar. Luke wasn't in a position to see that, however.

'Good!' Luke snarled, right on cue. 'I only came here to tell you that you're shit and I'm glad I don't know you.'

I rolled my eyes, abandoned the tea, and marched towards the ridiculous pair. Honestly. Some humans just needed a damned good shake.

I jabbed Luke's shoulder with my finger. 'This boy has been looking for you for months. He's desperate to get to know you as a person, regardless of what's happened in the past.' I turned to Mark and jabbed him. 'You failed as a father fifteen years ago. That doesn't mean you have to fail now. If you don't want anything to do with your son then the kindest thing to do is to say so now and Luke can move on with the rest of his life. But be damned sure that's how you feel. You won't get another chance at this.'

Mark stared at me. His hands twisted together and his jaw worked. He didn't say a single word though.

'Well, fuck off then,' Luke said. He spun away as Mark's eyes filled with tears.

'Wait,' I said. I walked past Mark, reaching down past the chair behind him and picking up the small wooden chest that had been lying there. 'Here, Luke.'

Mark didn't protest although his face did spasm with fear when I passed the chest to his son. Luke flipped it open and gazed at the contents. I reached past him and scooped up the scrap of paper with my phone number on it, crumpling it in my hand. Luke barely noticed.

'That's...'

Mark put his hands in his pockets. 'A lock of your hair.'

Luke pulled out a small, worn stuffed rabbit. 'Mr Floppy. I thought he'd gotten lost.'

I clenched my fists in delight. Without knowing exactly what was inside the chest, I'd been taking a gamble. When Mark Countman hadn't thrown away my phone number, however, and had dropped it into that box I knew that whatever else was in there, it pertained to Luke, for good or for bad. As it turned out, it was most definitely for good.

'These are letters,' Luke said wonderingly. 'They're all addressed to me.'

'I wrote them. I didn't post them,' Mark said, his voice gruff. 'You had a new family. You didn't need me. And as your girlfriend here said, I'd already failed you once by walking away. I should never have done that. I was young and selfish and I thought I didn't want a family.' A single tear rolled down his cheek. 'It was the biggest mistake I've ever made.'

I stepped back, sidling out of the room. Luke didn't need me now. Neither did his father. This could have gone very differently. Perhaps it still would in the future. I'd gotten them to this point though. That would be enough. What happened from here on it would be down to them alone. Besides, as soon as the two stopped hugging and Luke told his father that I wasn't his girlfriend at all then things would become remarkably problematic. It was definitely time to hot-foot it back to the office. Anyway, the Metafora magic was already tugging me away–and this time I knew it was because I'd properly succeeded.

I was still beaming when I stepped into the bustle of the faery godmothers' office. Billy glanced at me from across the room. I winked at him and he seemed to relax. I didn't hold a grudge against him for all the petty sanctions pushed upon me. My future was looking too bright and rosy for anything like that. Even the prospect of more trouble from the remaining trolls couldn't dampen my joy. I felt like I was becoming a proper faery godmother. Two wishes granted. Plenty more to go.

Alicia glided past me. 'There are some weeds on your desk,' she sniffed. 'You should get rid of them quickly. Some of us get terrible hayfever.'

I frowned. Weeds? I could feel my good mood evaporating. Despite it all, I still wasn't fully accepted by my work colleagues then. I was still being targeted and put into my place. I gritted my teeth and stomped over to my desk. I'd find out who put weeds on my fucking desk and I'd make sure they regretted it. No more playing little Miss Nice. I would show them who was boss. I would...

I stopped. There, in a stunning cut crystal vase, was the largest bunch of golden dandelions I'd ever seen. I couldn't see a card. I didn't need one. I leaned across and plucked one out of the vase, holding it up to my nose and inhaling its sweet green scent.

Delilah raised her head and glanced at me. 'Everything alright, Saffron?'

I just smiled at her. 'Fabulous.'

ABOUT THE AUTHOR

After teaching English literature in the UK, Japan and Malaysia, Helen Harper left behind the world of education following the worldwide success of her Blood Destiny series of books. She is a professional member of the Alliance of Independent Authors and writes full time, thanking her lucky stars every day that's she lucky enough to do so!

Helen has always been a book lover, devouring science fiction and fantasy tales when she was a child growing up in Scotland.

She currently lives in Edinburgh in the UK with far too many cats – not to mention the dragons, fairies, demons, wizards and vampires that seem to keep appearing from nowhere.

OTHER TITLES

The complete *FireBrand* series

A werewolf killer. A paranormal murder. How many times can Emma Bellamy cheat death?

I'm one placement away from becoming a fully fledged London detective. It's bad enough that my last assignment before I qualify is with Supernatural Squad. But that's nothing compared to what happens next.

Brutally murdered by an unknown assailant, I wake up twelve hours later in the morgue – and I'm very much alive. I don't know how or why it happened. I don't know who killed me. All I know is that they might try again.

Werewolves are disappearing right, left and centre.

A mysterious vampire seems intent on following me everywhere I go.

And I have to solve my own vicious killing. Preferably before death comes for me again.

Book One – Brimstone Bound

Book Two – Infernal Enchantment

Book Three – Midnight Smoke

Book Four – Scorched Heart

Book Five – Dark Whispers

Book Six – A Killer's Kiss

Book Seven – Fortune's Ashes

A Charade of Magic complete series

The best way to live in the Mage ruled city of Glasgow is to keep your head down and your mouth closed.

That's not usually a problem for Mairi Wallace. By day she works at a small shop selling tartan and by night she studies to become an apothecary. She knows her place and her limitations. All that changes, however, when her old childhood friend sends her a desperate message seeking her help - and the Mages themselves cross Mairi's path. Suddenly, remaining unnoticed is no longer an option.

There's more to Mairi than she realises but, if she wants to fulfil her full potential, she's going to have to fight to stay alive - and only time will tell if she can beat the Mages at their own game.

From twisted wynds and tartan shops to a dangerous daemon and the magic infused City Chambers, the future of a nation might lie with one solitary woman.

Book One – Hummingbird

Book Two – Nightingale

Book Three – Red Hawk

The complete *Blood Destiny* series

"A spectacular and addictive series."

Mackenzie Smith has always known that she was different. Growing up as the only human in a pack of rural shapeshifters will do that to you, but then couple it with some mean fighting skills and a fiery temper and you end up with a woman that few will dare to cross. However, when the only father figure in her life is brutally murdered, and the dangerous Brethren with their predatory Lord Alpha come to investigate, Mack has to not only ensure the physical safety of her adopted family by hiding her apparent humanity, she also has to seek the blood-soaked vengeance that she craves.

Book One - Bloodfire

Book Two - Bloodmagic

Book Three - Bloodrage

Book Four - Blood Politics

Book Five - Bloodlust

Also

Corrigan Fire

Corrigan Magic

Corrigan Rage

Corrigan Politics

Corrigan Lust

The complete *Bo Blackman* series

A half-dead daemon, a massacre at her London based PI firm and evidence that suggests she's the main suspect for both ... Bo Blackman is having a very bad week.

She might be naive and inexperienced but she's determined to get to the bottom of the crimes, even if it means involving herself with one of London's most powerful vampire Families and their enigmatic leader.

It's pretty much going to be impossible for Bo to ever escape unscathed.

Book One - Dire Straits

Book Two - New Order

Book Three - High Stakes

Book Four - Red Angel

Book Five - Vigilante Vampire

Book Six - Dark Tomorrow

The complete *Highland Magic* series

Integrity Taylor walked away from the Sidhe when she was a child. Orphaned and bullied, she simply had no reason to stay, especially not when the sins of her father were going to remain on her shoulders. She found a new family - a group of thieves who proved that blood was less important than loyalty and love.

But the Sidhe aren't going to let Integrity stay away forever. They need her more than anyone realises - besides, there are prophecies to be fulfilled, people to be saved and hearts to be won over. If anyone can do it, Integrity can.

Book One - Gifted Thief

Book Two - Honour Bound

Book Three - Veiled Threat

Book Four - Last Wish

The complete *Dreamweaver* series

"I have special coping mechanisms for the times I need to open the front door. They're even often successful..."

Zoe Lydon knows there's often nothing logical or rational about fear. It doesn't change the fact that she's too terrified to step outside her own house, however.

What Zoe doesn't realise is that she's also a dreamweaver - able to access other people's subconscious minds. When she finds herself in the Dreamlands and up against its sinister Mayor, she'll need to use all of her wits - and overcome all of her fears - if she's ever going to come out alive.

Book One - Night Shade

Book Two - Night Terrors

Book Three - Night Lights

Stand alone novels

Eros

William Shakespeare once wrote that, "Cupid is a knavish lad, thus to make poor females mad." The trouble is that Cupid himself would probably agree...

As probably the last person in the world who'd appreciate hearts, flowers and romance, Coop is convinced that true love doesn't exist –

which is rather unfortunate considering he's also known as Cupid, the God of Love. He'd rather spend his days drinking, womanising and generally having as much fun as he possible can. As far as he's concerned, shooting people with bolts of pure love is a waste of his time...but then his path crosses with that of shy and retiring Skye Sawyer and nothing will ever be quite the same again.

Wraith

Magic. Shadows. Adventure. Romance.

Saiya Buchanan is a wraith, able to detach her shadow from her body and send it off to do her bidding. But, unlike most of her kin, Saiya doesn't deal in death. Instead, she trades secrets - and in the goblin besieged city of Stirling in Scotland, they're a highly prized commodity. It might just be, however, that the goblins have been hiding the greatest secret of them all. When Gabriel de Florinville, a Dark Elf, is sent as royal envoy into Stirling and takes her prisoner, Saiya is not only going to uncover the sinister truth. She's also going to realise that sometimes the deepest secrets are the ones locked within your own heart.

The complete *Lazy Girl's Guide To Magic* series

Hard Work Will Pay Off Later. Laziness Pays Off Now.

Let's get one thing straight - Ivy Wilde is not a heroine. In fact, she's probably the last witch in the world who you'd call if you needed a magical helping hand. If it were down to Ivy, she'd spend all day every day on her sofa where she could watch TV, munch junk food and talk to her feline familiar to her heart's content.

However, when a bureaucratic disaster ends up with Ivy as the victim of a case of mistaken identity, she's yanked very unwillingly into Arcane Branch, the investigative department of the Hallowed Order of Magical Enlightenment. Her problems are quadrupled when a valuable object is stolen right from under the Order's noses.

It doesn't exactly help that she's been magically bound to Adeptus Exemptus Raphael Winter. He might have piercing sapphire eyes and a body which a cover model would be proud of but, as far as Ivy's concerned, he's a walking advertisement for the joyless perils of too much witch-work.

And if he makes her go to the gym again, she's definitely going to turn him into a frog.

Book One - Slouch Witch

Book Two - Star Witch

Book Three - Spirit Witch

Sparkle Witch (Christmas novella)

The complete *Fractured Faery* series

One corpse. Several bizarre looking attackers. Some very strange magical powers. And a severe bout of amnesia.

It’s one thing to wake up outside in the middle of the night with a decapitated man for company. It’s another to have no memory of how you got there - or who you are.

She might not know her own name but she knows that several people are out to get her. It could be because she has strange magical powers seemingly at her fingertips and is some kind of fabulous hero. But then why does she appear to inspire fear in so many? And who on earth is the sexy, green-eyed barman who apparently despises her? So many questions ... and so few answers.

At least one thing is for sure - the streets of Manchester have never met someone quite as mad as Madrona...

Book One - Box of Frogs

SHORTLISTED FOR THE KINDLE STORYTELLER AWARD 2018

Book Two - Quiver of Cobras

Book Three - Skulk of Foxes

The complete *City Of Magic* series

Charley is a cleaner by day and a professional gambler by night. She might be haunted by her tragic past but she's never thought of herself as anything or anyone special. Until, that is, things start to go terribly wrong all across the city of Manchester. Between plagues of rats, firestorms and the gleaming blue eyes of a sexy Scottish werewolf, she might just have landed herself in the middle of a magical apocalypse. She might also be the only person who has the ability to bring order to an utterly chaotic new world.

Book One - Shrill Dusk

Book Two - Brittle Midnight

Book Three - Furtive Dawn

www.ingramcontent.com/pod-product-compliance
Ingram Content Group UK Ltd.
Pitfield, Milton Keynes, MK11 3LW, UK
UKHW042004190726
13854UKWH00005B/2156